"Can you sing to me, like your mama did?" Mattie asked.

With a half-apologetic glance at Dawson, Isabelle sat on the edge of the bed.

Why should she feel sorry? To his regret, he admitted he'd given her every reason to feel he didn't want her spending time with his daughter. To his shame, he'd even suggested she was unsuitable simply because she was…what? A city woman? A newcomer? Beautiful?

All those things could mean danger. Or they could mean nothing.

He wasn't sure he had changed his mind, but it became harder and harder to remember his reasons.

Isabelle crooned a song in Spanish.

He sat as mesmerized by her sweet voice as Mattie. In the distant corner of his brain, a warning voice called, reminding him how caring for Isabelle could end in disappointment and wrenching pain. The voice was drowned out by the sound of her voice and by the blossoming of his distant dreams.

Mattie's eyes drifted shut.

Isabelle leaned close and kissed each cheek. "Sweet dreams, little princess."

The word jolted clear through Dawson. *Princess.* Was that how Isabelle saw his child? His throat tightened. His eyes burned. So many people loved and cared for Mattie, but something about Isabelle's tender touch and sweet words felt different.

Linda Ford lives on a ranch in Alberta, Canada, near enough to the Rocky Mountains that she can enjoy them on a daily basis. She and her husband raised fourteen children—four homemade, ten adopted. She currently shares her home and life with her husband, a grown son, a live-in paraplegic client and a continual (and welcome) stream of kids, kids-in-law, grandkids, and assorted friends and relatives.

Books by Linda Ford

Love Inspired Historical

Big Sky Country
Montana Cowboy Daddy

Montana Cowboys
The Cowboy's Ready-Made Family
The Cowboy's Baby Bond
The Cowboy's City Girl

Christmas in Eden Valley
A Daddy for Christmas
A Baby for Christmas
A Home for Christmas

Journey West
Wagon Train Reunion

Montana Marriages
Big Sky Cowboy
Big Sky Daddy
Big Sky Homecoming

Visit the Author Profile page at Harlequin.com for more titles.

LINDA FORD

Montana Cowboy Daddy

HARLEQUIN® LOVE INSPIRED® HISTORICAL

Recycling programs
for this product may
not exist in your area.

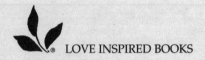

LOVE INSPIRED BOOKS

ISBN-13: 978-0-373-28378-1

Montana Cowboy Daddy

www.Harlequin.com

Printed in U.S.A.

As the mountains are round about Jerusalem,
so the Lord is round about His people
from henceforth even for ever.
—*Psalms* 125:2

This book is dedicated to my dear friends. You know who you are. Thanks to each of you for keeping in touch over the years, for sharing the ups and downs of my life and for always standing with me. Without you my life would lack color and depth and joy. Thank you and God bless.

Chapter One

Bella Creek, Montana, 1890

Weary from the long journey and tired of the cramped quarters, Isabelle Redfield was the first to step from the stagecoach to the dirt street of Bella Creek, Montana. A group of people stood about as if waiting for the arrival of the travelers.

Isabelle glanced around at the fledgling Western town where she hoped to start a new life—one of purpose and acceptance. Before her was a wooden-structured hotel, to her left, a wide street with bare-limbed trees and a welcoming bench. Past the hotel to her right, a café, Miss Daisy's Eatery. Her gaze went farther. Her heart slammed into her ribs at what she saw.

"No." She couldn't tell if the word left her mouth or stayed trapped in her mind as she watched a little girl, blond hair flying about her head, dash across the street. Did no one notice her? Or see the freight wagon bearing down on her, the horses' huge hooves ready to trample the child? Were they all too interested in looking over those who had traveled to their town?

She lifted her skirts, intending to run toward the child. Instead, her petticoats caught and she stumbled. Righting herself, she reached toward the child but she was too far away. Could she do nothing to prevent the disaster she saw coming? Must she watch helplessly… uselessly?

In a clatter of racing hooves, a horseman galloped into the scene. The rider reached down and snatched up the little girl and thundered out of the way.

Isabelle breathed a prayer of thanks for the rescue of the child.

The wagon driver shouted, "Whoa." The horses reared and pawed the air and the wagon careened to a stop farther down the street.

Isabelle stared at the big man who had rescued the girl and was clutching her to his chest, his expression fierce.

She couldn't hear his words as he spoke to the child, couldn't see his face, hidden as it was beneath the brim of his hat, but from the defensive look on the little one's face, she guessed he scolded her.

"Yes, Papa. I'm sorry."

What kind of place had she arrived in where children played untended in the street? Then were scolded for the neglect of the adults? It should not be.

Indignation burned through her veins as she continued on her way, closing the distance between herself and the pair seated upon the horse. She didn't slow until she reached their side. The warmth and smell of horseflesh greeted her as she reached up and ran her hands along the girl's arms. "Are you hurt?"

The child shook her head, still looking frightened.

"You're safe so long as you don't play in the street."

Her smile seemed to encourage the girl. But how safe could she be if no one watched her?

She lifted her head to face the man. "You're this child's father?" Having heard the child call him Papa, she knew he was. She only meant to remind the man of his responsibility.

His gaze hit her with such force she pressed her hand to her throat as if she could calm the rapid beating of her heart...caused, she reminded herself, from marching across the street. Certainly not from the power of piercing blue eyes in a tanned face.

She didn't wait for his reply. Nor did she heed a sense of warning that this was not a man accustomed to having someone suggest he was wrong. "I advise you to take better care of her before she is injured."

His blue eyes grew glacial. His lips pressed into a frown. "I don't believe I've had the pleasure of meeting you nor you of meeting me. I would think that makes you quite incapable of having a knowledgeable opinion of what I should or shouldn't be doing." His gaze bored straight through her.

She lifted her chin another inch. She was Isabelle Redfield and her opinion was generally considered worth taking note of. With a little sigh, she released her anger. He didn't know who she was nor did she want him to. "I would be remiss not to point out the child was in grave danger. Surely you could see that."

"I saw her." His clipped words warned her to drop the subject.

She lowered her gaze to the child and, not wanting to upset her, chose to let it go.

Her traveling companions had left the stagecoach and watched the proceedings from the hotel veranda.

She climbed the three wooden steps to join them. Isabelle's friend and fellow traveler, Kate, rushed to her side. "That was too close for comfort. Quite an introduction to Bella Creek." Kate's father, Dr. Baker, joined his daughter. Sadie Young, the new teacher for the community, stood nearby.

A white-haired old man leaning on two canes stood in the forefront of the gathered townsfolk, as if the official greeter. Each of those who had traveled with her introduced themselves and spoke of their plans. Dr. Baker and his daughter to help the ill and injured, Sadie Young to teach the children. And Isabelle to—

Well, she wasn't sure what she could do, but she'd find something that mattered.

Praying no one in this group would recognize her name, Isabelle brushed her skirts, smoothing them as best she could before she introduced herself. "Miss Isabelle Redfield." She adjusted her gloves. "I'm here to help, as well." *Please don't ask me what I plan to do.* The breeze tugged at her silk scarf, whipping the ends about.

Kate pulled her to her side. "Isabelle is my friend. She's with us."

When Kate said she would go with her father to the mining town, Isabelle had asked if she could accompany them. She'd grown weary of life in St. Louis, where for the past eleven and a half years, since her parents died when she was twelve, she'd shared the home of her second cousin by marriage, Augusta. Not that her home life was unacceptable, but everyone knew Isabelle was the sole beneficiary of both the Redfield and Castellano fortunes. It seemed most people sought her out, pretended friendship, even asked for her hand in marriage, simply because of her inheritance. Kate was the rare exception.

Perhaps she could start over here without that knowledge classifying her. As they'd approached their destination, she'd asked Kate not to tell anyone she was an heiress, which had brought a smile to Kate's lips as her gaze skimmed Isabelle's dress. "You should have taken that into consideration when choosing your gowns. Even your traveling outfit shouts money."

Isabelle had glanced dismissively at her sapphire-blue suit and long protective matching coat lined with warm wool. Her bonnet matched, as well, but the long silk scarf holding her bonnet in place was bright and cheerful with pink poppies all over. Clothes meant far less to her than they did to Cousin Augusta, who saw every occasion as an excuse to bring in a seamstress or two and discuss the latest styles.

"This is all I have, though I suppose I could have ordered different things." The gowns in her trunk were mostly new—suitable for a trip, according to Cousin Augusta. It had never crossed Isabelle's mind to suggest otherwise. She smiled as she thought of the fine silk and crisp satin of her gowns. It had been rather exciting to help select the fabrics and then watch them be transformed into beautiful outfits. She loved beauty wherever she saw it.

It was too late to prepare simpler clothes. Hopefully she would not be judged by what she wore.

"Good to see you all," the white-haired man said. "We need all the help we can get. I'm Allan Marshall, the one who sent for you. Welcome to Bella Creek." He shifted to lean on one cane in order to shake hands with the doctor and bend over each of the ladies' hands.

Many in the small crowd called out their greetings.

"Most people call me Grandfather Marshall, seeing as

there are so many Marshalls around. Like my grandson here. Dawson, get down and say hello to these folks."

The man Isabelle had recently scolded lowered the girl to the ground, swung off his horse and joined the older man. Tall and broad, so upright and strong looking…a marked contrast to his stooped grandfather.

"This is Dawson Marshall." The elder Marshall man chuckled softly. "You'll have to forgive him his manners. Sometimes he forgets he's not out with a bunch of rough cowboys."

Isabelle raised her head to meet the gaze of the man before her. She stilled herself to reveal none of her trepidation. Only a few minutes in town and already she'd managed to step on the toes of what appeared to be the biggest family in Bella Creek. Not that knowing would have stopped her from speaking her mind.

Grandfather Marshall continued. "Dawson's a widower in need of a woman to settle him down."

"Grandfather, I am not in need of a woman." The protesting words rumbled from the man's lips.

Isabelle managed not to show any sign of her alarm at the way the older man eyed her, then slowly—almost reluctantly—let his gaze slip toward the other two women. She dared not look at them to see their reaction. Would either of them be interested in the prospect?

From behind Dawson peeked out the little blonde girl, her blue-green eyes wide.

"Papa, she's beautiful," the child whispered, as she stared at Isabelle.

Amusement tickled Isabelle's insides but she decided it was wise to disguise it in view of the frown on Mr. Marshall's face.

"Welcome to Bella Creek." Dawson greeted each of

them. His expression cooled considerably when he met Isabelle's gaze. "Thank you for coming in answer to our appeal for help."

His latent displeasure didn't bother her except to refuel her indignation that a child had been in danger.

The various trunks and crates had been unloaded from the stage and with a "Hey, there" from the driver, the horses pulled away, leaving a clear view to the sight on the other side of the street.

Isabelle stared. The whole of the block had been burned to the ground. Blackened timbers and a brick chimney stood like mute, angry survivors. One section had been scraped bare except for remnants of spring snow clinging to the corners. And in the midst of it stood a new building, so fresh and out of place amid the rubble on each side that it looked naked. Shock chilled Isabelle's veins at the sight. She pulled her scarf closer around her neck.

Dawson Marshall strode over to stand nearby as they both studied the scene. "This winter a fire destroyed the dry-goods store, the lawyer's office, the barbershop, the doctor's office and residence, and the school. We're grateful it didn't jump the street and burn the church."

She'd read the news of the fire. Knew it to be the reason they needed a doctor and a schoolteacher, but to see the stark evidence gave it a whole different meaning. "Was anyone hurt?" She shuddered at the thought.

Kate and Sadie joined Isabelle at the edge of the veranda, crowding her closer to Dawson and his daughter.

He answered her question though he addressed the entire group. "Doc burned his hands trying to save his equipment. It will be some time before he can resume his duties, if he ever does. He said it was time to retire. He and his wife moved to California. The teacher wept profusely at the loss of her precious books and left town on the next stage, saying she would never return."

"Hence your need for replacements." Her scarf was tugged. She reached to contain it but stilled her hand when she saw the little girl behind Dawson fingering it.

She bent and smiled at the child. "What's your name?"

"I'm Mattie. I'm six."

"Pleased to meet you, Mattie."

Mattie's face lit with a smile.

Dawson moved away to speak to the doctor, Mattie firmly in hand.

Isabelle watched him. A big man with a strong face. Raising a child on his own. How did he manage?

Not that it concerned her.

Shifting her attention away, she met Grandfather Marshall's eyes. He grinned at her, his gaze darting to Dawson and back.

Goodness. Did he think she had an interest in his grandson? If only he knew she had no interest in men at all. No, she'd learned her lesson. They never saw beyond her inheritance. She'd allowed herself to believe Jamieson Grieve cared for her. After all, he had no need of her money. His father owned a successful bank. But then had come talk of how he'd invest Isabelle's inheritance in establishing more banks. Once started on the topic of Isabelle's money, it seemed he could talk of nothing else. She'd broken off with him, wanting to be seen as more than the source of a large bank account.

It had taken one more failure in the shape of Andy Anderson for the lesson to be embedded. A humble store clerk who daily espoused the evils of money as the root of all vices, he'd said a man ought to work for what he had and take pride in doing so. Believing he loved her for herself, she'd agreed to a betrothal. That was when she felt she must tell him about her inheritance.

Turned out he'd always known—why should she have believed otherwise? The man would have to be blind and deaf not to know. After their betrothal, he had wanted her to contact her lawyer and, as her future husband, have himself named as trustee of her estate. He said he knew how to put the money to good use.

That was when she'd said goodbye, a sadder but much wiser woman. From now on, she would not trust that a man's affections were not influenced by her inheritance. Perhaps by hiding the truth about herself, she could learn the real meaning of a person's interest in her.

"Doctor." Dawson's voice brought her back to the present situation. "You have patients waiting. Three men were injured by falling machinery. Which of these are yours?" He indicated the stack of crates and trunks.

"I'll need those and those right away," the doctor answered, pointing to several crates.

Dawson waved at the nearby men. "Let's get these over to the doctor's office." He turned to Sadie. "Miss Young, I'm afraid I don't have time to see you settled right now. Nor do we have your quarters ready. You'll be staying in the hotel until we do. If you don't mind going in and introducing yourself…"

"I'll manage just fine," Sadie said and made her way to the hotel entrance.

"I'll take you to your new office and your patients." Dawson nodded to the doctor, scooped Mattie into his arms and strode across the street.

Isabelle followed Kate and Dr. Baker. She didn't mean to miss this opportunity to prove she was an ordinary, everyday, useful sort of woman. Would she ever truly know acceptance as such rather than as a rich woman? Yes, she'd been blessed with it and unfettered love when her parents lived. Her mother, especially, lavished it on her. Isabelle didn't doubt Cousin Augusta's affection was genuine. But apart from Kate, every other friendship had been tainted by the color of her money.

They crossed the rutted street and Isabelle had to concentrate on where she put her feet. It helped her avoid thinking of the fact that she meant to step into a doctor's office…something she'd managed to avoid since her parents' deaths. They entered a narrow room with benches on either side. A couple of dusty men sat clutching their hats and sprang to their feet as Dawson entered.

"He's here? The new doc?" one asked.

Dr. Baker stepped forward. "I'm the doctor. Where are the injured men?"

Two heads tipped in the direction of another door. Dr. Baker and Kate crossed toward it.

Isabelle followed. The wood of the place being new, there were no sickroom odors. Nothing to remind her of when her parents were ill.

She crossed the threshold into the other room, and after a fleeting glance at a mangled hand on one man and the blood-soaked rag around the head of a second, she averted her eyes from the third man stretched out on the examining table. Every muscle in her body tensed, just as they had back then. Perhaps if she concentrated on the supplies, she could manage to forget the sights and smells and fears she recalled from watching her parents die.

She went to Kate's side as her friend pried open one crate and quickly arranged an array of bottles and instruments on the shelves as Dr. Baker bent over the man on the examining table.

Isabelle didn't hear what the doctor said to Kate or if Kate knew what he needed without words. Kate uncorked a bottle and poured some liquid on a cloth and handed it to her father.

The odor assailed Isabelle with revolting familiarity. The smell of sickness and death.

The room tilted. Her stomach churned. Clasping a hand to her mouth, she fled back to the waiting room and sank to the nearest empty spot on a bench. She sucked in a deep breath to calm her stomach and slowly righted her head to meet the challenging look of Dawson Marshall. He'd removed his hat to reveal thick blond hair. A fine-looking man but one who—if she was to guess from the way his pale eyebrows knotted together—wondered at her sudden exit from the examining room.

Unable to explain herself, she lowered her gaze to Mattie, who offered her wide-eyed wonder and then a shy smile.

Isabelle armed herself with that sliver of a welcome.

There must be something useful she could do in this town that didn't require her presence in the doctor's office. Something to prove to herself and everyone else that she was more than a rich heiress.

A moan came from the doctor's office and she bolted out the door.

Dawson stared after the woman. Had she taken such a dislike to him she couldn't bear to be in the same room? He leaned his head back against the wall, ignoring the two miners who watched him, their eyes wide with curiosity. She had no right to scold him about Mattie's safety. He'd seen the wagon bearing down and would have died before he let his daughter be hurt. He'd gently admonished her to look both ways before she dashed across the street…exactly what a good parent should do.

Isabelle's criticism of him reminded him sharply of Violet. She, too, had picked holes in everything he did. His now-deceased wife, a city woman who thought to find adventure and satisfaction on the Marshall Five Ranch, had instead found boredom and disappointment. A fact she never ceased to bemoan, saying she should have remained in the city. He totally agreed.

Isabelle's clothes and manners screamed the fact she, too, was a city woman. Her words had accused him of being a blundering father. Violet had called him a bumbling cowboy. He guessed one was pretty much the same as the other.

"Papa, she sure is pretty but why is she afraid?"

He ground down on his molars. The last thing this town or Dawson Marshall or his daughter needed was another woman like Violet—a fancy city woman who couldn't or wouldn't accept the demands of life in the West. He should never have married Violet. But he'd been a dewy-eyed nineteen-year-old. When she learned life on a ranch was hard work, she'd sought excitement elsewhere and ended up dying in a reckless horse race against some cowboys from Wolf Hollow, the nearby mining town, leaving him with a three-year-old daughter to raise.

Now a wiser twenty-six-year-old, he knew enough not to be blinded by a woman's beauty. Nor her gentle manner. Not even her concern for his daughter's safety.

Such a woman was not equipped to live out here.

"Come on, Papa." Mattie tugged on his arm. "Where are we going?"

"After her."

"I expect she is about her own business." He could only hope and pray that business, whatever it was, would not attract any more of Mattie's interest.

Mattie got up and tugged at Dawson.

He didn't budge as Mattie did her best to pull him to his feet. She tugged. She jerked. She turned her back to him and leaned into his outstretched arm like a stubborn mule, grunting under the strain.

He laughed at the accurate comparison. If Mattie set her mind to an idea, she would not easily give it up. His smile flattened. Reason enough to divert her attraction from the beautiful newcomer.

He curled his arm about his daughter's waist and drew her to his chest. "You know you will never be strong enough to move me." He bussed a kiss on her neck.

She giggled. "There's more than one way to get you to move."

"Really? Who told you that?"

"Aunt Annie."

Yup, his sister would feel free to tell Mattie her opinion. His little sister was only nineteen but had been taking care of Mattie for three years now. And the rest of the family even longer. She'd developed some very strong notions about things.

Mattie gave a decisive nod. "And Grandfather. He knows everything."

She, like everyone else, called the eldest Marshall Grandfather. Dawson's father was known to her as Grandpa Bud.

"Grandfather might not know everything. After all, he's just a man." The words almost stuck to his tongue. No one, least of all Grandfather, would look kindly on such a statement. After all, Bella Creek had been built by the Marshall patriarch to provide a safe and pleasant alternative to the ramshackle collection of buildings in the wild mining town known as Wolf Hollow. Many of the businesses had been created by him. Before that, he'd started the ranch. It was Grandfather who'd insisted the Marshalls were responsible for rebuilding the section of town the fire had destroyed and seeing to the replacement of the doctor and teacher.

"I'd do it myself if I could." Grandfather had slapped at his legs as if to remind them all he could barely walk, let alone ride or do carpentry work. A wreck with a horse had left him badly crippled. But it wasn't beneath him to use his regrettable condition to guilt them all into complying with his wishes.

For the most part, Dawson didn't object to helping rebuild the destroyed buildings. He hadn't known it would mean so many hours in town dealing with construction, finding materials and personnel. And why it had fallen to him to write out the advertisements for a new doctor and teacher and then sort through the applications, he could not say.

He smiled mockingly. Not that there'd been a lot of applicants. Not too many people cared to locate to the far northwest corner of Montana at the tail end of winter.

Mattie squirmed free of his grasp and grabbed both his hands. "Papa, she'll disappear if you don't stop her."

"No one disappears." Though he recalled the futility of trying to make a three-year-old believe that when her mother had ridden out of their lives and soon after died. As far as Mattie understood, her mother had disappeared. Thankfully, she was now old enough to understand a little better, though Dawson wondered if he would ever find words to adequately explain Violet's restless behavior.

"But what if she does?" Her voice dripped with concern. "I could tell she was really afraid."

Likely already realizing this rural life was more than she'd anticipated.

Ignoring the curious miners listening to every word, he planted his hands on Mattie's shoulders to still her movements. "Listen to me, Mattie. She's not the sort of woman you should be getting too friendly with." The moment Miss Isabelle Redfield had stepped from the coach in her fancy clothes, fine shoes and flimsy scarf, he'd recognized her as a city woman through and through. He knew enough to be cautious around city women. But Mattie didn't, and she'd eyed Miss Isabelle with far too much interest. "I doubt she'll be staying here long."

The excitement in Mattie's eyes died, replaced with hurt. He wished he could change that but far better to be warned now than burned later.

One of the dusty miners shuffled his feet. "Begging your pardon, Mr. Marshall, but she looked to me to be exactly the sort of gal a man would do well to be friendly with. It's been a long time since I seen anyone half so classy looking."

Mattie nodded vigorously. "That's what I thought, too."

Dawson chewed his lips. The precise reason he knew she wouldn't stay. Life here was rough and challenging. Not what well-heeled city ladies cared for. Like the miner said, there weren't many like that around here.

Mattie's voice grew dreamy. "She's a real lady. Her scarf is as smooth as a kitten's fur." She rubbed her thumb and fingertip together as if still feeling the fabric. "Just like her voice and smile." Mattie rubbed her arm. Dawson knew it was where Isabelle had touched her. "She was so kind."

If only the woman would leave before his innocent little daughter grew any more interested in the fine lady and her silky scarf. "We need to get back to the ranch." Hand in hand they left the doctor's house.

"Dawson, over here." Grandfather beckoned from in front of the hotel.

Dawson and Mattie crossed the street to join the older man.

"I'll get the wagon and take you home," Dawson said.

"No need. Annie's coming." Indeed, his sister drove the wagon toward them.

"When did you get to town?" he asked when she drew up beside them.

"Thought I'd have a look at the newcomers but I've missed them. Grandfather has fixed that by inviting them to the ranch for supper."

"I haven't had a chance to extend the invitation. Dawson, you can look after it," Grandfather said.

"Me? I thought I was done here and could go find my cows." He'd purchased his own herd last fall. They'd barely been moved to Marshall Five Ranch before snow fell. He'd checked on them periodically, hoping they wouldn't wander off to more familiar pastures. Several times he'd had to herd them back from the boundaries of the ranch.

"The others can take care of it." Pa and Dawson's brothers had gone out to check on the cattle. But they meant to go north to where they expected to find the main bunch and Dawson's cows always headed south.

Dawson opened his mouth to protest but Grandfather

shook a cane at him. "Annie is going to make a meal for Doc and the ladies. You will bring them out."

Dawson shut his mouth. There was no arguing with his grandfather when he was in one of these moods. Not for the first time, and likely not for the last, Dawson wished he had not been the one selected to greet the newcomers and get them settled. But his grandfather had insisted he was the eldest of the three brothers and so should be on the welcoming committee, and then he'd insisted he would ride along. And now it had come to this…inviting them out for supper. Doc, his daughter and the schoolteacher, he didn't mind. But the fancy city gal? He wanted to keep Mattie as far from her as possible.

"That Miss Isabelle is a fine-looking woman." Seemed Grandfather wasn't about to let Dawson forget his opinion.

It was useless to dispute the matter. Besides, she was more than fine looking. She was beautiful. He'd noted so the first glance he had of her. Black hair tucked beneath a bonnet that matched her sapphire-blue coat, ebony eyes that gave a sweeping glance to those gathered to welcome the newcomers and ivory skin that would likely melt beneath the Montana sun.

"Puts me in mind of my own Annabelle. Even their names are alike." Grandfather's eyes grew watery.

Dawson figured it best to ignore the comparison. Probably the only way Isabelle was like his grandmother was the similarity in names. Nothing more.

Grandfather cleared his throat and brought his piercing gaze to Dawson. "A man would be fortunate to win the heart of such a gal."

Dawson snorted softly, not wishing to offend the old man. "Don't you think I've learned my lesson about city women?" A woman such as that would be forever restless on the ranch.

"Mattie needs a mother." Both Dawson and Grandfather glanced over their shoulders to where Mattie kicked a hardened clump of dirt, oblivious to the conversation between the two men.

"I've no interest in marrying again."

"It's high time you got over Violet. Besides, it's not fair to judge every woman by Violet's actions."

Dawson thought it was completely fair. And not just because of Violet. He could name half a dozen other instances where a family or community had been upset by the discontent of a city woman. One especially came to mind. Violet's friend had come to town, turning upside down the life of one of Dawson's good friends, Johnny, and then she'd moved on. Leaving his friend flat broke and emotionally shattered. In fact, he could think of no city woman who had adjusted to life on a ranch. But he kept his opinion to himself. No point in wasting words when he knew Grandfather wouldn't listen.

Grandfather patted Dawson on the arm with his knotted fingers. "Give her a chance. You might be surprised to discover inner beauty to match her outer beauty."

Dawson shook his head. "You've seen her, what? Fifteen minutes? Half an hour? And spoken less than a dozen words to her. How can you make any sort of judgment about her?"

"I might ask you the same thing. Now help me to the wagon. Annie needs to get home and prepare a meal."

Dawson assisted the man to the seat beside Annie. As much as possible Dawson, his brothers or their father gave Grandfather what help he needed, but Annie managed when she was alone with him.

The pair drove off and Dawson called Mattie to him.

"Why did we stay here?" she asked.

"We are going to take the doctor and the ladies out to the ranch for supper."

"Oh, goodie." She did a happy skip and jump. "Miss Isabelle, too? Right?"

Grandfather would accept no excuse if Dawson showed up without her. "Somebody will have to feed them. There's no food in the house yet." He'd meant to have the pantry stocked by now but had fallen behind in that task. He'd left a notice at the store for people to contribute if they cared to. In the meantime, he would have to give in to Grandfather's plans despite his better judgment. At least, the part of the old man's plan where Dawson invited the newcomers to the ranch. Not the part where he tried to win the heart of one of them. And, for some reason, Grandfather had chosen Isabelle as the one Dawson should pursue. Dawson simply wasn't interested. "Let's invite them for the meal."

They looked to the right and the left but he saw no sign of the fancy city lady.

"You said she wouldn't disappear." Mattie's words accused him of being responsible for the lady's absence. "Now I'll never get to feel her soft scarf again." She *tsked*. "Hardly think losing someone is going to meet with Grandfather's approval."

Mattie had been surrounded by adults all her life, except for the few months she'd spent in school before it burned to the ground. It had turned her into a small adult. But she was correct about Grandfather's opinion. Dawson had unfinished business to attend to.

"Let's go find the schoolteacher." After that they'd look for Isabelle. She couldn't have gone far. Probably in Uncle George's general store being dismayed at the array of farm tools and the smell of turpentine.

Mattie marched along at his side as they stepped into the hotel lobby.

"She's here," Mattie whispered and hid behind him.

Indeed, Isabelle stood before a window as if studying the scene. He could tell her that what she saw was as exciting as life got around here. "I thought you couldn't wait to find her."

"I couldn't."

He had to bend to catch her whisper. "So why are you hiding?"

"'Cause she's so pretty."

He caught Mattie's chin and tipped her face upward, waiting for her eyes to meet his. "You are pretty, too. Don't ever forget it."

She brushed her gray pinafore, giving it a mighty frown, and kicked out one scuffed black boot. "I'm not pretty. Look at this old dress."

Dawson's heart rent at yet another pain his daughter endured. She'd known far too many for one so young. But as to her clothes...well, she ran about freely at the ranch and wore clothes that allowed her to do so. The last thing Annie needed was more laundry and fancy dresses to take care of.

He squatted to Mattie's eye level and caught her by the shoulders. "Honey, never let anyone judge you by the clothes you wear, how much money you have or what you do. Those are outward things. Remember the verse Grandpa Bud says so often. 'Man looketh on the outward appearance, but the Lord looketh on the heart.' It isn't the outside that matters. It's who you are on the inside." He tapped her chest.

Mattie's eyes widened as she looked at him. "Who am I?"

He stroked her cheek. "A sweet, kind, cheerful little girl who likes to make others happy." When she smiled, he would have hugged her right then and there, but she'd warned him she was too big to be hugged in public.

He straightened. "Now let's take care of those invites." He held out his hand to her and she took it, squeezing it as hard as her little fingers allowed.

They crossed to where Miss Isabelle stood looking out a window.

"Miss."

She turned.

He swallowed hard. The miner was right. They didn't often see such beautiful ladies. Nor one with such patient eyes. They revealed no sign of restlessness. That would come later. "You and the others are invited to join us at the ranch this evening for supper."

She tipped her head in acknowledgment. "Thank you but I cannot accept or decline until I consult with Dr. Baker and Kate as to a method of conveyance."

"That won't be necessary. I'll take you all there."

She nodded. "Then if it suits the others, I accept. Thank you." She stood before him, her hands folded, that silly scarf caught between her palms. Smooth as a kitten's fur. Though he wasn't sure if he meant the scarf. Or her manners. Or something else entirely.

He slid his gaze past her shoulder. "Where might I find Miss Young?"

The schoolteacher descended the stairs. "Are you seeking me?"

He extended the same invitation to her then hurried outside, where he filled his lungs with cool mountain air.

"Are you okay, Papa?" Mattie asked.

He settled his mind. Of course he was fine. Never again would a beautiful *unsuitable* woman be allowed to upset his world. He would ignore Grandfather's match-making plans because he didn't need or want a wife, and despite Mattie's fascination with Isabelle, he knew she would be most unsuitable.

Chapter Two

Isabelle couldn't help overhearing the conversation between Mr. Marshall and his daughter. Not that she tried very hard to ignore them. There was something appealing about the big man bending over his little girl. She was such a pretty thing and yet it seemed she wasn't certain of it. How sweet to hear him remind her it was her inner qualities that mattered.

Those words made her press her lips together as a great yearning emptied her insides of every rational thought. Her mother and father had likewise doted on her. Cousin Augusta was genuinely fond and caring. Why couldn't it be enough? *Oh, Father God, why do I search for more when I have Your love?* If only she could persuade herself it was all she needed.

Dawson Marshall and little Mattie left the hotel. Isabelle watched them standing on the sidewalk outside. He bent low to hear something Mattie said. And Isabelle's chest grew tight. She rubbed at her breastbone.

Sadie joined her at the window. "Does that man frighten you as much as he frightens me?"

What an odd thing to say. "*Frighten* isn't the word

I'd use." Intrigue? Confuse? How silly. Of course he didn't confuse her.

"Really?" Sadie continued as they watched the man and his daughter. "He's so big and I get the feeling he'll tolerate no nonsense."

"Maybe." Isabelle didn't see that as a negative. "He's certainly fond of his little girl."

Sadie agreed. "I wouldn't want to do anything he might construe as harmful to her."

"But you surely wouldn't."

"Not intentionally. But I have learned that parents often have a different view of things than a lowly teacher."

At least Sadie had a place in society as a teacher. Though Isabelle did, too—as the heiress. Not a position she cared for. Her resolve returned. She intended to find for herself a role that proved her usefulness. A sigh eased past her lips at the enormity of the task.

Across the street, Mattie and her father stepped into the doctor's house and Isabelle shuddered. She must conquer her feelings about sickrooms if she meant to help Kate and her father. Unless...

She turned back to Sadie. "When will you start teaching?"

Sadie wrinkled her nose. "I have no idea. The school isn't built yet. The clerk over there—" she indicated the man at the desk watching them curiously "—says the town plans to start work on the new school next week. Says it won't take long to complete with many hands on deck." The way Sadie said it, Isabelle knew she quoted the man. "I don't know what I'm expected to do while I wait."

The poor girl rocked her head back and forth.

"I'm sorry." So much for thinking she could help with the teaching. *Lord, there must be something I can do to prove my usefulness.* She'd keep her eyes and ears open. In the meantime...

"Supper. The evening meal." She'd learned the correct terminology in the days it took to arrive at Bella Creek. "What does one wear?"

Sadie chuckled. "From my limited experience I would say most ranch families don't dress in evening wear for the meal. What you're wearing is fine."

"Oh, but I'm all dusty from traveling. I must change." Her trunks had been carried to the doctor's house and she hurried across the street. In her haste she rushed through the door and straight into the chest of Dawson Marshall. She staggered backward.

Dawson grabbed her arm and steadied her. "Begging your pardon, miss."

She shook her head. "My fault. I apologize." His fingers burned a trail straight to her heart. No, that wasn't possible. Putting a healthy distance between them, she pulled her thoughts together.

"Come, Mattie. We have things to do. I'll be back in an hour to take you to the ranch." Dawson practically dragged the child away, leaving Isabelle as out of breath as if she'd run the full length of the rutted street. She folded her hands together as a war of emotions raged through her. The certainty that Dawson did not approve of her. Determination to fit in. A chance to prove she had more to offer than a sizable inheritance. She would prove it once and for all.

She glanced about at the stacks of crates and travel

bags. This would be the sitting room. The wine-colored sofa would fit nicely against the far wall, allowing a view out the windows—two faced the street, and another revealed the side view of ashes and bare ground. There were two armchairs. They should be placed between the front windows allowing good light for reading. A small stove warmed the room.

Doing her best not to think of the motherless Mattie and her doting father, Isabelle wandered through to the kitchen with its table and chairs, cupboards and a shiny stove radiating heat. Someone had wanted them to feel welcome. Or at least they meant to welcome Kate and her father, seeing as they hadn't known she'd arrive with them. What would their opinion have been if they'd known? Some would immediately plan how many worthy projects they could persuade her to donate to. Others would be ready to dislike her solely because she had more money—much more money—than they. Very few would welcome her for no other reason than she was a young lady with a desire to prove she had something to offer other than her inheritance.

She stepped to a little room off the kitchen—a pantry that held only a few empty containers. Good thing they weren't expected to make supper for themselves tonight.

There was something she could do right now...start organizing this household.

By the time Kate returned to the living quarters, Isabelle had put the dishes in the kitchen cupboard, a cloth upon the table with a lamp in the center, and a kettle full of water on the stove should anyone want tea.

"Wow. You've been busy," Kate said with an approving look. "I appreciate your help."

"It's the least I can do. You're in there helping your

father. I surely want to do more than sit around and look ornamental."

Kate chuckled. "Whether you sit or scrub dishes, you can't help but be ornamental."

"Far better to be useful. Here, help me move these things." With Kate's help, they rearranged the furniture in the sitting room and carried the trunks to the appropriate rooms.

Dr. Baker stepped from his office and sank wearily into the nearest chair. "I'm about spent. I wish we weren't expected to go out this evening."

Kate knelt at her father's knees. "I can stay home with you if you'd rather."

"Unfortunately," Isabelle felt she must point out, "there's no food in the house."

"I think I saw a restaurant beside the hotel." Kate looked out the window. "Yes, Miss Daisy's Eatery. We could go there."

"No," the doctor said. "We'll go. I'll be fine."

Kate did not look relieved. She had not quit worrying about her father since he'd been hurt when thrown from his wagon. He had lain unconscious for three days. Kate's mother had died when she was young, so she was especially close to her father.

Isabelle turned away to stare out the window. In part she and Kate had become friends because they were both motherless. It had quickly grown beyond that.

Mattie was motherless, too. Isabelle's heart went out to her. An idea blossomed in her mind. Perhaps God wanted her in this place for the purpose of befriending a motherless child. She knew a little how Mattie must feel and would willingly offer what comfort and assurance she could to the child.

* * *

Dawson wanted nothing so much as to ride out of town clear to the southern border of the ranch. He could assure himself his cows were safe and put from his mind the few fleeting images of Isabelle. He knew she spelled danger for him and his daughter. He'd leave right now but he had been tasked with taking the newcomers to the ranch, so instead he went to the livery barn and rented a carriage so they could ride in comfort. With Mattie beside him, he returned in an hour to the doctor's house and stepped down to knock on the door.

Dr. Baker opened to greet him. Behind him stood the two young women. Miss Baker neat and tidy and rather ordinary looking. Miss Isabelle anything but ordinary looking. She'd changed into a dress that made her dark eyes seem larger and her skin more fair. The gown was blue—he supposed Violet would have called it royal blue. Violet's memory served to bring his thoughts under control.

Doc already wore a heavy coat and the others reached for theirs. Isabelle's was black wool with gold-colored frog closures.

The only reason he noticed such things, he assured himself, was that they had figured importantly in Violet's life. The thought was filled with bitter regrets. The sooner he got this evening over with, the sooner he could shake the dust of town from his boots and head for the hills.

He assisted the young ladies to the backseat. Doc would sit in the front and he'd keep Mattie right beside him.

"We'll get Miss Young and be on our way." They stopped at the hotel and he assisted the new schoolteacher aboard.

"How far is the ranch?" Miss Young asked.

"The buildings are only four miles from town but the ranch lands extend far to the west and south." Less distance to the north but they wouldn't care about specifics. He glanced over his shoulder to speak to the ladies. And met Isabelle's gaze. His thoughts stumbled and righted, and he remembered what he meant to say. "Have any of you been on a ranch before?"

"No. I'm anxious to see it." Perhaps Isabelle spoke for all of them.

He couldn't help wondering if she would be amused and entertained for a time or immediately bored by the realities of ranch life, much of it plain hard work, often repetitive and boring.

"Can you tell us a little about your ranch?" Miss Young asked.

Was she the only one who was curious? "My grandfather moved here just over a dozen years ago. He brought with him his two sons, my father and my uncle, as well as me and my two brothers—Conner is twenty-two, four years younger than me, and Logan two years younger than that—and our sister, Annie. My mother came, as well, but she passed away four years ago. My father took over the ranch and Uncle George runs the mercantile in town. According to Grandfather, he fought the elements, the Indians, the government, rustlers and gold miners to build a successful ranch."

"And your grandmother?" Kate asked, gently.

"She died before we moved out here. Grandfather has never remarried." He continued telling about the ranch. "We raise horses and cattle. The discovery of gold has given us a ready market for many of our animals."

Mattie turned around to face the ladies. "You'll like

the ranch. It's the best place in the world. Too bad you have to live in town."

All the ladies chuckled at Mattie's comment.

"Teachers have to live in town," Miss Young said.

"So do doctors," Kate added.

Dawson waited for Isabelle to say something. When she didn't, he turned to look at her. She wore an expression he could only describe as both surprised and hopeful.

She blinked as she realized he watched her. "I have never lived anywhere but a city. I don't even know what to expect."

Mattie clapped her hands. "You are going to like it so much. It will be lots of fun."

No one corrected her assumption that Isabelle would be living on the ranch. Or maybe Mattie only meant visiting.

He turned the corner where the trail climbed up an incline. They reached the crest, allowing them to see the ranch buildings in the hollow beyond. Pride filled his heart. "I was twelve when we moved here, full of excitement and expectation as only a young lad could be."

Isabelle's soft response came from the back. "I would say your grandfather was full of the same emotions."

He'd never thought of that, but it was no doubt true. He pointed out the buildings. "The house greets you as you approach the ranch." A two-story log-and-timber structure, it was big enough for many Marshalls, Grandfather had said on several occasions. "Barns, storehouses, harness room…" Dawson indicated the various buildings. All except the smaller house tucked into a copse of trees to the right of the main house, which he didn't wish to discuss. Unfortunately, he hadn't had an opportunity to warn Mattie and she pointed directly at it.

"That used to be our house before Mama died."

A pall of silence fell over the occupants of the buggy.

"Now I live with Grandfather, Grandpa Bud, Aunt Annie, Uncle Logan and Uncle Conner."

Doc recovered first, perhaps more accustomed to dealing with death's consequences. "It would appear you have lots of people to love you and take care of you."

"Yup. I surely do. Though Aunt Annie says sometimes I'm more nuisance than I'm worth." She paused and Dawson held his breath, hoping his daughter wasn't preparing another verbal explosive to drop on them. Now everyone would think she was neglected and maybe worse.

As if to prove his fears, a gasp came from the backseat. Dawson wouldn't allow himself to turn and see which of the ladies was the most shocked.

"But then," Mattie continued in a cheerful voice he hoped indicated she was well loved, "she kisses me right here." She touched the top of her head. "And says she doesn't regret it for a minute. She says life would be boring without me. That's right, isn't it, Papa?"

"Indeed it would." Though at the moment he could do with a little boredom. Dawson had heard Annie teasing Mattie about being a nuisance, usually when she'd gotten into mischief, but his guests did not have that information. He spoke to them all but his eyes went only to Isabelle.

"Mattie makes it sound like my sister resents her but that's not the case. She adores Mattie."

He broke from Isabelle's gaze to smile at his daughter. "Isn't that so, little one?"

"Uh-huh. She says she doesn't know what she'd do without me."

"That's sweet," Isabelle murmured. "It appears to be a fine arrangement for all involved."

"It is." He glanced over his shoulder again, saw Isabelle and Mattie eye one another with what he could only describe as longing. His insides twisted.

"Mattie, face front before you fall."

"Yes, Papa."

As his daughter turned around, he caught on her face an expression he hadn't seen before and was at a loss to interpret. But a shudder crossed his shoulders. He must protect Mattie from being hurt by dreaming impossible dreams about Isabelle. How was he to do that when he had cows to check on? And a town to rebuild? And a hundred details to take care of?

Isabelle wanted to pull little Mattie close and hug her. A motherless child surrounded by adults who put up with her, yet, at the same time, loved her. Something in Mattie's eyes convinced Isabelle the child wanted more...needed more. Though she had no reason to jump to such a conclusion. Nothing but the echo of her own heart.

However, they arrived at the ranch house and Isabelle didn't have time to dwell on it. She looked about. This was her chance to see ranch life, and if she used it to observe Mattie's home life, as well, who could judge her for that?

The house rose before them, solid and large as if built to withstand the challenges of nature. A wide veranda provided protection from the elements.

Dawson held his hand out to assist her to the ground. She meant to avoid looking directly at him but her gaze drew toward his and halted there. His blue eyes blazed a warning. Why? What had she done? She stumbled and he gripped her hand hard until she got her feet under her.

She hurried to the veranda, dismissing the moment as imaginary. He had nothing to fear from her and she wanted nothing from him. Turning to study her surroundings, she enjoyed a wonderful view of the treed mountains to the west. Her heart filled with strength and joy, and a Bible verse sprang to her mind. *As the mountains are round about Jerusalem, so the Lord is round about his people from henceforth even for ever.* Calmness filled her. She might find it impossible to trust mankind, but she knew and loved God, whom she could trust. A smile tugged at the corners of her mouth.

Dawson reached around her and pushed open the door. "Please, everyone, come inside." He waited for the others to precede him, Mattie leading the way. They entered a cloakroom with a low bench along three walls. Under the bench were several pairs of well-worn cowboy boots with toes tipped upward. Above the benches, hooks held coats and hats and odd bits of leather strapping and goodness knew what else. She longed to ask the use of everything she saw.

"So this is what a ranch house looks like." She hadn't meant to say the words aloud and hoped they indicated her fascination.

But Dawson had already stepped through one of the two doors leading from the cloakroom and indicated they should follow.

Grandfather Marshall hobbled toward them with the aid of his canes.

"Welcome to the Marshall Five Ranch. Come right in." They were in a large dining room. Leather-clad window seats circled the room beneath wide windows that allowed a generous view of the outside scene. A large table, covered with a white lace tablecloth and set for the meal, stood in the middle of the room. A wide archway opened to the sitting room and another, narrower door revealed a kitchen from which came the delicious aroma of a meal.

"Annie," Grandfather Marshall called. "Our guests are here."

A woman scurried into the room. A very young lady. This was Aunt Annie? She couldn't be more than eighteen or nineteen. Somehow Isabelle had expected a much older woman, wrongly assuming she was the eldest Marshall sibling. Dawson introduced his sister and the likeness was unmistakable—she was probably as tall as Isabelle herself, blonde with striking blue eyes.

A much smaller young woman waited in the doorway.

Isabelle couldn't help but stare at the second woman, who was in trousers and a shirt, her blond hair in a long braid down her back. She'd never seen a woman dressed in such a fashion and barely managed not to gasp. This was the West, she reminded herself. The Wild West, obviously.

Dawson introduced her. "Carly Morrison, Annie's friend and fellow troublemaker."

Isabelle wasn't sure he teased or was serious but both Carly and Annie laughed.

"We aren't troublemakers," Annie insisted.

Dawson's eyebrows reached for his hairline.

Carly grinned at Annie. "We just like to have fun."

Isabelle immediately liked the two girls. She and Kate used to have fun together until Dr. Baker's accident. She missed those times.

Annie took their coats, then indicated where they should sit.

"Can I sit by Miss Isabelle?" Mattie asked.

"I think you should stay beside me." Dawson guided her around the table to the chair beside him.

Isabelle refused to look at him or try to guess if he meant to keep his daughter away from her—he had no reason to think she would harm his child—or if he simply preferred to have Mattie beside him, where he could guide her manners. She looked at Mattie, though. "I can see you better this way."

Mattie favored her with a beaming smile. "I like that."

Sadie didn't immediately take her seat. "I can help with the meal."

"As can I," Kate added.

Isabelle was already seated. In her world, the cook served the food, but this wasn't her world and she needed to remember it. She pushed to her feet. "I'll help, as well."

Annie waved their offers aside. "We have it under control. Sit and relax. I know you've had a long, tiring day." She gave Carly a mischievous glance. "All we did was hang around the house cooking supper."

The elder Marshall chuckled as the girls returned to the kitchen. "After you get to know this pair you'll realize the unlikelihood of that story."

The girls in question carried in platters and bowls full of food and then sat down.

Grandfather Marshall signaled for attention. "I'll ask the blessing." In reverent, deep tones, he thanked God for all the blessings He'd bestowed. "Good food and new friends. Thank You. Amen."

There followed a flurry of passing bowls and platters from hand to hand—roast meat, turnips, creamy mashed potatoes, rich brown gravy and beets in a sweet-and-sour sauce. The food tickled every taste bud in her mouth. "Excellent fare. Annie, you are a good cook. If you ever want a job as such, I will gladly give my recommendation."

Conversation ground to a halt. Had she committed a faux pas? She glanced across to Dawson. He scowled.

She quirked her eyebrows questioningly but he offered no explanation and she slowly faced Annie.

Annie held her fork suspended above her plate. "I have a job here as cook, dishwasher, laundry lady to my brothers, my father and grandfather, plus caring for Mattie."

Isabelle sensed Dawson's silent disapproval but figured she might as well continue what she'd started. "It seems like a lot of work. Does Carly help you?"

Carly chuckled. "I live with my father and take care of him."

"And ride like a man," Annie added.

Carly shrugged. "One must do what one must do." She turned back to Isabelle. "Sometimes Annie needs help to keep this lot of men in line. That's where I come in."

Dawson snorted.

Grandfather Marshall grinned. "I do believe her father sends her over here in the hopes we'll teach her to be a lady."

Carly choked. "Don't ever give him such an idea." She shuddered visibly.

Isabelle couldn't tell if it was real or make-believe, but it brought laughter from those around the table and she allowed herself to relax. She might put her foot into things once in a while, but not out of malice. Only because she didn't quite know how to fit in with these people.

As if sensing her uneasiness, Kate squeezed her hand under the table. "It's a little hard to understand where everyone belongs in the picture, what with meeting so many people today."

"I expect that's true," Grandfather Marshall said. "But you'll soon have it figured out."

"I got it all figgered out already," Mattie said. "You—" she nodded toward Sadie "—are Miss Young, the teacher."

Sadie nodded. "That's right and I intend to start classes as soon as possible. All I need is a few tables and chairs and some books."

Mattie waited until Sadie finished then turned to the man at her father's other side. "And you are the new doctor."

Dr. Baker smiled. "I hope you aren't sick."

Mattie giggled. "Nope." She moved on to Kate. "You're the nurse. You help your father."

Kate tipped her head in acknowledgment. "That's correct."

"And you." She gave Isabelle wide-eyed study. "You…" She looked puzzled. "You're pretty and you're nice," she blurted out.

Isabelle's hands dropped to her lap and she stared at Mattie. Her throat closed off. She feared tears would burst free if she so much as opened her mouth. Was that all she was? Pretty but useless.

Dawson sat back as Annie and Carly removed the plates and serving dishes and brought out generous slices of chocolate cake. "Among the many things Annie does well is bake a chocolate cake that exceeds any I've ever tasted." Why did he look at Isabelle as he said those words? Why did he feel like he must defend their way of life?

"Thank you, big brother. Mama taught me how to bake."

He continued to watch Isabelle as she tasted a mouthful of the cake. Her eyes widened and she met Dawson's gaze. "This is very good. Indeed, as you say, the best I've ever tasted."

He released a gust of air as she shifted her attention to Annie to compliment her on her baking. He immediately informed himself that he wasn't hoping for some sign of appreciation of ranch life. He jammed an invisible fist into his thoughts.

"Annie, would it be possible for you to teach me how to make this cake…?" Isabelle paused. "Or is the recipe a family secret?"

Annie laughed. "I'll be happy to show you how to make it so long as you promise to keep the recipe to yourself."

Dawson had never before realized how much she sounded like their mother.

Isabelle held up her hand in a solemn salute. "I promise." She and Annie smiled at each other. A shiver raced across Dawson's shoulders. Bad enough Grandfather had decided Isabelle was like Grandmother. Even worse that Mattie was awestruck, but if Annie took a liking to her, he would have his hands full fending off their interest.

They finished the meal with tea and the ladies moved to the kitchen, Mattie trailing behind them. Dawson, his grandfather and the doctor, who asked the men to call him John, retired to the sitting room. John leaned his head back and soon snored. Poor man had had a long day.

Seeing their guest slept, Grandfather opened his current book and began to read. Dawson tried to do the same but his attention kept drifting to the sounds of talk and laughter from the kitchen. And why he should notice Isabelle's voice more keenly than the others didn't make sense. It wasn't as if she talked loudly. Or that he wanted to be aware of her.

"Papa?"

He jerked his head up at his daughter's voice. She stood in the doorway, holding Isabelle's hand.

His insides crackled.

"Papa, Miss Isabelle said she would put me to bed." Mattie left Isabelle's side to kiss her father's cheek. "Good night."

He held the child close. He could not let Isabelle do this. But how could he stop her without hurting Mattie? "I'll take you upstairs."

Mattie stiffened. "But, Papa, I asked her to. That's okay, isn't it?"

He could hear the tears building in her shaky voice.

"Allow the child this little pleasure," Grandfather said. "What harm can it do?"

Dawson could have reminded Grandfather of the sorrow Mattie had suffered when Violet left. But one look at his grandfather and he knew he would not win this one without making a scene. So he kissed Mattie on the cheek and slowly released her. "Good night, little one."

Mattie went to Grandfather for a hug and a kiss, then returned to Isabelle's side, took her hand and led her upstairs to the bedrooms.

Dawson followed with his eyes and listened until the bedroom door squeaked. Still he looked upward wishing he could intervene.

"She's a beautiful woman," Grandfather said.

"So you've said repeatedly."

"Seems Mattie is taken with her."

"I don't think that's a good thing."

Grandfather considered Dawson so long Dawson struggled not to squirm. Just when Dawson thought he might have to jerk to his feet to get away from the old man's study, Grandfather spoke. "Son, you can't use the same ruler to measure every woman."

"I have no idea what you mean." He could only hope his cold tone would discourage the older man.

Grandfather made a dismissive noise. "I know you well enough to know when you look at Isabelle, you see Violet. Or at least tell yourself you should."

"Grandfather, I have no opinion on her. I just met her. Time alone will determine what sort of woman she is."

"Time doesn't stand a chance against your preconceived ideas."

He would not respond. If he had preconceived ideas it was with good cause. He didn't take in a satisfactory breath until Isabelle descended the stairs and returned to the kitchen. Surely that would put an end to this ridiculous conversation.

"Like I said, Mattie needs a mother." Grandfather's words fell into the silence like an explosion.

Dawson jerked to his feet. "If I marry again, it will be an ordinary ranch woman. I don't intend to repeat a very bad mistake."

He didn't slow his steps until he reached the kitchen.

The women huddled together around the table and laughed about something.

He recognized the gleam in Annie's eyes. She was up to something. She and Carly often did things their fathers and brothers disapproved of. They'd even been known to visit Wolf Hollow, the rough mining town up the creek, until Pa had put a stop to it.

He shifted his gaze to Carly. Yes, they were up to something. His attention moved onward to Isabelle. The same spark of mischief filled her eyes. He'd seen that look before. In Violet's eyes as she outlined some adventure meant to relieve the boredom of her role of wife and mother. Despite what Grandfather said, there was something frighteningly like Violet in Isabelle.

"I need to take our guests home." He heard the sharp tone of his voice but hoped no one else would notice.

Annie rose. "I'll get the coats."

Kate headed for the sitting room. "I'll inform my father."

Carly stretched. "I best get home, too, before Father starts to worry." She slid her chair back but made no other move toward leaving.

Annie returned and Dawson waited for them all to don their outerwear, then led the guests out to the buggy and helped them aboard. He told himself it made no difference whether he helped Sadie, Kate or Isabelle. It was only common courtesy. But he had to stifle his reaction when Isabelle's hand rested in his.

Annoyance at Grandfather's suggestion he should be interested in this woman intermingled with the bitter memory of the years he'd spent married to Violet. In hindsight he realized he should never have married her. He hadn't known her long enough. He'd been flattered by her attention and mesmerized by her beauty and self-assurance. He'd been thrilled when she agreed to marry him. Too late he'd realized she saw him as another adventure.

Sadie kept up what little conversation there was during the trip home, talking about her plans to set up a temporary schoolroom. The others settled back, weary from their long day.

Dusk wrapped about the town as he reached Bella Creek. The air grew colder. He let Sadie out at the hotel and escorted her inside, waiting until she reached her door before he returned to the buggy. A few yards farther, he pulled up in front of the doctor's house. A figure stepped from the shadows.

"Doc?"

"What can I do for you?" Dr. Baker climbed down and went to the man.

"Got a bad hand."

"Come along."

Kate didn't wait for Dawson to help her down but hurried after her father. Soon a lamp glowed inside the examining room.

Isabelle took his hand as she stepped to the ground. She stared at the unlit living quarters and shivered. "It's dark."

He fought a brief mental war between his desire to keep his distance from this woman and the dictates of gentlemanly manners. The latter won out. "I'll go ahead and light a lamp."

Entering the house, he groped toward the kitchen, where he'd earlier noticed a lamp on the table. He lit it then went to the stove, stirred up the embers and added some wood.

"Thank you. I will handle it in the future."

He hadn't heard her step into the room and jerked about to face her. In the glow from the lamp, her features were golden, her smile gentle. She removed her hat and set it on the table. The light touched her hair, filling the dark strands with a fiery glow.

Why was he staring? He shook himself and bolted for the door. Forced himself to stop and face her. Now he could say all the things he hadn't been able to with Grandfather listening and dreaming an old man's dream on Dawson's behalf. "Miss Redfield, I must warn you not to encourage my daughter's fascination with you." He rushed on, ignoring the shock in her eyes. "She's young and vulnerable. I don't want to see her hurt."

Isabelle's eyes snapped. "You're suggesting I mean to hurt her?"

"Not on purpose but—" How did he say all he felt in a word or two? "She belongs here in the West, on a ranch."

"And I don't? And may I ask how you've come to that conclusion?"

His gaze lingered on the fur collar of her coat, then went down to the fine leather boots, also with fur lining.

She nodded, her expression icy. "I see."

"I doubt you do. But you're city and we're country." Before he could say more, he turned on his heel and strode away.

Chapter Three

Isabelle tossed and turned half the night. She was *city*. Perhaps that was a step up from being an heiress but ultimately it left her struggling with the same sense of frustration and rejection.

In the morning, Kate confronted her. "You seemed restless last night. What's bothering you?"

She told her friend what Dawson had said. "Even without knowing of my inheritance, he sees me as useless...worse, as a threat to his child's happiness."

Kate sat beside her on the bed. "We both know that isn't true."

Isabelle turned her palms upward in a sign of helplessness. "I *am* useless."

Kate hugged her. "I think you can do anything you set your mind to and you know it."

Slowly, Isabelle let the truth of Kate's words settle into her thoughts. She didn't have quite as much faith in her abilities as did Kate but neither was she prepared to let Dawson's opinion deter her.

"I want to help you. I thought I could take care of the house while you assist your father."

"I'd appreciate that."

Her resolve firmly in place, Isabelle went to the kitchen to prove her usefulness. But it was easier said than done. She had no idea how to prepare breakfast. Their pantry had been stocked while they were out at the Marshall Ranch. Only because of those generous gifts did Kate and the doctor have a satisfying meal.

"I need help." She didn't mind confessing her inability to Kate.

"Let's pray about it." Kate took her hand. They bowed their heads and took turns praying aloud. When Isabelle first learned this practice of spontaneous prayers from Kate, she'd been surprised but soon embraced the idea. Kate called it "letting go of things and letting God take care of them."

The door to the doctor's waiting room opened and closed, and Kate and her father left to see to the caller.

Isabelle went to her trunk and removed her Bible. She'd been raised to attend church and say her prayers. Her mother had taught her to trust God, but not until she met Kate four years ago at a church event did Isabelle's faith begin to grow. Over the years, with Kate's patient teaching, she'd grown to see that God wanted to be part of every day, every action. Her Bible fell open to a passage she frequently read. *Whatsoever ye do in word or deed, do all in the name of the Lord Jesus.* She closed her eyes as the familiar lonesome ache sucked at her insides. *God, I feel so useless. What can I do to Your honor and glory? Show me. Oh, please, show me where I fit.*

What did she mean? She was the heiress Isabelle Redfield. According to her lawyer, who was trustee of the funds, she had a lot of money and taking care of it took a lot of work. But somehow her lawyer had done it without her input for years. She saw no reason he couldn't continue to do so. She wouldn't have access to the money she'd inherited until she turned twenty-five or married. But being in charge of a vast amount of money meant nothing to her.

She wanted to do something that had meaning for *her*.

She managed to make a satisfying lunch…again because of the food supplied by others. It didn't take long to sweep the floors and dust the shelves. As she worked, she tried to think what she would make for the next meal. If only she had a book…

That gave her an idea. Surely there would be one at the store. With money in her pocket, she headed across the street to the Marshall Mercantile store and stepped inside. At once, a myriad of smells assaulted her. Most of them she couldn't identify but they carried hints of men at work. Her gaze lit on an array of hammers, shovels and axes.

Immediately she pictured Dawson swinging an ax as he deftly chopped wood. Had he been the one, or one of those, who'd filled the woodshed at the doctor's house? Maybe he would come by again to replenish their supply. No. She was certain he wouldn't. At least, not if he thought she'd be there. He'd made his opinion of her quite evident. She shook her head, trying to drive away those foolish thoughts, and shifted her gaze to a different display. Several oil lamps and, farther along, tins that would be used to carry the coal oil.

"May I help you?" A man's voice drew her attention to the other side of the store where household items filled the shelves. She knew him to be Dawson's uncle George. They'd been introduced yesterday. He was another big man.

She made her way to the counter. "I expect my request is rather odd." After all, the women out here would know how to prepare meals and baked goods. "Is it possible you have a book to help me learn how to cook and bake and all those other things I need to know?"

The man gave her a kindly look. "Your mother didn't teach you?"

"No. She died when I was young and my cousin gave me a home." No need to add that neither home saw the need for her to learn such skills. Instead, her lessons had included doing fancy needlework, reading the classics, proper etiquette and learning to be a refined young lady. Of course, those lessons were of value, but they left her ill-equipped to manage a household on her own, and she was determined to run the house for Kate and her father.

"I'm sorry about your mother but I might have a book that will help you. If I can just remember where I put it." He ducked down to paw through the contents of the cupboard beneath the counter. "Never thought I'd be able to sell the book, so I stuck it away somewhere." His voice echoed as he dug further into the shelves. "Ah, yes. Here it is." He straightened, turned to one side to blow dust from the book. "*A Guide to Practical Housewifery*. Think that will do?" He handed her the volume.

She opened it to the index and read some of the chapter headings. *Soup. Fish. Oysters. Meat.* Several kinds of cakes. *Food for the Sick. Remedies. Other Practical Matters.* She flipped through a few pages. The instructions looked easy to follow, as if written for someone in her situation. "It's perfect. I'll take it. How much?"

He named a sum that she found more than satisfactory, and she counted out the coins to pay him.

From the back room, Isabelle heard the murmur of Sadie's voice. Sadie had convinced everyone that a temporary classroom could be set up in the back room of the store and within a couple of hours the transformation had been wrought.

"Did all the expected students come for classes?" Isabelle asked.

"Only a few showed up this morning but she has a full house this afternoon. It's rather pleasant to have the children traipse through the store and to hear their voices."

A child's voice reached them and Isabelle cocked her head toward the sound. "Is that Mattie?"

Mr. Marshall nodded. "She's a special little girl." He studied the door leading to the temporary classroom. "We've all done our best to give her a good life but the child needs a mother."

"Doesn't she have Annie?"

"Don't get me wrong. Annie does well. But doesn't she deserve a life of her own? That girl is barely more than a child herself and has spent four years taking care of her father and brothers, not to mention Grandfather. And Mattie on top of it."

He shook his head. "You know, a number of unmarried women have tried to earn Dawson's interest but he rebuffs them. That man needs to forget how his wife treated him and realize not all women are like that. But then, I shouldn't be gossiping like an old woman, should I?" He turned his attention back to her purchase. "Would you like this wrapped?"

She started to say no, but a horse rode by and she automatically glanced out the window. She didn't care to have everyone in town know what she'd bought. "Yes, please." It took but a moment for Mr. Marshall to wrap the book and hand it to her.

"I wish you all the best," he said with a kindly smile.

As she made her way across the street, she mulled over the storekeeper's words. What did he mean about Dawson's wife?

Not that it was any of her concern. She had other things to occupy her mind, and she hurried into the house, where she went immediately to the kitchen, sat down and began to study her new book.

Thankfully, the kitchen windows faced the alley, so she couldn't see Dawson and the other man working on the school.

But with every ring of a hammer, every shush-hushing of a saw cutting through wood, with every muted sound of one man talking to the other, she thought of him and wondered about his marriage.

Forcing her attention back to the book before her, she chose what she meant to make and gathered together the ingredients.

Later in the day, a tray of oatmeal cookies cooled on the table and Isabelle smiled with satisfaction. She'd prepared vegetable soup for supper and it simmered on the stove.

If only she had someone to share her success with, but Kate and her father had gone out of town to attend an injured miner. A glance at the clock over the doorway showed the time had come for the children to be released from school, and she hurried to the window overlooking the street and watched as, one by one or in groups of two or more, the children ran from the store, laughing and calling to each other.

Mattie exited, chattering away to the girl at her side. Isabelle curled her hands. All these cookies should be enjoyed by a child returning from school.

She turned away and carefully put the cookies into containers. She tried not to think of Mattie and how much she'd enjoyed putting the child to bed, tucking her in just as her mother once tucked her in. For a moment she'd dreamed of spending more time with Mattie, but Dawson's warning made that impossible. Isabelle was not the kind of woman he wanted Mattie to associate with. What had she done to make him judge her so harshly?

School was over and Mattie ran across the street to join Dawson.

When he rose this morning he had hoped he could escape to the hills but Grandfather had had other ideas.

"Miss Young suggested she start holding classes in the back room of the store. Seems a reasonable idea. Ride on in and let George know. Help him arrange things. And seeing as your brothers are away, get back to construction on the school."

He'd protested, reminded his grandfather of the cow herd he needed to look after, pointed out that the work didn't require the presence of a Marshall. He might as well have talked to one of the empty chairs. In the end he did as Grandfather said simply because he figured the sooner he did so, the sooner he could ride out to check on his cows. Mattie had demanded to go with him to town because she didn't want to miss the opening of school.

Uncle George thought turning his storeroom into a classroom was a good idea. He, Dawson, Sadie and a couple of others hanging about the store had the room cleaned out in less than an hour and set six tables and a dozen chairs in place. Uncle George had arranged some empty shelves and Sadie placed her books on them.

There hadn't been time to notify everyone, but word got around, and after lunch the town children were all in attendance.

He should be pleased at the resumption of classes, but it meant Mattie would be in town, where she would see Isabelle Redfield far too often. His brows knotted. Why did that name seem familiar? He searched his memory but could think of no reason.

Dawson had spent the day working on the school, which, unfortunately, stood next door to the doctor's house, allowing him plenty of opportunity to observe the coming and going of people seeking medical attention. Doc and Kate would be busy. How did Isabelle spend her time? His gaze went often to the wooden wall.

He'd pretended not to watch when she dumped wash water on the two bushes someone had planted to replace those destroyed by the fire. He told himself he needed to stretch his back when he straightened to observe her fetch some pieces of wood for the stove. He had to order his feet not to run over and offer to help. But when she went out the front door and crossed the street, his hands grew still. His eyes followed her every step. Did she look both ways to make sure no wagon or horse bore down on her? He eased out a sigh when she stepped into the store. Someone needed to keep an eye on her.

With a groan of frustration he realized he had been doing exactly that and bent over his work. But mentally he counted the moments until he heard the door across the street squeak open and had to check and see if Isabelle returned.

She'd stood on the steps of the store, smiling at the package in her hand. What had she purchased in Uncle

George's store that brought such a pleased look to her face? Not that he cared. He hoped he'd made himself clear on that matter.

Then she'd picked up her skirts and stepped into the street, pausing to let a wagon go by.

Dawson had waited until she disappeared into the house then measured the board for the schoolhouse wall. He measured again to be certain then turned to mark the piece of wood on the sawhorse. What were the measurements? He took the tape and again stretched it out. This time he promised himself he would not be distracted by wondering what Isabelle did all day long behind the walls of the house next door.

He cut the wood, more than a little relieved when it fit perfectly, and nailed it into place. Only one other man had joined him in the work and the sound of his hammer echoed Dawson's. He let that thud drive all wayward thoughts from his head throughout the afternoon.

Now that school was out and Mattie with him, he would be able to concentrate better.

He swung Mattie in the air. "Hey, little one. How was school?"

"Fun. I like Miss Young. You know what she said?" Mattie rushed on with her own answer. "If I do my work well and keep my shelf tidy, there will be a surprise for me. Well, for all of us. She put a gold star on my printing. Said it was very neat. And she read us a real nice story about a crippled boy and his horse. She said she would read a chapter every day." Mattie let out a long sigh as if she had been holding back this information for a long time.

"I'm pleased you had a good day. Now play out of the way while I finish work." He could put in another two hours before it was time to go home and Mattie was good about amusing herself.

"Can I go over to the doctor's house?"

She meant could she go see Isabelle. They'd had this discussion on the way to town. He did not want Mattie going there. He now reiterated what he had told her earlier.

"You haven't been invited, so you have to stay here."

With a little sigh, she went to the corner of the yard that butted up to the doctor's yard and sat cross-legged on the scraped ground. Soon the grass would grow back but, for now, the ground was bare. Mattie would get dirty but he couldn't expect her to keep clean while she played here.

He turned his attention back to the construction, glancing up often to check on Mattie. She collected an assortment of wood chips and charred wood and arranged them around her, then sat and stared at the doctor's house. He studied her. Could she see in the kitchen window? Did she see Isabelle? He could hardly forbid her to watch the house…though he would if it was possible. Having to work beside the doctor's house provided far too many opportunities for Mattie to hope for a glimpse of her.

Isabelle had been all Mattie talked about on their ride to town. "Miss Isabelle tucked me in real good. She pulled the covers to my chin and snuggled them tight to my side. She said I was like a little cocoon. She said her mama used to do that for her. She sounded sad when she said that because both her mama and papa are dead." Mattie had grown quiet.

He hadn't known that, and for a moment his feelings softened.

A lonely note filled Mattie's voice when she spoke again. "I think she's sad. She told me she never quit missing her mama. It's like a little shadow that follows her everywhere."

He wondered if Mattie had absorbed some of Isabelle's sadness. His determination rebounded. He must make sure the woman never again got a chance to talk to Mattie alone, but before he could think how he would stop it, Mattie laughed. "She tickled me and made me giggle."

He should never have let Isabelle put Mattie to bed and wouldn't have except for the glowering presence of his grandfather.

He glanced up and stared. Mattie had disappeared.

His heart kicking into a gallop, he straightened and looked around. His lungs released suddenly as he saw her picking through the sack of nails. They tightened again when she put nails between her teeth.

"Mattie." He kept his voice much calmer than he felt for fear she'd suck in a nail. "Please don't put nails in your mouth."

"Why? You do."

"I'm an adult."

She gave him a look he had not seen before. He could only describe it as disbelief laced with accusation. Then she stalked back to the corner, where she planted her arms over her chest with a little huff.

A minute later, when he again checked on her, she had again disappeared.

He circled the building and found her climbing on the stack of lumber. A board slipped and she teetered. He crossed the remaining few feet in seconds and caught her.

"Mattie, please stay off the wood. You could be hurt." He set her on the ground.

She dusted herself off and, with head high, marched

away to the far corner of the yard and he returned to his work.

He barely took his eyes off her before she was again out of sight. He closed his eyes and calmed his frustration before he went in search of her. He circled the school twice and didn't see her. This was so unlike his daughter he didn't know what to make of it.

"Have you seen Mattie?" he asked of the other man, who had nailed a whole lot more boards to his side of the building than Dawson had on his.

"Yeah, she just went by." He nodded in the direction he meant.

Dawson continued circling the building. But Mattie stayed ahead of him or behind him, purposely avoiding him, causing him to waste time.

He changed direction and waited at a corner hoping to catch her. He heard a little giggle and tensed. As soon as she stepped into sight, he scooped her up.

She squealed. "You scared me." But rather than laugh, she frowned.

"Mattie, I have work to do. Stop playing games." He set her down and returned to the piece of wood he meant to saw into the proper length.

A few minutes later he wasn't surprised to glance up and find her gone. Instead of looking for her, he put his tools away and went to speak to the other man.

"I'm headed home."

The man looked at the sun. "Early, ain't it?"

"Gotta take Mattie home."

"We ain't getting much help on this, are we?" He tipped his head to the partially finished building. "Teacher and kids deserve a schoolhouse, wouldn't you say?"

"I'm doing my best." No reason he should feel he had to defend himself and yet he did.

"Maybe you could find someplace for your daughter to go after school."

"I'll see what I can do." He'd ask Annie to come to town and pick her up. "I'll be back tomorrow."

He found Mattie hiding behind the lumber. "Come on. We're going home."

Without a word, she fell in at his side but shied away when he reached for her hand. "Mattie, it isn't like you to act this way." She didn't answer and remained surprisingly quiet on the way home.

Over dinner, he asked Annie, "Could you ride into town and pick up Mattie after school so I don't have to leave off work until later?"

She stared at him. "I could if I had nothing else to do but I'm rather busy that time of day. And every day," she added softly.

Guilt stole up his insides, especially when Grandfather looked at him so accusingly.

Annie continued. "I'm sure there is someone in town who could help you out."

Grandfather nodded. "Why not ask that nice Miss Isabelle? I like that gal. She's got spunk. I could tell that the first time I saw her."

"Why, that's an excellent idea," Annie said.

Dawson took note of the way she and Grandfather smiled at each other. Had they been conspiring together? He could tell them not to bother but what was the use? Neither would change their minds on his behalf.

"Oh, please, Papa. I'd like to stay with her."

He hated that Mattie sounded so hopeful. "I'll find

someone in town. Maybe one of the older girls." He returned to his meal.

"You know, Miss Isabelle reminds me of your grandmother."

"So you said." Dawson barely remembered his grandmother but had grown up listening to tales of her efficiency and bravery. How she raised the finest chickens in the country and butchered two every Saturday for Sunday dinner. He could not see a city girl like Isabelle doing that. Grandfather had told the boys how Grandmother had helped him put in the crop one year when he'd injured his hand badly and other stories, like— Well, never mind. "Grandmother was no city girl."

Grandfather chuckled. "You're wrong. She'd never been on a farm until we married and I took her home. We did all our courting in the city. But she never once balked. Whatever needed to be done, she dug in and did it."

Why had Dawson never heard before that his grandmother was a city woman? Was Grandfather making it up? But he'd never known the old man to be anything but painfully honest.

He said nothing more, though he could tell Grandfather would have liked to discuss it further. No doubt he would have liked to point out how well Grandmother had adjusted. That was a different era. Grandmother might have been raised in the city but likely had learned how to work.

Tomorrow, he'd make arrangements for someone to care for Mattie.

The next day, he arrived a little early for school and waited at the door for the students to arrive. The oldest girl was Tom Shearer's daughter, Kitty. Far as he could remember of what he'd heard, the girl would be perhaps thirteen. He'd seen her often enough, thought her rather placid, frequently at the tail end of a group of kids. But she would be old enough to watch Mattie.

She approached now and he called her. She jerked to a halt and stared. "Oh, hi, Mr. Marshall."

"Hi, Kitty. I wonder if you might take Mattie home with you after school until it's time for me to leave. I'd pay you a few cents. You can ask your mama at noon if it's okay."

The information seemed to seep in slowly and then she nodded. "Sure. Ma won't mind."

He turned to Mattie. "You go home with Kitty after school and I'll pick you up there. Okay?"

"Okay." Mattie skipped away cheerfully, Kitty plodding along behind her.

Dawson stared after the pair. He'd expected resistance on Mattie's part, so this quick compliance was a pleasant surprise.

Relieved that his problem was solved, he returned to work on the school.

Isabelle spent the day pretending she didn't hear men working next door. And if she glanced in that direction when she went outside for something, it was only because she liked to see the progress on the building. When the time came for the children to be released from school, she hurried to the window overlooking the street, hoping for a glimpse of little Mattie. The girl had stolen her heart. It hurt to know Dawson didn't want her to spend time with his daughter.

She watched as one by one, or in groups of two or more, the children ran from the store, laughing and calling to each other.

The rush ended but she hadn't seen Mattie. Had she missed the child? Or did she remain at the store with her great-uncle?

She began to turn away when the door opened again and Mattie exited in the company of an older girl. Mattie chattered away. The older girl nodded once or twice but seemed bored with Mattie's conversation.

Isabelle thought of the jar of cookies. Kate and her father had certainly appreciated them, but how she longed to share them with a child.

It was not to be and she turned her attention to supper preparation, though some of the joy of serving the Bakers had leaked out of the work.

She had potatoes prepared to cook, carrots scraped and a jar of canned meat from the amply supplied pantry ready to heat when banging on the door surprised her. She opened it. "Dawson, you startled me."

"Is she here?"

She shrank back from the anger in his voice. She guessed he must mean Mattie but she could be mistaken. "Who are you looking for?"

"Mattie, of course." He pulled open the door and strode in without waiting for an invite.

She stood back and watched him, wary of his ire.

He glanced around the kitchen, saw Mattie wasn't there and tramped through to the sitting room. Of course, she wasn't there either, and he faced her, a scowl darkening his features. "Is she in your bedroom?"

Her cheeks burned. The man was far too bold and overbearing. "She isn't here. Why would you think she is?"

He scrubbed at his chin. "I don't know what to think.

She never acted like this before you—" He seemed to think better of finishing his sentence.

"Before I came?" She didn't wait for an answer. Didn't need to. His eyes said it all. "You're blaming me for her behavior?" Her anger flared to match his. "I've spent only a matter of hours with her. You've spent six years with her. How could I have that much influence?"

"I don't know." He didn't shout but it felt like he had.

"I can see you're upset about something. Perhaps if you told me why, I could help."

"How?"

She understood what he didn't say. What could she—a city woman—do in any situation out here in the West? But she wouldn't let him know how much his judgment hurt. "I don't know. Maybe I could say who I saw her with. Or at least defend myself." Her calm exterior seemed to get through to him and he let out a blast of air as if he'd forgotten to breathe.

"Who did you see her with and when?"

She described the older girl. "They left the store when school let out."

"That's Kitty. I arranged for her to watch Mattie after school so I could work. We need to get the school built as soon as possible," he said as if defending himself.

She saw no need to say otherwise because she agreed.

He continued. "When I went to Kitty's parents' house to pick her up, Kitty was in her room reading. She came out when her mother called. I asked where Mattie was and Kitty looked surprised, like she'd forgotten she was supposed to watch her. She said, 'I guess she went to find you.' But she isn't at the school, so I thought she might have come here." He groaned and grabbed the back of the nearest chair as if he might collapse without its support.

Mattie was missing! Isabelle couldn't help but recall the child playing in the street the day of her arrival. Was this how she was cared for? And yet he saw Isabelle as a danger to his child?

"Sit down and let's think about where she might have gone."

He sank to the chair. His hands dangled between his knees.

Dawson looked so dejected, she longed to offer him comfort, assure him she shared his concern about his daughter, but she guessed he wouldn't welcome it, so she sat across the table.

"Where would she go in town? Perhaps to some friends?"

"I suppose she might have gone to visit a friend." His head came up and his eyes found hers, his full of despair. She hoped hers offered comfort and encouragement.

"I need to go see."

She felt his worry clear through her body. It tensed every muscle, stung every nerve. "Do you want me to come and help you look?" Not that she could offer much in the way of assistance, but a missing six-year-old was frightening. She couldn't allow herself to even think of what might have happened to her.

Hope filled his eyes, replaced quickly with doubt and uncertainty and then hardness.

She knew before he answered what he'd say.

"I'll manage on my own. But thanks for the offer." He pushed to his feet.

Even though she'd expected his reply, the words still hurt. She schooled her face to reveal nothing of what she felt. "If she happens to show up here, I'll keep her until you return."

He hesitated before he murmured, "Thanks."

She stood in the doorway as he left, his long legs eating up the distance. She watched until he was out of sight. Still she stared down the street, praying Mattie was safe and sound, had simply been distracted in her play and forgotten she had been told to stay with this Kitty girl.

Until you return. Why did her words ring in his ears like a welcome when he'd been anything but welcoming? And he wasn't about to change his mind. He was only doing what he thought best, even if it was hard and Mattie felt it unfair.

Where was Mattie? Her name echoed endlessly in his head. She'd never before disappeared like this. People didn't disappear. Hadn't he told her that often enough?

He went from home to home asking after her. No one had seen her since school.

He turned back to the center of town, taking a different route, watching for his daughter. *Dear God, reveal her to me.*

Searching on foot took far too long and he headed for the livery barn and his horse. He'd left Jumper in a small corral with hay. He called the horse to him and led him into the barn to saddle him.

The interior was dim, so he heard Mattie before he saw her huddled in the corner.

He squatted down. "Mattie, what are you doing here? Do you know how worried I've been when you weren't with Kitty?" Relieved and angry at the same time, he didn't immediately reach for his daughter, but at the watchful, waiting look on her face, his anger fled and he held out his arms.

She didn't move.

He sat on the dusty floor and lifted her to his lap. "Care to tell me what's going on?"

She allowed him to hold her but didn't snuggle close. He closed his eyes against the pain this stiffness brought to his heart.

"Kitty didn't want to do anything. I was bored."

"I see." He knew there was more to it than that. Mattie had always been good at amusing herself.

"She doesn't talk to me at all. I decided to wait here until time to go home."

He smiled at the irony of her sitting in a dark corner in preference to Kitty's company. "Seems a little boring."

One shoulder came up to indicate she didn't care. "I'll wait for you here after school."

"Oh, little one. That's not a good idea."

"It's okay."

"No, it's not. You need to do more than sit in the dark." He felt like his little girl was fading into the shadows. He wanted to hold her tight and protect her from every threat. Including Isabelle? His answer should be a sure and certain *yes*, but all he found was uncertainty.

Without trying, she had turned his world into chaos.

Mattie sat up and faced him. "I could go to Miss Isabelle's. She'd let me stay with her. I know she would. And I'd be so good and so happy." She poured drama into her plea. "Please, Papa. I'd like that and so would she."

"How can you be so certain she would agree?"

She jumped up and grabbed his hand, trying to tug him to his feet. When that didn't work, she put her back to him and leaned forward, her weight pushing at his hands.

Loving this return to normal, he curled his arm about

her waist and drew her to his chest. "You know you will never be strong enough to move me." He bussed a kiss on her neck as he always did when they played this game.

She giggled. "There's more than one way to get you to move."

"So you said, but you can't always believe Aunt Annie and Grandfather."

"Don't let them hear you say that."

He laughed outright at her droll sense of humor. "You can be sure I won't." He pretended to let her pull him to his feet and lead him from the barn. He told himself it was all part of the game for her to continue pulling him along the street and right to the back screen door of the doctor's house, where Isabelle stood as if watching and waiting for them to come. *Until you return.* Like coming home, he thought. A smiling woman to welcome him.

"You found her." She threw open the door and ran out to hug Mattie.

Mattie clung to her neck.

Dawson watched, confused by the way his resistance mingled with relief.

"Papa wants to know if I can stay here after school while he works." The words burst from Mattie before Dawson could think to warn her he hadn't agreed to such an arrangement.

His mind raced. Spending time with Isabelle was not a good idea. Mattie would grow more interested in the woman. What would happen to his little girl when Isabelle grew tired of living away from the city?

Her gaze came to his, questioning, going from disbelief to wonderment. "Really?" The word seemed to come on a gentle breeze.

Mattie tugged on his hand. "See? I knew she wouldn't mind."

He tried to think how to extricate himself from this situation. But on the other hand, it might provide the perfect solution. Mattie would be where he could see her and she'd get this infatuation out of her system. "It will only be for two or three hours." Then, as if he needed a more reasonable explanation, he added, "It's important to get this town rebuilt."

Mattie squealed her delight.

Isabelle smiled brightly.

Dawson felt his world wobble. He knew he would regret this choice.

Chapter Four

Isabelle stared out the window long after Dawson and Mattie had disappeared. After a few moments, Kate came to her side. "I couldn't help but overhear your conversation. Are you sure it's a good idea for you to let her stay here?"

Isabelle jerked about to stare at her friend. "Do you think I'm a bad influence on her? Like Dawson does?" She had no illusions. He'd asked for her assistance simply out of necessity and because Mattie had frightened him by disappearing.

Kate gave Isabelle a sideways hug. "I was thinking of you. I'm afraid you'll get hurt."

Isabelle shivered. She'd already been hurt once by Dawson's comment that she didn't fit in. He hadn't changed his mind about that. "I like little Mattie."

"I know. Promise me you'll be careful not to get too involved."

"I'll just have her after school for an hour or two." She knew that wasn't what Kate meant. But her warning had come too late. Isabelle's heart had gone where it wasn't welcome, and whether she got a chance to spend time with Mattie or not, she would not come away from this without more hurt, if only from the knowledge that she didn't fit in.

Sighing softly, she turned from the window. "I want God to use me to help Mattie. Nothing more. Nothing less." Because she must confine herself to what was possible.

"Then let's pray for that." Kate took Isabelle's hand and bowed her head. "Our Father who art in heaven. Thank You for giving Isabelle this opportunity, especially after Dawson made it sound like he'd never allow it. We ask You to use Isabelle. Give her wisdom and words to help a little girl deal with the facts of her life. And, God, I ask You to protect Isabelle's heart. I don't want to see her wounded again. Amen."

Isabelle's lungs filled fully for the first time in the last hour. "Thank you." She squeezed Kate's hand. She'd gladly go ahead with this plan even knowing she might be hurt in the end. One thing her life had taught her— she could survive pain. And she'd gladly bear such in exchange for the opportunity to spend time with Mattie. Yes, she would also see more of Dawson, but she had yet to decide if that was a good thing or not.

Why did she feel this attraction to him when he saw her as unsuitable and someone who would never fit in?

The only answer she could give herself was that she'd seen tender moments in him, in how he dealt with Mattie. A man of honor and integrity with a capacity for deep, enduring love. And, she warned herself, a man who had high expectations of others.

She shook off the warning and set supper on the table. No patients required the doctor's attention that night, so Kate helped her clean up the kitchen then suggested a walk.

They roamed the streets of the town, pausing often to speak to people sitting on their porches or working in their yards. The town's people welcomed them, asked how they liked the place and made comments about the un-seasonably warm weather...usually following it up with a dire warning that it wouldn't last. A man with a star on his chest stopped as they walked on the path across from the church. She would guess him to be about her own age or a little more. He had brown hair, brown eyes and a deep, grooved smile. A strong-looking man, though she began to think all men in western Montana were strong and handsome. The sign on the building behind him read Sheriff.

"Howdy, ladies. Pleasant evening, isn't it? Allow me to introduce myself. Jesse Hill. How are you liking Bella Creek?"

"It's so peaceful and quiet," Isabelle said. "I've always lived in a city and there is constant noise." She chuckled. "I suppose it's your job to keep it peaceful and quiet."

"I do my best," Jesse said. "Saturday nights are the busiest and noisiest but most of the rowdies head on over to Wolf Hollow, where they're free to carouse." He fell into step with them as they continued on their way home. "Dawson is supposed to make sure you folk are feeling welcomed and have everything you need. Is he doing his job?"

Kate jabbed Isabelle in the ribs with her elbow. Isa-belle looked at her friend in surprise. What was that for?

Her expression innocent, Kate answered the sheriff. "He's doing his job just fine."

Isabelle still didn't know why Kate was so amused.

In her opinion, Dawson had failed completely at making them feel welcome, though he'd perhaps offered her a second chance by allowing Mattie to spend time with her.

The sheriff escorted them across the street to their door. "Good night, ladies. If you need someone to remind Dawson of his responsibilities, let me know." He laughed as if he'd told a good joke. "Might not do any good but I can try. Dawson is as stubborn as a long-eared mule."

Isabelle watched him stride away, her heart sinking like a rock. Seemed she had little hope of making Dawson see her as more than a city woman.

The next day, Dawson continued to work on the schoolhouse. Still just one man showed up. The expected help always had excuses. Had to get firewood. Needed to milk the cow. A pig to butcher. Company coming. Perhaps when his father and Conner and Logan got back, there would be a little more manpower on the scene.

What had they found out about the cows? Had they found his herd? He could only hope and pray they'd survived the winter.

He lifted his head and sniffed. His mouth watered at the ginger aroma. If he wasn't mistaken, someone had gingerbread fresh out of the oven. He glanced across the street to Miss Daisy's. Her customers would be lining up for generous slices for dessert. He'd brought a lunch prepared by Annie, but he mentally added a trip to the restaurant after he'd eaten the sandwiches.

As noon hour drew closer, the delicious aroma caused his stomach to growl. Working across from Miss Daisy's made it hard to put off dinner.

The doctor had a steady stream of patients. Several

times he heard Kate speak to someone in the waiting room as the door opened and closed.

She worked hard as her father's assistant.

He tried to picture Isabelle reading in one of the big chairs he'd helped put in the front room but she refused to stay there, even in his thoughts. Instead, she stirred something on the stove and turned to someone at the table, smiling with such warmth he almost swallowed the nail he held between his lips.

No, he informed himself. He did not see himself at the table sharing the meal with her. Besides, she didn't know how to cook. He knew that because Annie had told him she said so.

All this smelling food and thinking about food proved too much to resist. He set aside his measuring tape and called to his coworker. "I'm knocking off for dinner."

"I'll head home for my meal, then."

Dawson hunkered down against the raw wood of the wall and opened the lunch sack. Roast-beef sandwiches on thick slices of Annie's bread. She was a fine cook. She did a good job of caring for all of them. But something nagged at the back of his thoughts. Did he and the other men in the family expect she would continue to care for them? She was young, only nineteen. Wouldn't there come a time she would want her own family?

Then what would he do? Who would take care of Mattie for him?

And why did his gaze go to the wall of the doctor's house only a few feet away from where he sat? For that matter, why had he sat facing that house when he could have gone to the other side of the school and perched on one of the benches in the town square?

It wasn't as if he thought Isabelle—or someone like

her, he determinedly inserted into the thoughts—would provide Mattie with the love and care she deserved.

Though she was obviously fond of Mattie and Mattie of her.

He jolted to his feet, stuffed the rest of his sandwich into his mouth and strode across the street into Miss Daisy's Eatery. A half a dozen customers sat at the tables as Miss Daisy's sister, Dorie, bustled about carrying full plates out to the tables and taking empty ones back to the kitchen.

"Good day, Dawson," Dorie called. "Find yourself a chair. I'll be right with you." She ducked out of sight before he could tell her all he came for was a huge piece of that gingerbread. The spicy scent still filled his nostrils. It half drove a man mad.

He sat at an empty table, politely refusing several invitations to join others. As soon as Dorie returned, he made his request.

"No gingerbread today, I'm afraid," Dorie said. "Our dessert is rice pudding."

"Fine. Bring me that." He could hardly say it wasn't what he'd had in mind.

As she went to get it, Dawson wondered if his nose had lied to him. The pudding was fine, served with a generous amount of thick cream, but rather bland compared to what he'd been smelling half the morning.

He finished and paid the bill, thanking both Dorie and Daisy, who stuck her head out of the kitchen to greet him, and then he returned to the school. The spicy smell again called to him. He sniffed, turned full circle to pinpoint the source and followed his nose right to the back door of the doctor's house. Before he could think to stop himself, he knocked.

Isabelle opened the door and stared at him. He wished

he could tell if he saw surprised welcome or surprised unwelcome in her eyes. Or perhaps he saw only guardedness. After all, he'd warned her to stay away from Mattie and him, and then days later he'd asked if Mattie could stay with her after school. It was enough to convince her he didn't know his own mind.

The overwhelming smell of gingerbread and the sight of generous portions on three plates at the table made him forget all the warnings he'd given himself. "Something smells mighty fine in here."

Isabelle blinked back all emotion from her eyes and stepped aside to wave him in. "Would you care to join us for dessert?"

"Don't mind if I do." He flipped his hat to the hook by the door and sat beside the doctor as Isabelle cut him a piece of gingerbread.

Kate passed him a pitcher of cream and he poured on a generous amount.

"Can I offer you coffee, as well?" Isabelle hovered by the stove.

"I'd appreciate it." He waited until she set a steaming cup in front of him and sat down across the table. He delayed until she picked up her spoon to eat her own dessert before he allowed himself to taste the food that had been teasing him for half the morning. "Umm, this is delicious."

"Thank you." Isabelle regarded him solemnly.

"You made it?" Did he have to sound so surprised? Not that he wasn't, but did he have to show it? "I—"

"You can't believe I'm capable of making anything?"

The doctor concentrated on his food but Kate watched Dawson with interest.

He felt like he walked on soap bubbles and any movement would burst them, leaving him floundering for footing. "I suppose I am a little surprised."

"I made this without help." No doubting the challenge in her voice. Then she smiled, wreathing her face in humor. "I'll admit it's my very first attempt at making a cake."

"You did well." He ate another mouthful to show his approval and carefully avoided looking directly at her. His gaze slid past her to the stove. A pot held a rich-looking stew. She'd made that, too? He shifted his attention further to the cupboard. A bit of brown store paper lay folded with the string beside it and on top was a book. He tilted his head slightly to read the spine. *A Guide to Practical Housewifery.*

Was this what she had purchased at the store? And what did it mean? That she meant to learn some practical skills? He tried to think how such a decision would affect him. A flash of his earlier forbidden thought came to mind. Isabelle at the stove…a man at the table. He would not put himself in that chair. No, nothing had changed and he needed to ask the doctor for some kind of medicine if he thought it had.

He finished his piece of gingerbread, resisted the urge to lick the plate and managed to say "No, thanks," to the offer of a second helping. Satisfied as he hadn't been after Miss Daisy's rice pudding, he leaned back in his chair and savored his coffee.

"Father, why don't you rest while there are no patients?" Kate said to her father.

The doctor pushed his chair back. "Excuse me, Dawson, while I grab some shut-eye. As a doctor I've learned to sleep when I can. Nice of you to join us. I understand you're working on the school, so you'll be in town often. Feel free to drop in anytime."

Silence followed the doctor's departure, making him wonder if the ladies were as comfortable with offering such an invitation. He tried to think how to ease their concern.

"Perhaps you ladies would care to join me Sunday after church and I'll give you a tour of the town and the surrounding area. Miss Young and the doctor, too, of course. I'm sure they'd all like to see more of the place."

"That sounds like a fine idea," Kate said.

"Indeed," Isabelle said, but her expression could best be described as watchful.

Not until he'd excused himself and returned to work did it hit him and he banged the heel of his hand to his forehead. Despite Grandfather's constant pushing for Dawson to give the city woman a chance, to accept that she might not be like Violet, he fully meant to keep a wide distance between himself and Isabelle. Instead, what had he done but offer to spend an afternoon with her. At least they wouldn't be alone. Sadie, Kate and the doctor would be with them. He'd exclude Mattie, but it would break her heart. He'd simply make sure to keep her as far away from Isabelle as possible, though how he'd do that in a crowded buggy remained to be seen. And what was the use of it when she would be spending the after-school hours with Isabelle?

He pounded in a nail. Or, at least, that was his intent. Instead, he hit his thumb and jerked back, shaking the offended digit. That was what came of having such muddled thoughts.

Isabelle looked at the clock, wondering if it had stopped, but the steady tick-tock assured her it counted off the minutes. The afternoon had gone by with stubborn slowness. By three o'clock, time had slowed to a crawl. Mattie would soon be there. Isabelle set cookies out on a plate, planning to serve them with a glass of milk. She stared at the plate. Were cookies considered the proper after-school snack or would bread and jam be better? She had no idea. What had *she* eaten?

Well, for one thing, her tea was served in the nursery by the governess. Her mind flew back to those days as a truth dawned. She couldn't remember what she'd eaten because it was the company that mattered. Mama would always come to share tea with her, and Isabelle would tell her every detail of her day.

She wanted to offer the same to Mattie. Her undivided interest.

She went to the window to watch for the children to get out of school. But she was so anxious to see Mattie that she walked across the street to stand by the doorway. She turned to look at the schoolhouse. Dawson rested one foot on a chunk of wood, his sleeves rolled up, his hat pushed back. A bit of sawdust clung to the brim of his hat. And his blue eyes found hers.

She smiled and waved, determined to prove she wasn't affected by his opinion of her.

He gave a one-fingered salute. And no smile.

She understood his guardedness. He was understandably wary of leaving his daughter in her care. Except it wasn't okay. Why must she prove herself all the time? Back in St. Louis she was seen as rich and very suitable, but for the wrong reasons, in her opinion. Here no one knew she was rich and they still found her unsuitable. Again, for all the wrong reasons.

She tilted her chin and met him look for look across

the dusty street. She couldn't say what he saw in her firm gaze, perhaps her promise he wouldn't be sorry, perhaps her sincerity, perhaps something more, something that mushroomed from deep inside—the need for acceptance and value. *I just want to be seen for who I really am.* She might have mouthed the words or only thought them. Either way, he couldn't have heard or known, yet he smiled and nodded and she turned away feeling he finally understood.

Of course, he didn't, and she knew that.

The door flew open and a half a dozen little boys burst into the open, running up the street yelling at each other about a ball game and chores.

Two older girls hurried out, each carrying a book and talking about exams.

Then Mattie dashed through the door. She skidded to a halt as she noticed Isabelle and practically threw herself at her. "You came to get me."

"I got impatient waiting for you." She leaned over to hug the child. "Are you ready to go home with me?"

"Yes, yes, yes." Mattie jumped up and down in time with the words and took Isabelle's hand, half dragging her off the step. "Can I go say hi to Papa first?"

"Of course." She wondered if she would see approval in his eyes or regret that circumstances had forced him to ask for her help.

Hand in hand she and Mattie crossed to the school yard. At their approach, Dawson took off his hat and slapped it on his knee, sending bits of sawdust dancing. Grinning widely, he held out his arms. Mattie raced into them and Dawson lifted her high in the air, bringing pleased giggles from the child. He hugged her and rubbed his chin against her.

"Stop, Papa. You're giving me a whisker burn." But even though she said stop, Mattie's voice begged for more.

Dawson tickled her and growled into her neck then perched her on one hip. "How did school go today? Did Miss Young have to make you stand in the corner?"

Dawson winked at Isabelle to indicate he only teased Mattie. Isabelle felt included as never before. Like the two of them shared an interest in Mattie's well-being. Like they shared even more. Her throat tightened and tears pressed against the backs of her eyes at the futility of such an idea.

Mattie got huffy. "Of course not, Papa." She cupped his cheeks to bring his attention back to her. "I really like the story she's reading to us after lunch. You know what she said? She said her papa used to read to them every evening. Isn't that something? Maybe you need to do that."

Dawson chuckled and his gaze again came to Isabelle. "That sounds like a fine idea."

"Maybe that's what real families do."

His expression darkened.

"Are you saying we aren't a real family?"

Mattie hung her head. "Guess I don't mean that."

"I hope not. I think Grandfather, Grandpa Bud, your uncles and aunt would be a little surprised to hear they aren't part of your family. And a little hurt."

Isabelle could see Dawson was more than a little hurt and sought a way to make him understand that Mattie simply meant she felt different because she was motherless. She stepped closer and pressed her hand to Mattie's back.

Her arm brushed Dawson's but she did not let the

sudden quickening of her pulses show. "You are a fortunate little girl to have so many people to love you. More than most."

Mattie nodded. "And I got the best papa of all." She gave Dawson a loud kiss. "Am I right, Papa?"

"It's me who is fortunate to have the best girl in the whole world."

Isabelle heard the tightness in his voice and smiled encouragement at him.

Something in his gaze shifted as they looked at each other. It was as if a barrier between them had crumbled and they had each opened their heart to the other. Later, she promised herself, she would tell herself it was all in her imagination, but for now she floated on the moment.

Dawson pulled away first. "Now, you go along with Miss Isabelle so I can get this school ready for you and your friends." He lowered Mattie to the ground.

"Yes, Papa." She claimed Isabelle's hand.

Isabelle didn't immediately move but waited for Dawson to straighten and meet her eyes once again. "We'll be waiting for you at the end of the day, and be assured, Mattie will be well taken care of."

"Thank you." His gaze again reached into her heart and caught pieces of it.

Only then did she let Mattie drag her to the house.

How could she possibly feel like she fit into Dawson's heart—or rather that he fit into hers—when he made it clear she didn't?

Dawson returned to his work. Mattie would be okay, he told himself over and over. It was for only a couple of hours. Besides, Isabelle had a window open and several times as he paused in his labors he heard Mattie laughing and stopped to listen. What were they doing? How much influence would Isabelle have?

Was she like Violet? More interested in fine clothes and the proper use of six different kinds of forks than in responsibility?

A truth seared through him. Isabelle wanted to spend time with Mattie. Violet had resented the time Mattie's care required. He shook his head as if the motion would drive away the thought. He could not let such a tiny realization influence him. He spent the next hour thinking of his quandary—allowing a city woman to spend time with Mattie all the while fully aware of the risk it meant to her future happiness. Would she grow so fond of the woman that she would be devastated when she left? And leave she would. Like he'd said to her, she was city. Through and through.

Finally quitting time came and he put his tools away. "See you tomorrow," he called to the other man, who likewise made his way homeward.

He strode up to the back door of the house next door and knocked. All the windows were now closed against the cold afternoon wind.

Isabelle opened the door, and Mattie stood with a red, pink and orange scarf draped about her neck…the very same scarf Isabelle had worn the day she arrived, if he wasn't mistaken. Soft as kitten fur, Mattie had said. Something about that scarf flashed a warning in his brain. A deep, dark fear surfaced. Would knowing Isabelle make Mattie yearn for a life that took her away from him? How soon before Mattie decided she wanted to have fancy clothes and no longer wanted to be part of the ranch? All of a sudden this arrangement filled him with anxiety.

"Feel it, Papa. I told Miss Isabelle it was like kitten

fur. She said she'd like to feel kitten fur and find out. Do you know she's never seen baby kitties? I told her we would show her ours. Don't you think we should, Papa? I think she could climb to the loft to see them." But Mattie looked doubtful.

Dawson relaxed. This was his Mattie, wanting everyone to enjoy ranch life.

"Seems like a fine idea." Not until he'd spoken did he realize Mattie had somehow tricked him into agreeing to take Isabelle to the ranch again when everything inside him warned it wasn't a good idea. Only it wasn't everything. His head warned against it but his heart wondered at the possibilities. Somehow he had to sort that out.

"How did your afternoon go?" He meant the question for Mattie but he looked at Isabelle.

Isabelle answered. "We had a good time."

"What did you do?"

"Mattie, why don't you show him?"

Mattie ran to the table, grabbed a piece of paper and brought it back to him. On it she had drawn what surely was meant to be a mommy cat and three kittens. "I have named them Orange, Blackie and Stripes."

"Is that the name of the kittens at home?"

Mattie nodded. "Is it okay if I leave the picture here? Miss Isabelle says she'll make a scrapbook of my drawings."

"It's okay." The last vestige of his worry over this arrangement disappeared. "Let's go get my horse."

Mattie put the picture back on the table and scampered from the house.

"Does she ever walk?" Isabelle asked with wonder.

Dawson laughed. "She usually runs. I'll have to hurry to catch up." He didn't immediately leave as he searched for a way to let her know he hadn't changed his mind about her. But to point out again that she would never belong while asking her for the favor of watching Mattie seemed extremely rude. So he thanked her and trotted after his daughter.

Chapter Five

Isabelle lay in bed enjoying a few minutes of laziness. It was Sunday. Time to get up and prepare for church. She looked forward to her first attendance here in Bella Creek. The church stood across the town square from the school and kitty-corner to the hotel. She'd studied it from several angles, liking the clean, simple lines of a clapboard church with a steeple and pebbled glass windows. Something about the building's simplicity made her heart swell with anticipation.

Kate scrambled from bed and stretched. "I hope no one needs Father today. He should rest."

Isabelle sat on the edge of her bed. "Let's pray he gets the whole day."

They did so, then dressed and prepared the meal together. Kate's father joined them. He said little, obviously tired.

A little later the three of them walked down the street toward the church. Sadie joined them, linking her arm with Isabelle's.

"Dawson has offered to take the four of us on a drive to see more of the country," she told Sadie.

"Oh, I'm sorry. I can't go. I have already accepted an invitation to visit the home of two of my students— a sister and a brother."

People came from every direction, the town people walking and those from farms and ranches arriving in wagons, buggies and on horseback. Most of them called out a greeting to the doctor and the ladies, making conversation between them impossible, but Isabelle wished she could convince Sadie to change her arrangements. She needed all the company and support she could muster if she were to spend the afternoon in Dawson's presence.

Would he bring Mattie? Part of her said of course he would. The child would want to accompany her father. Another part—one with a more strident voice—said he would not, if only to keep the child from any more contact with Isabelle than necessary. She hadn't missed the warning look on his face yesterday when he came for Mattie. No, he hadn't changed his mind about her, and having to ask her for help only made it more difficult for him.

A wagon trundled past and pulled to a stop. Annie and Mattie hopped down and joined them, leaving their grandfather to ride on.

"Where's Dawson?" Why did she blurt out the question? It didn't matter to her if he'd forgotten the invitation to take them for a drive. In fact, she would be relieved. His very presence reminded her of how he viewed her and put her nerves on edge.

"Here he comes now," Mattie said, waving to her father as he rode a horse down the street.

They wouldn't be going anywhere with him on horseback. Her disappointment surprised her, and she would have denied it, but it was too real. It came only from a longing to see more of the town and country, she told herself.

She gladly let Annie usher them through the gate and up the steps into the church. Mattie skipped ahead of them until they entered the building and then she grew appropriately subdued as if she'd been taught to respect the house of God.

Isabelle would have slipped into one of the back pews so she could listen to the service without being observed, but Annie led them all forward to the pew fourth from the front and they slid in.

Mattie ended up between Annie and Isabelle, and she gave Isabelle a huge smile.

Isabelle rubbed the little one's back.

Dawson escorted his grandfather inside and they sat beside Annie.

Three people sat between Isabelle and Dawson, and yet she felt crowded by him. Knowing he disapproved of her, solely on the basis of her being from the city, made her muscles tense.

Then the organist began to play and a dark, ruggedly handsome man stood behind the pulpit.

Annie leaned close to whisper, "Our new preacher, Hugh Arness. He's only been here a month. He doesn't like being called 'reverend.' Says that title belongs to God. We're to call him 'pastor' or just plain 'mister.'"

Pastor Arness announced the opening hymn and everyone reached for a hymnal. Annie and Isabelle shared one with Mattie between them, sitting so ladylike. The preacher had a deep, resonant voice and led them in song.

Isabelle joined her voice to those around her, smiling

as Mattie did her best to sing the words. For the moment Isabelle felt like she belonged.

They sang two more hymns and then Pastor Arness opened his Bible and read a passage.

Annie shifted about as the man spoke, but Mattie sat very still, her hands folded neatly in her lap just as Isabelle folded hers. Isabelle smoothed her skirt. Mattie did the same. Isabelle's throat tightened and tears pressed at the backs of her eyes as she realized Mattie imitated her every move. Never before had anyone wanted to be like her. What an awesome privilege and responsibility.

On the other side of Grandfather Marshall, Dawson's long legs almost touched the back of the pew in front of them.

Isabelle pressed hard against the wooden seat. Not that he could see her unless he turned sideways, but she didn't want him to notice Mattie's behavior. Somehow she knew he would object and she had no intention of letting him take this honor from her.

She concentrated on the sermon, blessed by the exhortation to do one's best, the preacher's text being, "I have set before thee an open door, and no man can shut it."

She needed those words. She was here because of God's leading and she would use every opportunity He put before her. *Thank You for Your direction, Lord.*

It took a long time to get out of the church as people crowded around them for introductions and to welcome them. Dawson and his grandfather exited several minutes before Isabelle and the others made it to the door.

She fully expected he would have ridden away and blinked in surprise to see him waiting at the gate by his horse, Mattie beside him. Grandfather sat in the wagon.

"Who's coming with me?" Grandfather asked.

"I'm going with Carly," Annie said. "Enjoy your outing." She grinned at Dawson as if she knew something Isabelle didn't. "Make the most of every opportunity."

If Isabelle wasn't mistaken, Dawson's face darkened and he scowled at his sister. "You stay out of trouble."

"Always do." She waved and followed Carly and a tall, angular man who had been introduced as Carly's father, Mr. Morrison.

"I'll be by with a buggy in an hour for the rest of you," Dawson said.

"Thank you," Kate said.

Dawson didn't move. It took a moment for Isabelle to realize he waited for her response.

"Thank you," she managed.

"Later, then." He swung into the saddle, lifted Mattie up behind him and rode away.

Dawson took Mattie and Grandfather to Uncle George and Aunt Mary's home for dinner. Their children were all grown and moved on, so only they remained and were always glad to have any of the other Marshalls join them.

Twice, during the meal, he warned Mattie to slow down. "What's your hurry?" As if he didn't know. What was he going to do about his daughter's fascination with Isabelle? He couldn't see anything but hurt in store for her.

"We're taking Miss Isabelle for a drive in the country," Mattie informed their aunt and uncle.

"Don't forget the doctor and Miss Kate and Miss Sadie."

Mattie nodded. "They're coming, too. Papa says we'll take them to see the falls. Isn't that right, Papa?"

"That's the plan."

"Aren't you done yet, Papa?" Mattie's plate was clean clear down to the pattern.

"I said we'd be an hour." He sipped from his cup of coffee.

"But we need to get a buggy from the livery man."

"That's true." Still, he didn't move as he fought an internal war. If only he could find some excuse to cancel the afternoon. But that would disappoint Mattie and he didn't care to do that.

A pain in the left side of his jaw made him realize how tense he'd become.

Mattie pulled on his sleeve. She looked at him, correctly interpreting the way he pulled his lips in, and her voice quivered. "Papa, aren't we going?"

Grandfather grunted. "What does the Good Book say about a child leading? Listen to the child and stop branding certain young ladies." He headed for the big overstuffed armchair where Dawson knew he would soon fall asleep.

Mattie blinked hard. "You're gonna brand someone? Why?"

Aunt Mary chuckled. "He's not going to brand anyone. Your grandfather simply means…well, he means…" She tossed her hands in the air. "I suppose he means your father should give everyone a chance to prove their worth based on their actions."

"Oh." Mattie shrugged. "Guess I don't know what that means." She grabbed Dawson's hand. "Come on."

He could not disappoint his daughter and he pushed to his feet. "Let's go get a buggy."

She rewarded him with a wide smile and skipped along beside him as they headed down the street toward the livery barn.

In a few minutes they sat in a buggy and returned up the street to stop in front of the doctor's house. He didn't jump down, too confused to know whether to go to the door or drive away. Not normally an indecisive man, today his thoughts warred with each other. He didn't know how long he would have sat trying to make up his mind if Mattie hadn't jumped up.

"I'll go get them."

"No, that's my job."

She sat back with a pleased smile on her face. "That's what I thought."

He climbed down and made his determined way to the door. This was not a good idea. He knew he would regret it but he was trapped. He sighed and knocked. Might as well make the best of it. All he had to do was show them the town and take them to the falls. If he felt a little trickle of excitement it was only because he would be out in the open and this would be the first time to see the falls this spring. What if Isabelle thought them ordinary and wondered why he chose to take her there? No doubt she would. Why should he care either way? The others would surely enjoy the drive.

He rearranged his expression to reveal nothing just as Isabelle opened the door. Her gaze darted past him to the buggy and Mattie, and if he wasn't mistaken, she looked relieved, even pleased to see his daughter.

He didn't care for her reaction. How was he to keep them apart?

"Are the doctor and Miss Kate ready?" He saw no sign of them.

"They got called away and Sadie had a prior invitation."

He stared. "Just you and me and Mattie?"

She took a step back. "Is that a problem?"

Yes. He'd counted on the presence of the others to ease his unwelcome awareness of Isabelle.

She backed up farther and began to unbutton her coat. "I understand if you've changed your mind." Her cool voice revealed nothing. Giving him no indication as to whether she felt relief or regret.

"I haven't changed my mind." His confused feelings caused him to say things he regretted as soon as he spoke. "But if you don't wish to go, I understand."

Her fingers stilled on the second button. Her gaze went past him. Her fingers left the button and returned to the first and pushed it through the buttonhole. "I'd like to see more of the country."

Just the three of them. He could hardly ask her to sit in the back. They would have to share the front bench. He could sit in the middle and keep that much distance between her and Mattie but Mattie wouldn't like that, and the thought of rubbing elbows with Isabelle for the duration of the trip caused him to swallow hard.

She wore a questioning look. "Make up your mind."

"I have. Shall we be on our way?"

He helped her into the buggy, climbed up with Mattie in the middle and then released the brake. With a flick of the reins to start the horse moving, they drove down the street. "I expect you've seen the main street, but what you can't see and won't until spring is how the trees in the center square provide shade. The ladies usually plant flowers. Grandfather insisted on the benches so people can relax or visit or have their lunch in a pleasant spot." Why did he ramble on about a town square that was nothing more than a wide spot at the intersection of two streets?

Hardly worthy of comment in comparison to the things Isabelle must have seen in St. Louis.

Isabelle looked from side to side. "I noticed the benches, of course, and thought them a very pleasant addition. I imagined people sitting and visiting, catching up on news from friends and neighbors, but I can hardly wait to see the trees leafed out and flowers blossoming. Maybe I can help with the flowers."

He stared at her. He hadn't expected she'd pay any heed to his description, dismissing it as unworthy of notice, yet she'd already considered the very things Grandfather hoped to encourage—neighborliness.

She noticed his study and her smile flattened. "Did I say something wrong? Are only certain people allowed to tend the flowers?"

He shook his head. "Any and all help is welcome."

She nodded, a pleased look in her eyes. "Then I look forward to it."

Did she really plan to be around long enough to plant flowers? Or would she tire of country life before then? His thoughts all muddled by her eagerness to be involved, he turned onto Silver Street. "Once past the school and church we begin to enter the residential area." He pointed out the houses and told her who lived in each. She studied each house with interest.

"What do these people do?"

"Some work at the mines but prefer to live in a better place than Wolf Hollow. Some work in the various businesses in town."

"Some of the people go to school," Mattie added. "Eric and Lisa live there. They have two little sisters." She shifted and pointed to the house across the street. "Mary Jane lives in that house. She's like me. She doesn't have any brothers or sisters. Except she has a mama and a papa, though her papa is gone lots at the mines." She let out a long sigh. "Mary Jane is sad sometimes. I suppose it's because she misses her papa." Another long dramatic sigh. "Like I miss my mama even though I don't recall what she looks like." She turned to Isabelle. "Will I always miss my mama?"

Dawson forgot to breathe. He'd never heard Mattie mention missing Violet. He hadn't thought she could remember her at all.

Isabelle wrapped her arm about Mattie's shoulders. "I don't think you'll ever get over missing your mama. I know I won't. But the missing doesn't always hurt. It can comfort us or encourage us or help us remember to do the right thing, knowing that's what our mamas would want."

Dawson couldn't have been more surprised at Isabelle's words even though he wondered if Violet would have cared what Mattie did. She'd shown little interest in the child. Far better for Mattie if she didn't know that.

They turned down the cross street, passed more houses. "There are a few empty houses beyond here."

"Empty? What happened to the occupants?" Her calm voice seemed to say she only made conversation, but whether she tried to hide it or not, he detected a slight tremor as if she feared personal pain or loss had driven them away.

This hint of tenderness brought a queer mingling of surprise and pleasure in his thoughts.

"A few moved away after the fire. Others never found the gold they dreamed of and gave up to return to their former lives."

"I would think going back would be equally disappointing."

He stared at her, knowing his eyes likely said far more than he intended. How could her words carry both regret and hope?

She met his gaze, her eyes shuttered.

He was convinced she knew how to hide her feelings.

"Look." Mattie pointed to his left and thankfully drew his attention from Isabelle and his irrational thoughts. "Pussy willows." A tree in an abandoned yard hung heavy with the furry catkins. "Stop. I want to get some."

Dawson pulled the horse to a halt. "Hang on," he warned, as Mattie tried to edge past him while the wagon still rolled. He jumped to the ground and lifted her down.

She grabbed his hand and leaned away in an attempt to drag him across the street.

Dawson didn't move and turned to Isabelle, who sat patiently on the bench, smiling widely at Mattie's eagerness.

"Do you want to come with us?"

Her smile faltered as her gaze came to him and then it beamed from her eyes. "I'd love to see the pussy-willow tree."

How could her simple response fuel such a pleased reaction in his heart? It was only a tree—a pussy willow, a simple reminder of spring.

She reached for his hand and carefully, elegantly, stepped to the ground.

Elegant! The word reminded him of the need for caution. No reason to read anything more into her words and reactions than simple good manners.

Mattie grabbed Isabelle's hand on one side and Dawson's on the other and urged them forward. "You ever seen a pussy-willow tree?" she asked Isabelle.

"I have in passing."

They stopped under the sweeping branches.

Isabelle reached up and touched the catkins. "Soft as fur," she murmured.

"Soft as kitten fur." Mattie looked at Dawson as if to remind him it was how she'd described Isabelle's scarf.

He didn't need a reminder and dug his knife out of his pocket to cut off some of the branches—a handful for Mattie and another for Isabelle.

She bent over the willows, her eyes peeking at him from under the fringes of her dark eyelashes. "Thank you."

"It's nothing. I expect you get lots of bouquets of hot-house flowers. These are just cuttings from a tree in someone's yard." He meant to remind himself that she was a city girl, a rich one if he took into account her wool coat with attached hood. But at the way her eyes widened and then shuttered, at the way her smile fled and the slight tensing of her hands, he wished he could pull back every one of those words. He had no call, nor wish, to hurt her feelings. "Of course, many times, things of nature are superior to what man can produce." It hardly made sense but he could think of nothing else.

Her smile returned, filling her eyes. "'The heavens declare the glory of God; and the firmament sheweth his handywork.'"

Surprise and something akin to pleasure jolted through him at her response. Who would have expected her to quote the same verse his grandfather often used?

Mattie grinned up at Isabelle. "That's the Bible verse

Grandfather always says." She turned to Dawson. "Isn't it, Papa?"

He nodded, too startled to speak.

Mattie danced back to the wagon, and Dawson and Isabelle followed, side by side but not touching, though the breeze brushed her coat against his leg and brought to him the scent of something sweet and subtle. Not like the heavy perfumes Violet had preferred.

There had to be some reason he kept aligning Violet and Isabelle in his thoughts. Perhaps a subconscious knowledge he needed to remember the similarities. Not that he would likely forget. Especially when he saw the way Mattie gazed admiringly at Isabelle as he helped the fine lady into the buggy and how she fingered the material of Isabelle's coat as they sat side by side. Everything about her shouted *city* and *money*. He did not wish Mattie to learn to value those above the simpler things of ranch life. He shuddered. Being drawn by such attractions might lead her away from him.

They continued passing houses. Not until they were almost abreast of the Garrisons' house did he think he should have chosen a different street or even gone around the block. He gritted his teeth and hoped none of them looked out the window. Especially Betsy. Seemed that was too much to hope for, because even before he finished the thought, Betsy flew from the house, almost tripping over her skirts. "Dawson." Her screech made the horse toss his head and whinny.

"Papa, why did you come this way?" Mattie whispered her protest.

"It's the street out of town." Though not an excuse for such forgetfulness.

Betsy reached the side of the buggy and grabbed at it, leaving him no choice but to stop.

"Whoa." Anyone who knew him would hear the barely constrained impatience.

Betsy batted her eyes and gave a wide, generous smile. "Hi, Dawson. Where ya goin'?"

He smiled back, though it felt a whole lot more like a grimace. "Good day, Miss Garrison. It's a beautiful Sunday, isn't it?"

Mattie drummed her hand on his arm.

"What?" he asked her.

She rocked her head back and forth, her eyes flashing a warning.

He understood her concern. Betsy had managed to invite herself along on more than one occasion. And she always hung on to his arm and pushed Mattie away. "We're going for a drive. If you'll excuse us, we must be on our way."

Betsy pouted. Apparently someone had told her it was appealing.

It was not.

He waited for her to step back and not until she did could he fill his lungs. He half expected her to bolt to the buggy and push both Mattie and Isabelle into the back so she could crowd to his side.

"That was Betsy Garrison," Mattie informed Isabelle. "She likes my papa. But she doesn't like me."

Isabelle's look met his over his daughter's head. Hers faintly accusing, as if demanding to know why he would encourage such an interest.

"It's entirely one-sided," he murmured.

She tipped her head fractionally and shifted her attention to Mattie, her expression softening as she squeezed the child's shoulder.

"I don't understand why she wouldn't like you. I do." She spoke so softly he barely heard her words.

"I like you, too." Mattie rested her head against Isabelle's arm.

Dawson's teeth creaked. How could he protect his little girl from this city woman who would admire everything she saw, weary of it and go back to the city leaving Mattie hurting? Why had he suggested an outing? Or, at least, why hadn't he canceled it when he saw Isabelle would be the only one accompanying them?

He wasn't blind to how both he and Mattie could be hurt if he wasn't extra cautious. Even now he could turn back and end this trip. But he knew he wouldn't. And no amount of telling himself it was only for Mattie's sake erased the truth that he did this willingly, albeit with fear and trembling. Surely he would pay a price, and so would his daughter.

Chapter Six

Isabelle couldn't miss the tension in Dawson's face as they proceeded down the street, but she could only guess its cause. Did he regret that she was the only one to join him and Mattie, or did he regret that she sat on the buggy seat and not this Betsy person? But Isabelle didn't regret it after Mattie said Betsy didn't like her. Surely that would be reason enough for Dawson not to consider such a relationship.

The truth was, Isabelle didn't know him sufficiently well to make that assumption, though everything she'd observed and her own reaction to the man suggested otherwise. But she knew better than to trust her heart when it came to men. Her experience with Jamieson and Andy had surely taught her that.

She nudged the pussy-willow bouquet at her feet, where she'd put it for safekeeping until she returned home. He'd made it sound like she'd prefer the hothouse flowers that filled her cousin's house on a regular basis, some sent by suitors and would-be suitors. What would he say if she told him he was mistaken? There was something touching about a man cutting a bouquet and handing it to her, even if it had been done only out of kindness.

No one spoke as they left the town behind them. The trail led north. To the west she saw snowcapped mountains. "They look like jagged teeth," she said, hoping to ease the tension that, she admitted, might exist only in her own mind.

Mattie giggled. "I used to say I know why they're called 'peaks.' It's 'cause you can always see them peeking at you."

Isabelle chuckled. "That's rather clever." She had no intention of looking directly at Dawson but smiled down at Mattie. However, when she lifted her head, their gazes collided. She jerked her attention forward. He'd already made it clear he didn't approve of her, but to see the message in his eyes again shattered any enjoyment of the afternoon. Not that she meant to let his opinion influence her. She would learn how to do something useful and beneficial while she was here and had the opportunity.

"Know what else I said when I was little?" Mattie asked.

"You're still little," Dawson teased, his tone making it clear how much he enjoyed his daughter.

Mattie huffed up straight. "I'm old enough to go to school."

"Ah, yes. I'd forgotten you're now an old lady."

"Papa!" With a toss of her head, she faced Isabelle. "Want to hear?"

"I'd love to." Her heart warmed at the way Dawson and Mattie teased without rancor.

"I used to think my grandfather meant something to see when he said he found an Indian camp*site*. I 'member asking him where are the eyes. I figured it had to have eyes to have sight." She covered a little giggle.

Again Isabelle chuckled and met Dawson's amused look over his daughter's head.

"She was so literal."

"What's that mean?" Mattie demanded.

Dawson considered his answer a moment. "It means you see things in black and white."

Mattie crossed her arms over her chest in a gesture that plainly spoke disbelief. "I do not. I like colors." She waved her hand. "The blue sky. The dark green pine. The purple crocuses. Can we look for some?"

"Don't see why not, though I've not seen any yet." Dawson kept his attention on the road ahead, but even so, Isabelle caught the hint of a smile on his face. He obviously enjoyed his little daughter.

She forced her hands to remain folded neatly in her lap when she ached to twist them into a knot. How could she hope she might fit in this world?

The ruts in the road led onward. The mountains stood solid and unmoving. Just as God remained faithful. She would trust Him to guide her to a satisfactory place.

The road climbed upward. The trees crowded close, shuttering the sun so they only got flashes of it on their faces.

"We're almost there." Mattie bounced up and down.

Dawson pressed his hand to her knees. "Careful or you'll fly away and then what will happen?"

"Then you'll catch me and bring me back."

Struck by the certainty in Mattie's voice, Isabelle studied the eager child. How amazing to be so completely secure in her father's love and care. She lifted her gaze to Dawson, her insides full of admiration and something more…something she couldn't identify but that came from a distant, seldom-visited part of her heart and felt strangely like loneliness.

"Stop, Papa." Mattie's sharp call drove everything else from Isabelle's mind and she looked about, alert to whatever had made the child call out.

Dawson pulled the wagon to a halt and grinned at Mattie. "You sure this is the place?"

Obviously he wasn't alarmed, so Isabelle relaxed.

"This is it. Listen, Isabelle." Mattie tipped her head, a rapt look on her face. "You can hear it."

Isabelle turned her attention to the sounds around her, uncertain what Mattie expected her to hear. Birdsong, the whisper of the breeze through the overhead branches and a distant sound of wind? No, not wind. A faint rumble. "Is that the sound of the waterfall?"

Mattie grabbed Isabelle's hand, her eyes wide with joy. "We always stop to listen before we get there."

Dawson regarded Isabelle with watchful interest. Did he wait for her response?

Having no idea what he expected from her, she gave a mental shrug and turned her attention back to the child. "Are we still a long ways off?"

"Almost there," Mattie answered. "It's real loud up close."

"Really? I can hardly wait."

"Let's go, Papa." The child leaned forward as if she could get to her destination faster that way.

Dawson moved on without saying a word, but his look suggested disapproval. She could not think why. Did he want her to seem more excited? Did he think she found the activity boring? Beneath her? Or was it a special place that he only shared with her reluctantly?

"One can never get tired of seeing nature's beauty and power," she said, hoping it would make him understand this outing was not beneath her and she enjoyed every minute.

"The falls are considered to be magnificent."

She noticed he spoke from a neutral point of view. And wanting to know his opinion, she asked, "Have you seen them so often they've become commonplace?"

"I don't believe a person could ever become complacent in the face of such power and beauty. But I'll let you judge for yourself."

The sound of rushing water grew louder as they climbed. They reached a small clearing and he pulled to a halt. "We walk from here. Mattie, wait for me," Dawson called as Mattie jumped from the buggy. "It will still be icy and slippery in places."

"Show her from here." Mattie rocked back and forth on her feet as she waited for Dawson to help Isabelle down.

"I will." He retained Isabelle's hand. "The rocks can be slippery."

As if to prove him correct, one foot slid out from under her.

His hand gripped hers. "Thank you," she murmured, heat stinging her cheeks. Not, she realized with some dismay, because of the way she clung to his hand, but because of the way her heart rushed up her throat at the warmth and strength and solidity of his grasp. And the way the simple touch went beyond her hand to that lonely place behind her heart, behind doors that had been closed, locked and barred since... With a start, she realized it had been since the deaths of her parents.

She righted herself. She would have pulled her hand

away but had no desire to lose her footing again without him to rescue her. But with quiet determination she again closed and barred those inner doors. This was not the time or place, and he was certainly not the man to make her open them.

Perhaps there would never be such a man. All the more reason to confine her enjoyment of this day to the thrills of nature and then return to town and resolutely set her face toward her goal.

"Come on," Mattie yelled, but when she would have rushed ahead, Dawson ordered her to his side.

With an impatient sigh, as if adults took far too long to do anything, Mattie obeyed her father and took Dawson's other hand.

They navigated the few yards to a high point. Through the trees she glimpsed foaming white water below.

"It isn't the falls," Mattie explained. "Just the crazy wild water after them. We have to go down that trail to see the falls." But she waited as Isabelle studied the high cliffs facing them and the wild water.

"It's awe inspiring," she said after a minute.

Still holding both Isabelle's and Mattie's hands, Dawson indicated the trail they'd take. It wasn't wide enough for the three of them to go abreast and he released them. Mattie would have rushed ahead but, again, Dawson stopped her.

"I'll lead the way," he told her and set out with Mattie at his heels.

Isabelle followed. The rocky path required them to concentrate on their footing. Several times Dawson reached back to help her over the rough terrain and she gladly accepted his assistance. In many places, where the sun didn't reach through the branches, snow lingered and she shivered in the cold air.

"Are you going to be warm enough?" Dawson asked.

"I shall indeed." She had no intention of turning back as the roar of water grew louder.

"It's just ahead." Likely he meant to encourage her, though it wasn't necessary. The growing sound of rushing water echoed in her heart, drawing her like a magnet.

They stepped to a rock embankment. Dawson pointed to the right, though she needed no one to indicate where the falls were. The rumble of them drew her attention immediately.

"We can get closer. Mattie, hold my hand." Dawson took Isabelle's, as well, though there was little danger of her falling from the flat, wide bank.

The sound grew in intensity as they moved forward. The breeze brought a gentle mist that landed on her skin. She licked her lips and laughed.

He looked at her, one eyebrow crooked in question.

She only laughed again, overcome with the pleasure of the moment—surrounded by the extremes of nature shared with a man and child.

At his continued study, she felt her enjoyment falter. Her smile slid from her face but he turned away and didn't see. If he thought her silly or useless it didn't matter. She hadn't come here looking for a man. Nor a family to replace the one she'd lost almost a dozen years ago. Not that anything could substitute for the love she'd lost.

Was a new love possible? A new family? One of her own?

She dismissed the questions as soon as they surfaced. Easily dismissed them as they reached a spot directly adjacent to the falls. They stood almost eye level with the water pounding between rocky protrusions and feathering over the edges of others. It was a series of falls, one after another, cascading into each other in a mighty, roaring rush. In many places, winter ice clung to the rocks, creating unusual sculptures.

"Amazing." She could think of nothing else to say. And she could do nothing but stare and enjoy. Air released from her lungs in a great sigh as if she'd unconsciously held her breath for hours…days…months. How long had it been since she'd felt so free and at peace? Maybe never. At least, not as an adult.

"Are you okay?" Dawson asked.

She turned to face him, not caring that her expression probably revealed her pleasure. "Something about this place—" Words failed her and she rubbed her palm across her collarbone and rocked her head back and forth.

Mattie pulled on Dawson's arm, jerking him backward, stretching Isabelle's arm. Was there really any need to be still holding hands? But when she tried to ease free, he tightened his grip. "Have you seen enough?"

She wanted to say no. She would never see enough. But no doubt he expected her to say yes. Still she hesitated, her gaze returning to the falls.

Mattie left Dawson's grip. "Don't go too far," he cautioned.

She perched on a nearby rock, her knees drawn up and her chin resting on the backs of her hands.

Dawson pulled gently on Isabelle's arm, leading her forward. He released her at Mattie's side and pointed to a spot by the girl.

Isabelle sat on one side of Mattie, Dawson on the other, all three content to watch the roaring waters. The damp coldness of the rock seeped through Isabelle but she didn't care.

Mattie slipped to her feet and moved away a few feet to stare at the waters.

Dawson touched Isabelle's arm and pointed upward. A bald eagle soared overhead, riding the wind currents.

Joy and something more—she knew not what to call it—flew from her, lifting skyward as if wanting to join the eagle's flight.

Mattie looked upward, too, then turned, her eyes sparkling and her mouth smiling. Then a look of surprise took over and she stared at Dawson, shifted her gaze to Isabelle and back to Dawson. Her face grew damp but not with the mist from the falls. Tears ran unchecked down her face.

Dawson was on his feet, reaching for his daughter. "Mattie, what's wrong?"

She held up her hands and waved them back and forth before her as if to keep him away.

How odd. From what Isabelle had observed, the child eagerly went to her father.

"I remember this." The words sobbed from Mattie's throat.

"You've been here many times."

"No, I remember coming with you and Mama. You sat with her on that rock." A sob shook Mattie. "I was afraid."

Dawson took a step closer but stopped as she edged back.

Isabelle held back a warning. If Mattie went too far, she would reach the edge with nothing but roaring water beneath her. Her heart stalled.

"Why were you afraid?" Dawson's soothing voice hopefully calmed the child.

Mattie blinked and shifted away from her father. Her gaze found Isabelle and, with a cry, she raced to her.

Isabelle opened her arms and folded the sobbing child into her embrace. "Shh, shh, shh," she crooned. Not because she thought Mattie shouldn't cry but because she wanted to offer comfort the only way she knew how.

Mattie drew in a shuddering breath and lifted her face to look into Isabelle's eyes. "Mama said bad things to Papa. Angry, loud things." She buried her head against Isabelle's shoulder and clung to her. Isabelle felt her fear clear through.

Dawson reached for Mattie, his hand suspended inches from his daughter's back, and then he dropped his arm to his side and ground about on his heel to stalk to the edge of the embankment and stare out at the raging waters.

Her heart ached for him…for them both…but she was at a loss. What could she do other than hold Mattie and long for a way to offer comfort to Dawson?

Dawson's insides felt like the tossing waters before him. In turmoil. Raging. He should never have come here. But he'd brought Mattie many times. It was one of their favorite places for an outing. Never before had she recalled that day, though it was blazoned in his memory. He'd brought Violet and Mattie when Mattie was barely three…talking enough to make herself understood. She'd been fascinated with the rushing water.

His hope and prayer had been that Violet would enjoy the time together and begin to see how they could be a family, enjoying each other's company, sharing dreams for their little girl.

Instead, Violet had paced back and forth on the rocks, scolding him for bringing her out in the wilds, as she called the place. "Wild and untamed. Not at all what I expect in the way of amusement."

Even at the time, he had wondered if the words also applied to him. He'd brought her to this same rock and tried to reason with her, make her see the beauty of the place, make her understand all that family had to offer. Her protests had grown more vehement until she'd shouted insults at him. "Boorish. Interested only in cows." Her final words had shriveled the last of his hope. "I should never have married you. I'm not interested in cows, family or life in this forsaken place." He knew then it would be only a matter of weeks before she left. Instead, she had died in her reckless race.

Mattie had cried when Violet yelled at him, and he'd scooped her into his arms and tried to comfort her.

He'd never thought Mattie would remember. Why now? His fists curled and uncurled. Was it because of Isabelle? Had her similarity to Violet triggered that horrible memory? He slammed his fist into his palm. He had only himself to blame. He'd known from the beginning the risks involved with friendship with another city woman. He hadn't expected Mattie to recognize the similarities. He'd hoped she'd see only the differences. Isabelle's dark hair and dark eyes. Her calmness. Calmness? Dawson blinked. Yes, she'd seemed content to sit and watch the waterfalls.

What difference did it make? Coming here with Isabelle had triggered Mattie's memory. Now what was he to do? Slowly he turned to study his daughter, clutched in Isabelle's arms. He could not rob his daughter of this small comfort. Not here. Not now. But from now on, he meant to keep a goodly distance between the two. He should have stuck to his intention in the first place— then this wouldn't have happened.

Even as he decided his course of action, he acknowledged how difficult it would be in a small town like Bella Creek. And what was he to do with Mattie after school? He accepted the only solution. He would take her home as soon as classes were out. Grandfather would object but Dawson would deal with that.

Or perhaps he should forget his family, his cows, his dreams of his own home and take his daughter and go elsewhere.

A groan pressed against his teeth. He would not release it. Would not give Isabelle any reason to pity him.

Her gaze met his, full of—

What did he think he saw? Compassion or accusation? He shrugged. Her opinion of him simply didn't matter.

The wind picked up, carrying with it a cold mist.

Isabelle wiped at her face and looked upward, as if surprised at the moisture. That hardly made sense. The spray from the falls had dampened their skin from the minute they arrived.

He turned into the wind, welcoming the sting of the cold spray. He licked the moisture from his lips, puzzled that it seemed to come from above rather than from the waterfall.

From above! The thought jolted through him. It didn't come from the river. It came from the sky. "It's raining. Hurry. We have to get off the mountain before the trail ices up." Or worse, the rain turned to snow. He'd lived in Montana long enough to know a snowstorm could engulf them in a matter of minutes.

He hoisted Mattie to his hip, took Isabelle with his other hand and hurried across the embankment. At the narrow trail, he had to go ahead of Isabelle but he didn't release her hand. They couldn't take their time. Several times, Isabelle slipped on the icy trail and his hold prevented her from falling. He struggled onward, breathing hard as he climbed the hill back to the wagon. The trees on the trail had protected them from the full force of the rain, but as they stepped into the clearing where they'd left the wagon, rain slashed increasingly at them.

He released Mattie to the buggy seat and lifted Isabelle aboard, not waiting for her to grab at a handhold. He jumped up beside them. A rolled-up fur robe rested under the seat and he took it out, flipped it open and draped it around Isabelle and Mattie.

Isabelle looked at him sitting exposed. "You'll freeze to death."

"I've been in worse weather and survived."

"Nevertheless." She pulled Mattie to her knee and opened the robe to invite him to share the warmth.

He knew he should refuse but he had no desire to be wet and cold, and he slipped the heavy fur across his shoulders, shutting out the elements. Isabelle and Mattie pressed against him on the other side. He adjusted the robe, pulling it up to form a hood over their heads. Isabelle had opened her coat so Mattie could burrow into its protection.

They rode down the mountain toward town. Before they reached the wider trail, both the wind and the rain increased and he was grateful for the shared protection of the robe.

"How much longer?" Mattie's voice was muffled against Isabelle.

"Soon." *Please, God, let us get back before this turns to snow.*

"Papa?"

"Yes? What is it?"

"I didn't mean to make you angry." Her uncertain tone stung worse than the icy pellets striking his face.

Did he imagine Isabelle pressing closer to him? That couldn't be so. He would expect her to stiffen in judgment for how Mattie perceived that day and for today's reaction.

"I wasn't angry, little one. I'm still not. I'm only sad that you have such a bad memory."

"Okay." Her tiny voice was almost lost in the wind.

They drove onward. He welcomed the stinging cold. Like whipcords slashing his face. He blamed himself for Mattie's fears every bit as much as he blamed Violet. He should have known better than to expect Violet to change her mind.

They reached town. He stopped at the doctor's residence and rushed Isabelle and Mattie indoors. The stove radiated warmth and he set Mattie on her feet before it, kneeling to look in her face. "Are you cold?" He longed to ask more important questions. Was she happy? Did she worry about the future? All things that were his responsibility to ensure.

"Not much." She held her hands out to the heat.

He rose and slowly brought his attention to Isabelle. Her cheeks were rosy. Drops of water clung to her lashes and the hair about her face. Almost like a halo, he thought, shoving away the foolish idea before he even finished thinking it. Then the truth hit him. She'd sheltered his child, protecting her from the cold at the expense of her own comfort. He lifted a hand, meaning to wipe the moisture from her face, caught himself in time and waved her toward the stove. "Get warmed up while I return the buggy."

Mattie turned big eyes toward him. "You're coming back, aren't you?"

His heart twisted cruelly. When Violet first left, Mattie had feared every time he went out of her sight. But he thought that was in the past. Now, because of an unfortunate trip to a place they'd visited many times, it appeared the fear had returned.

Kneeling before her again, he took her hands and waited until she looked directly into his eyes. "Mattie, I won't leave you."

"Unless something bad happens to you. Like it did Mama."

"In that case, you can know that my last thought would be about you. And you know there are lots of people who will love you and take care of you."

"I know," she said with resignation. "You told me before."

"Then maybe you should believe me."

She shrugged. "I do, but my heart doesn't always remember."

He chuckled softly. "We all have that problem from time to time." And before his heart could forget the lessons learned from Violet, he hurried outside, into the cold rain.

Chapter Seven

Isabelle stared at the closed door. He'd certainly left in a hurry before she could ask what his heart needed to forget. But he was right. She, too, had a heart that didn't always remember the lessons engraved on her brain.

She turned back to Mattie. "Would you like some hot cocoa?"

Mattie's eyes brightened. "Yes, I would, please."

Isabelle put water in the kettle and set it over the heat to boil then found cocoa, sugar and evaporated milk in the pantry. She paused as she prepared the mixture. How did she know to make it?

The memory washed over her and through her and filled her heart and soul. "My mama made me hot cocoa every Sunday at bedtime." The ritual had made her feel loved and secure. "I can still see her choosing our favorite cups."

"What was your favorite?"

"It was a china cup. The saucer had long since been broken but I didn't care. It had bright orange flowers on the cup and a yellow band around the top. My mama said it had belonged to my Spanish grandmother and she would tell me stories about her family." The water boiled and she poured it into the cocoa mixture and added the milk. She put the two cups on the table and Mattie sat across from her.

The girl sipped carefully of the hot drink and sighed her pleasure. "This is good."

"Thank you." Isabelle sipped her own, closing her eyes as warmth from the drink and a deeper warmth from her memories eased away the coldness from their trip back to town.

Sitting pressed to Dawson's side, she'd felt his hurt at Mattie's fear echoing in her heart at the thought of the poor child recalling such a frightful memory and the poor father feeling he was responsible. So much sadness to bear.

"What sort of stories?" Mattie's question brought Isabelle's thoughts back to her own situation.

"She said my *abuela*—"

Mattie frowned, not understanding.

"That's Spanish for *grandmother*."

"*Abuela*. That's pretty."

"Yes, it is. My *abuela* was a horsewoman. She raised fine black horses that were famous all over Europe and then America."

"My papa wants to raise his own cattle. He bought a herd of cows from England. Is that where your grandmother lived?"

"Close. She lived in Spain. Both of them are far across the ocean."

Kate stepped from the examining room area. "Hi, Mattie. I wondered who Isabelle was talking to." She glanced toward her father's bedroom door. "I thought my father might be up but it didn't sound like his voice."

Isabelle rose. "I didn't know you were back."

"Yes, for a couple of hours."

"Do you want a cup of hot cocoa?"

"Sounds wonderful." Kate watched as Isabelle expertly made another cupful. "You learn quickly."

"I always knew this. My mother taught me. I just haven't thought of it in a long time. Not until Mattie and I came home cold."

"Where's Dawson?"

"Papa took the buggy to the livery barn." Mattie looked anxiously at the door. "He said he was coming back."

Isabelle put the full cup in front of Kate then covered Mattie's hands. "He'll be back."

She nodded. "I know." She grew thoughtful. "Do you remember lots of stories about your mama?"

"Lots and lots." Half a lifetime of them.

Mattie studied her half-empty cup. "I don't hardly remember my mama. Sometimes I think I didn't have one."

Kate and Isabelle shared quick smiles, and then Isabelle turned back to Mattie. "Honey, we all have mamas."

"But what if I don't know who she was?"

The child's worry burrowed deep into Isabelle's heart. If she forgot her mother it would be like…well, like she never existed. No wonder the child was concerned. "Do you know her name?"

"Violet. But Papa doesn't like me to say it."

"I see." Except she didn't. "Do you have a picture of her?"

Mattie shook her head. "See what I mean? I don't think she was real."

A knock sounded on the door.

"I'll get it," Kate said and opened the door to let Dawson step inside.

He brushed off the moisture clinging to his face. "It's time to go home, Mattie."

"Can I finish my cocoa first?"

Dawson looked from Kate to Isabelle.

Isabelle went to the stove. "Why don't I make some for you, too? Hang your wet things on those hooks." She indicated the spot by the door.

Dawson took off his hat and coat and hung them. Water dripped to the mat below.

Kate paused at Isabelle's side to murmur, "Someone ought to tell him how his daughter feels."

Isabelle nodded then saw Kate's insistent look. "Me?"

"You're the one Mattie talks to." Kate returned to the table.

Isabelle took the cup of cocoa and set it before Dawson.

"Miss Isabelle says her mama used to make her cocoa every Sunday night. And now she's making us some," Mattie said.

Dawson nodded. "That's nice." He cradled his cup in his hands. "Sure hope it doesn't snow," he said.

Isabelle wondered why he worried so much about snow that surely wouldn't last long this time of year but she wasn't sure how to voice her curiosity.

Kate did, though. "Why is snow so bad?"

"Snowstorms always carry a risk to the cattle. They can be trapped, buried, and unable to get feed. But this time of year, they could have calves at their sides and the calves don't fare well. On top of that, spring storms are often heavy, wet snow that can really play havoc on the herds." He rubbed his chin with his fist. A furrow appeared between his eyebrows. "We've had significant losses this winter already."

Mattie leaned forward. "Isabelle knows Spanish. Her grandmother lived in Spain. That's kind of close to England."

Isabelle stayed expressionless. She did not want him to ask about her family. Thankfully, he had no reason to connect the Redfield name with her Castellano ancestors and likely wouldn't be aware of their prominence.

"That's interesting." He clearly didn't think so but meant to be polite. "How are you settling in here?"

Isabelle let Kate answer.

"The place suits very well, though Father is still tired from the journey. He'll recover soon."

Isabelle knew her friend well enough to catch the little note of concern that Kate tried to hide.

Kate drained her cup. "Mattie, do you want to see the doctor's office?"

"Is it scary?"

Kate chuckled. "Not at all. In fact, he has some books he keeps for children to look at. Do you want to see them?"

"Okay." Mattie followed Kate into the sitting room.

Kate paused at the doorway to glance back at Isabelle with a quick dart of her eyes in Dawson's direction. Isabelle couldn't mistake her friend's intention of providing her a chance to talk to Dawson about Mattie.

She filled her lungs and let her air push out the words she wanted to say before she could lose her courage. "Mattie says she can't remember her mother."

His jaw muscles bunched. "I don't want her to. She was an unsuitable woman."

"Unsuitable?" A dozen possibilities as to what he

meant flitted through her mind. "But you married her." How unsuitable could she have been?

"She didn't fit in. Didn't even try. She neglected the home and after Mattie was born, neglected her. If my mother hadn't lived close by I shudder to think what would have become of Mattie. I don't know how many times I came home to find Violet missing and the baby next door. After Ma died, Annie was doing her best to care for the others but most of Mattie's care fell on her. She was only sixteen."

He looked at her, anger, despair and regret racing across his face.

"Did you not realize what she was like before you married her?" Isabelle's words came out in agonized slowness. To think of such a marriage. And then to have a child in a home where she knew no security. How awful.

"Of course not." His shoulders rose and fell. "Or perhaps I let myself be blind to the facts. I was a nineteen-year-old pleased by her attention. I fancied myself deeply in love." He turned his cup round and round. "I don't want Mattie to know anything about her."

Isabelle breathed a silent prayer for guidance. Even if it would bring his wrath down around her shoulders, she would do her best to make Dawson understand Mattie's need to know about her mother. "May I have permission to say something?"

His gaze came to her, full of warning and something more. Likely only her imagination suggested she saw a longing for understanding. "Permission granted."

"Have you considered that by not allowing Mattie to remember her mother, she's lost her twice over?"

Eyes of blue turned stormy. "She's better off that way."

She forged on with what she wanted to say. "Like it or not, her mother is part of her. Don't you realize that if you teach her to hate her mother, you teach her to hate part of herself?"

His eyes darkened to midnight blue. His lips pressed together.

A trickle of fear skittered across her shoulders. She had never before been so bold and confrontational. Had she gone too far?

He shoved his cup away. "You don't know what you're talking about."

She caught his arm, stopping him before he could push from the table. "I have lost my mother. And my father. I can't imagine pretending they never existed."

"Did they love you?"

She nodded, her eyes filling with tears as the memory of being loved and cherished ached through her.

"Then it's not the same." He shook her hand from his arm and got to his feet. "You couldn't possibly understand."

Isabelle heard the door to the examining room open and close and tried to signal him to stop talking but he continued, ignoring her desperate looks.

"You're a city woman. You don't belong here any more than Mattie's mother did. I regret I ever met her. I wish she wasn't Mattie's mother. It would suit me fine if Mattie forgot her entirely."

"Papa." The agonized sound jerked his attention to his daughter standing in the doorway, a shocked look on her pale face.

* * *

Dawson's heart landed in his boots. He'd meant the warning for Isabelle's ears alone. He took a step toward Mattie, stopped at the look on her face. Like bone china about to shatter. "Mattie?" he whispered.

Big, unfocused eyes met his.

"Mattie?" He spoke more firmly, wanting to shake her from this state of shock.

Mattie's eyes left his, stared past him. She swallowed loudly and shuddered.

He reached for her but she twisted her shoulders away and he let his hand fall to his side, afraid to touch her lest she break into pieces. What had he done? He only wanted to protect his child. Instead, she looked as if he'd struck her. But why should his honest opinion of her mother upset her so? It had nothing to do with how he felt about Mattie.

She blinked. Her eyes narrowed and she looked at Isabelle. She reached out a hand to the woman, tears pooling on her bottom eyelids.

Isabelle half rose then darted a glance at Dawson and sat back down, shaking her head sadly at Mattie's silent plea.

Kate seemed the only one who knew what to do. She pressed Mattie to her side. "You only heard part of the conversation. I'm sure there's a good explanation for what your papa said."

Mattie rolled her head back and forth and drew in a sobbing breath.

"It's time to go home, little one." Dawson hoped she would respond to the gentle pleading in his voice.

She marched over to her coat, drying on the back of

a chair, and slipped into it without a word, without looking at any of them.

He donned his own outerwear in the same silent state,
feeling as if someone had driven a firebrand into his
heart. "Thank you for the cocoa. Good day, ladies." He
reached down to capture Mattie's hand and led her from
the house. He swung into the saddle and lifted her to
ride behind him. She sat stiff as a board.

"Hang on," he said.

She didn't move and he reached back to pull her arms
about his waist. Normally she hugged him tight and
pressed her face to his back, something that gave him a
lot of pleasure. The fact she did neither hurt like being
trampled by a bull.

"Let's get home." He turned the horse toward the
ranch. Surely she would snap out of her state once they
reached the ranch.

He could blame no one but himself for this. He'd
known from the first that he shouldn't allow her to get
too fond of Isabelle. He should have put his foot down.
But he'd been lulled along by the affection Mattie had
for her. By Isabelle's affection for Mattie. And his need
for someone to watch Mattie after school.

He sucked back the groan that rushed to his mouth.
Isabelle was too much like Violet. That was why Mattie remembered her mother and asked about her when
she had formerly forgotten her.

Isabelle's words rang in his ears—Violet was half of
Mattie. He didn't want it to be so but he couldn't deny
it. Surrounding her with people like himself—the Marshall family and others of the community—would ensure the Violet part of her would disappear.

The rain stopped. Snow did not follow. At least he

didn't have the added worry of his cows dealing with a snowstorm. What Bible verse did Grandfather quote when Dawson or one of the other members of the family fretted and worried? *Take no thought for the morrow.* Like Grandfather said, there was enough to be concerned with today without worrying about tomorrow.

Easier said than done with so many things on his mind. How had his cows fared? If only he could go check on them. It would ease his mind. At least he would know what he had to deal with.

And now Mattie. He wished he could think of something that would make her feel better, but apart from pulling the words back, which was impossible, he could think of nothing, so they rode on, tense silence thundering in his ears.

At the ranch, he reined in. "Want to come with me to the barn?" Normally, Mattie insisted on accompanying him and helping as he took care of Jumper.

"I want to go to the house," she mumbled, not a trace of enthusiasm in her voice.

"Very well." He rode to the door and let her down.

She didn't even wait for him to dismount before she went inside. By the time he reached the door, she had disappeared from the cloakroom. He followed her into the kitchen but she hurried through to the stairs and raced up to her bedroom.

Annie stared after her then turned to Dawson. "Something wrong?"

He slumped to the nearest chair and hung his hands between his knees. "I took her and Isabelle to the falls. No one else came along." He scrubbed at his chin. "I should have known better. Isabelle reminds Mattie of her mother and she's upset."

Annie crossed her arms and studied him. "You couldn't hope to push Violet out of her thoughts forever."

He jerked his head up. "Why not?" He held up a hand. "Never mind." Probably all women had the same senti-mental notion about the necessity of Mattie remembering Violet. But they hadn't lived with the neglect, the discon-tent and the criticism he'd endured day after day. They hadn't seen the way she refused to take care of Mattie. Like he'd told Isabelle, if not for his ma, he didn't know what would have happened to his wee daughter.

Grandfather limped into the room. "What sent little Mattie fleeing up the stairs like someone was after her?"

With a gut-deep sigh, Dawson sat back and explained it again.

Grandfather patted Dawson on the back. "Son, you can't wrap her up in cotton wool and hope she never has to face harsh realities. Could be it's time for her to learn who she is. Could be God sent Isabelle here to help the process along."

Dawson did not want to listen to Grandfather telling him that Isabelle was part of God's plan for Mattie's life. He bolted to his feet. "I forgot I left Jumper outside. I best go take care of him."

But if he thought going to the barn and tending his horse would ease his troubled thoughts, he discovered it wasn't so. Why had he taken Isabelle to the falls? He should have heeded the warning shouted by his brain. Instead, he'd pushed it away, choosing a few minutes of selfish pleasure over the need to protect both himself and Mattie from the momentary enjoyment of an outing. Now he had to find a way to undo the damage. And to erase the memory of the day's events.

He shook his head, trying to forget the way Isabelle

had clung to him on the trail to the waterfalls. And how she'd stared at the rushing water with an expression of joy.

Either she truly enjoyed nature or she was a very good actress.

He had no intention of trying to discover which.

A little later he returned to the house. Mattie sat at the table, Annie at her side, one arm around the child. They both looked up at his entrance and both wore matching looks of caution.

He slid to the chair across from Mattie. "I'm sorry you heard what I said to Isabelle. Those words were meant for her alone."

Mattie studied him long and hard. "But they were about me."

"No, little one. They weren't. You know I love you and would never hurt you."

Her expression remained unforgiving. "I know you don't like my mama. Annie told me about it a long time ago."

He gave his sister an accusing look.

She simply shrugged. "I answered her questions. That seemed reasonable and I never said you didn't like Violet."

Mattie sat up straighter and waited for the adults to look at her. "No one had to tell me that. I just know it. 'Cause she didn't love you like she should." She crossed her arms over her chest in a defiant way and puckered her mouth. "But why don't you like Isabelle?" A whole world of challenge rang from her.

Dawson opened his mouth to say it was because she reminded him of Violet. He closed it again without speaking. Because she didn't. Yes, she was a city girl and obviously one used to the finer things of life. That alone made her unsuitable for the Bella Creek area let alone ranch life. Or did it? Couldn't people from all walks of life embrace challenges? But why was he even thinking along those lines? It wasn't as if he meant to court her or even spend more time with her.

Mattie stared at him, waiting for his answer.

"It isn't a matter of liking her or not liking her. Sometimes you simply have to trust me to know what's best. I don't want you hanging around her anymore."

"You might be grown-up and my papa and all, but you are wrong about her." Mattie rose with unexpected dignity and stalked into the sitting room to join Grandfather.

Dawson let out a long, weary sigh. Sometimes being a father was hard.

Annie crossed her arms, too. Why had he never before noticed how Mattie imitated her? Of course, considering how much time they spent together, it was normal. "I have to say I agree with Mattie. You are judging Isabelle wrongly. I think she's good for Mattie."

How could Annie make such a judgment in a matter of a few days? He bit back his thought. She'd known Isabelle the same length of time he had, and he had made up his mind about her. "I want Mattie to stay away from her."

"Humph." Annie went to the stove, keeping her back to Dawson, but he could have sliced her disapproval into chunks large enough to fill the barn loft. "What do you plan to do with Mattie after school, then?"

He didn't answer. He had only one option but he knew

he faced opposition on every side, so he kept his thoughts to himself.

Sometimes doing what he thought was right was difficult.

Chapter Eight

Isabelle choked back tears as she explained to Kate how the conversation had deteriorated. "I haven't changed my mind about her needing to be allowed a connection to her mother. Even if Dawson found the woman unsuitable." A woman like herself. Someone who would never fit in. She straightened her shoulders. "Kate, is it true? Is there no place here for someone like me?"

Kate hugged her. "What do you think? Does it matter what we came from or does it matter where we're going?"

"Both, I suppose." Isabelle mused over the words for a moment. "Maybe it's like I said to Dawson about Mattie's mother. To deny our past is to deny a part of ourselves."

Kate patted her back. "You're right. I suppose the trick is to find a way to keep our past in its rightful place so we can achieve our goals."

Isabelle nodded. "I know what I want and I am going to do my best to get it."

Kate tipped her head and considered her. "What is it you want?"

"I want to be accepted for who I am. Not what I have." She looked about the kitchen. Her gaze stopped at her coat hanging by the stove to dry and she recalled Kate's words that she should have dressed more plainly. But her merit shouldn't be judged by what she wore or where she came from and certainly not by the amount of the money left to her. She turned back to Kate, her voice strong. "Promise me you'll keep my inheritance a secret."

Kate gave her a one-armed hug. "That's your secret to keep or reveal as you choose."

Dr. Baker came from his room. "My goodness. I believe I slept away most of the day." He glanced toward the examining room. "Are you sure no one has called for me?"

"Not one person," Kate assured him. "Are you feeling better?"

Her father gave Kate a kindly look. "I'm fit as a fiddle."

Kate made him tea and fussed over him until he waved her away. "Kate, don't you have something better to do than worry about an old man?"

Although Kate did her best to hide her feelings, Isabelle clearly read her friend's hurt and understood its cause. Kate did not care to hear her father talking about being old. Poor Kate had been so frightened when her father was injured. Knowing what it was like to be without both parents, Isabelle had offered sympathy and consolation. She and Kate had grown exceedingly close during those anxious days.

Since his recovery, Kate tended to hover over her father.

The good doctor must have noticed Kate's sudden

stillness. He reached for her hand. "Not that I don't appreciate your concern and I couldn't manage my office without you." His expression grew puzzled. "Did I do it on my own before my accident?"

Isabelle had observed the doctor's erratic memory of events before his injury.

Kate worried her lips before she spoke. "Father, there is nothing that gives me more pleasure than being your assistant." She bustled to her feet. "I better get a meal on the table."

Isabelle jumped up. "I said I would take care of preparing the meals."

Kate slowly faced her. "I don't want you to feel tied down."

"I need to be useful."

"Then let's do it together. But I want you to promise me one thing."

"Of course." Isabelle waited, knowing her friend would be kind and gentle.

"You remember you are always free to consider other possibilities. Don't feel you are obliged to stay here. You never know what God has in store for you."

Isabelle happily agreed. When she'd met Mattie, she'd hoped spending time with her was part of God's plans for her. As she'd accompanied Dawson and his daughter to the waterfalls, she'd even allowed herself to imagine she might have a place in both their lives. Before the afternoon ended, Dawson had made it unmistakably clear that he did not see it that way. She closed her eyes against the disappointment scraping her insides. "I don't expect there will be anything else to consider." She would do her best to be satisfied.

* * *

Dawson took a sullen, quiet Mattie to town the next day. "I'll take you home after school," he said as he dropped her off in front of the store.

"Goodbye." She marched away without a backward look.

With a heavy heart, he went to work. His movements felt sluggish as the day passed with agonizing slowness. He saw Isabelle leave the house to get firewood. She never so much as glanced his way. Wasn't that what he wanted? Yes, it was. But it didn't feel right. In fact, it felt downright awful. As if someone had erased the color from the sky.

Realizing he had to inform Isabelle not to expect Mattie after school, he set aside his tools and crossed to the woodpile. "I'm returning home early today so I won't need Mattie to come here."

She faced him, her expression impassive, but he noted the slightest puckering of her mouth. Something most people wouldn't even see but he'd noticed it a few times and knew it signaled displeasure.

"I see. Thank you for letting me know." She adjusted the pieces of wood in her arms and turned her feet toward the door.

If only he hadn't been able to hear the hurt in her voice. "It's—" He could hardly say it wasn't personal because it was completely personal. What could he offer in way of explanation? "I have things to take care of at home." Like explain to Grandfather how the school would get built if no one showed up to do the work. Grandfather wouldn't likely accept that a Marshall had a good excuse for not being there.

"You don't need to explain yourself to me." She didn't

even turn to tell him that but continued on her way, stepping into the house and closing the door behind her.

He clamped down on his back teeth. She was right. He didn't need to explain himself to her and yet he wished she would say she understood. Mattie did not need to know more about her mother. That knowledge held nothing but pain for his child.

And perhaps more pain for himself? The question came unbidden, likely planted there by something Grandfather had said because it certainly didn't come from Dawson's thoughts. He no longer felt any pain at Violet's behavior. All he felt was a gut-wrenching need to protect Mattie from knowing how little her mother had cared for them.

Returning to work, he bent over the saw, grateful the sound of cutting the board covered his moan. He had to do what was right for Mattie. He must protect her.

He waited on his saddled horse outside the store before school was dismissed.

Mattie exited last and stood on the wooden platform, not looking at him.

"Let's go home."

She didn't move. Simply stared into the distance.

He reached down for her hand. She shifted and crossed her arms. "Mattie!" When she didn't respond, he dismounted and lifted her to the back of his horse then climbed up in front of her.

Again, he pulled her arms about him and warned her to hang on. But her arms remained limp about his waist and he rode homeward with caution.

As soon as they reached the ranch, she hurried inside. He went to the barn, in no hurry to confront his grandfather. He brushed his horse, swept the floor and rearranged the tack room. Finally he could think of no more reason to delay going to the house.

He entered and took his time about taking off his jacket, then decided the cloakroom could use some tidying.

"Best get in here," Grandfather roared from beyond the door.

This was not going to be fun, Dawson thought as he stepped into the kitchen.

Grandfather sat facing the door. "Boy, what's your explanation for quitting work in the middle of the day? I'm counting on you to get that school built, but instead you're lollygagging about the place. Do I have to go in and do the work myself?"

"I had to bring Mattie home."

"No, you didn't have to. You decided to. Different thing entirely."

Dawson let the accusation go. What choice did he have? He certainly wasn't leaving Mattie with Isabelle again. "I'm about out of options."

"Ain't how I see it. What I see is a stubborn man unwilling to change his mind. You had a perfectly good arrangement with Isabelle. One, I might point out, that made Mattie happy. Now just because the girl remembers a sad incident involving her mother, you blame Isabelle." The old man snorted. "I suppose if she'd remembered out in the barn, you'd blame the cats."

"Don't be absurd."

Grandfather leaned over his canes and fixed Dawson with a piercing gaze. "Let me tell you how it's gonna be. You are going to go to town and spend the day working on the school. The whole day."

"I suppose you got it all figured out what I'm to do

with Mattie. Well, let me tell you how it's not gonna be. She is not going to stay with Isabelle."

They faced each other. Dawson could be as stubborn as his grandfather when it was called for.

Grandfather relented first, which gave Dawson a sense of victory. Edged with caution. The old man did not often give up a fight. Unless he had something up his sleeve.

"I tell you what. I'll send Annie in to get Mattie after school."

Annie appeared in the doorway as if she'd been waiting to be summoned.

Dawson looked from his sister to his grandfather. Why did he get the feeling there was something odd about this setup? "I thought Annie was too busy."

Annie shrugged. "I am, but seems I have little choice."

Dawson knew when to accept defeat graciously. "Then that's it."

The next morning, he took Mattie to the barn with him as he went to saddle the horse. She had not spoken to him except for a few necessary words and had turned her back to him when he tried to kiss her good-night.

"Mattie, this can't go on."

"Am I acting like my mama? Will you hate me if I do?"

He could barely stand, so great was his shock. He tried to settle his thoughts. When he could speak in a normal tone of voice, he squatted to her level to look into her eyes.

"Matilda Annabelle Marshall, I will never hate you. Never, ever."

Her gaze searched his a long time. "Do you hate Mama?"

"Oh, little one. It's not that simple." How did he explain to a six-year-old the feelings of rejection and disappointment and failure his marriage had produced in him? "I have never hated her. But she—"

"She was unsuitable. Like Isabelle."

The words, spoken with such decisiveness, cut a swath through his thoughts. He didn't know how to respond. "I guess."

"Then I don't understand. Isabelle is nice and you don't like her."

He straightened and continued toward the barn. "Some things are hard to understand."

"Or maybe you're wrong."

What had happened to the sweet little girl who had loved him so fully and freely until now? Knowing Isabelle only a few days had destroyed his relationship with his daughter. Already his opinion was being verified that the woman would not be good for them.

He left a sullen child at school and crossed the street to start work. He made sure he stayed on the far side of the building so he couldn't see the doctor's house. It didn't stop him from hearing the slap of the door. He stared blankly at the wall before him, refusing to satisfy his curiosity as to whether it was Isabelle who went out or one of the others.

A sigh of relief escaped his lips when, later in the day, he watched Annie ride by to pick up Mattie. The child would be safe at home.

His heart marginally more at ease, he continued sawing and hammering. The board he had didn't fit the space he needed and he made his way to the pile of lumber to find another. The sound of girlish laughter drew his attention toward the house next door. That sure sounded like Annie's voice. His nerves tensed and he stopped to listen. Someone spoke. Annie for sure. Had she taken Mattie home and returned? Another voice came through the open window. Mattie? A shudder raced across his shoulders. He tossed the length of wood back on the pile and strode across the yard. How dare Annie deliberately ignore his order to keep Mattie away from Isabelle?

He pounded on the door.

Isabelle opened and fell back before his scowl.

"I want to speak to Annie." His sister sat at the table, a look of defiance on her face. Beside her sat Mattie, with a matching look.

"I'm right here," Annie said.

"I'd like a word in private." He tipped his head to indicate he meant to talk to her outside…away from the listening ears of little girls.

Annie squeezed Mattie's shoulders. "I'll be right back." She followed Dawson to the far corner of the yard.

He confronted her, his anger burning through his veins. "What are you doing here? You know I don't want Mattie to be around Isabelle."

"The day I can't go where I want and see whom I want will never come." She jabbed her finger at him as she spoke. "If I want to visit Isabelle, I will."

He leaned back so her finger didn't poke his chest. "Not with Mattie, you won't."

"So now you're going to tell me what I can and can't do when I have your daughter? Me, who has looked after her for three years. If you don't care for how I am with her, I suggest you find someone else." Jab jab jab.

He caught her finger. "Stop doing that."

Brother and sister scowled at each other.

Annie released a whoosh of air. "Dawson, you know I don't have time to run into town every afternoon and get Mattie. Isabelle is the perfect solution for someone to watch her."

"You and Grandfather had this all worked out, didn't you?" He made no attempt to keep the disgust out of his voice.

She shrugged. "We thought it was time for a little prod in the right direction."

"Right direction?" The pair of them were so mistaken. He swung away and took a step toward the house.

Annie caught his arm. "What are you going to do?"

"I'm going to take Mattie home."

She planted herself in front of him. "You'll upset Grandfather and he's already got enough on his mind."

"Like what?"

"He feels helpless that he can't do anything to hurry the rebuilding along. He's worried about Pa and the boys. And he's worried about you." She jabbed him again.

"Why would he worry about me?"

"Because you're turning into a bitter, judgmental man."

"I am not."

She shrugged. "I won't let you upset Grandfather."

He didn't fancy another staring match. "Then what do you suggest I do?"

"Leave her with Isabelle."

"I can't do that."

"Do you think if Mattie doesn't see Isabelle she will somehow unremember Violet?"

"*Unremember* isn't a word."

"Nor is it possible."

He scrubbed at his chin. What was he to do?

Annie returned to the house. Was she going to take

Mattie home? It would be a relief. She opened the door. "Isabelle, Dawson would like to speak to you."

He would? Why?

Looking as confused as he felt, Isabelle stepped outside.

Isabelle understood that Dawson didn't want Mattie coming to stay with her after school. She knew he wouldn't be pleased by Annie bringing Mattie over and could tell by his body language and his scowl that he'd told Annie that very thing.

She'd watched brother and sister face each other, circling like wary opponents.

Then Annie had marched back to the house and told Isabelle that Dawson wanted to see her. "He does?" She could think of only one reason… Dawson meant to tell her again how unsuitable she was, how dangerous to Mattie just because he and Isabelle did not see eye to eye on the subject of the child's mother.

Stilling her trepidation, she crossed to where he stood looking stormy enough to send a grown man running away. She would show no fear.

"Yes?" Good. Her voice sounded calm.

He stared past her to the house. Perhaps imagining Annie watching. "I suppose you could tell I tried to find other arrangements for Mattie."

She almost laughed. "I could tell."

His gaze flickered to her. Surprised. Wary. "It isn't working out very well."

"I'm sorry?" But she wasn't. She only said what she thought he wanted to hear.

"Annie's too busy to come to town and get her every afternoon."

"Of course." Where was he going with this conversation?

"Grandfather is getting upset because construction is slow on the school and he can't do it himself."

"I see." Yes, she could understand how the older man would find that galling.

"I seem to have run out of options."

She waited. Whatever he wanted to say, he would have to say it without any prodding from her.

"What I'm saying…asking…is, can she continue to come here after school? You see, I'm rather stuck."

"That's hardly a way to convince me to agree." Stuck? The only reason he asked her. Not that she was surprised.

"I'll be right next door."

As if that made Isabelle a safe choice! He sure knew how to make a girl feel special. But she wasn't about to refuse his request. "I will gladly keep Mattie after school, on one condition."

"A condition? I guess I have to hear it before I can agree or otherwise."

She ignored the warning in his eyes and the way his jaw muscles clenched.

"I ask only that she be allowed to talk about her mother if she desires and you allow me to answer any questions she has." She stood with her hands clasped at her waist, hoping her expression revealed nothing of her nervousness. Would her request result in him changing his mind yet again?

"I don't see how you can answer questions about Mattie's mother, seeing as you never met her."

"I don't mean specific questions, but I simply want the freedom to allow her to grieve a very great loss."

He snorted. "It wasn't a great loss. Mattie is better

off without a discontent, always-ready-to-leave, always-complaining mother."

"Whether or not Violet was a good mother doesn't change the fact she was Mattie's mother." She rushed onward, determined not to let his anger deter her. "I believe the mother–child relationship is the most basic of human bonds. Losing it inevitably creates an emptiness and a sadness that only grows if not filled."

"Don't you think I've done my best to fill it?"

"Of course you have. That's not what I mean. I remember when my parents died. I was very close to my mother. Cousin Augusta, with the best of intentions, thought the way for me to deal with it was to push the loss into the background and never mention it. It's not the sort of pain a person can hope to bury."

How did she know this? She stared at the blackened ground that filled the empty yards beyond where they stood. She knew because of her own experience. "I had just turned twelve when I moved in with Cousin Augusta. I'm afraid I was a sad, weepy girl whose world had been ripped apart by my parents' deaths. Cousin Augusta, in what she thought was kindness, said I must put the past behind me and not talk about it anymore."

She shuddered a little at the remembered agony of those days. "I didn't want to displease my cousin and guardian, so I tried to obey. Every time a memory came to me, every time I felt sad and wanted to cry, I stuffed those things back until one day I couldn't contain it any longer. I started to cry and couldn't stop. I cried and cried." Great heaving sobs that sucked at her very soul. "My cousin called in the doctor to give me something to calm me down. Instead, the kindly old man sat on the edge of the bed where I lay sobbing my heart out. He talked softly and calmly. At first I didn't listen, didn't hear him over my sobs. Then slowly, his words made their way to my brain. I don't recall most of what he said except he told me there was healing in both crying and remembering and that talking about loved ones kept them alive. 'They'll forever be a part of you. One you can't erase. Nor should you want to.'"

She drew in a shaky breath. The memory and words had rushed from her without forethought. What must he think of her confession? All she'd wanted was to make him see that expecting Mattie to forget she had a mother was hurtful and potentially harmful.

"The doctor must have said the same thing to Cousin Augusta because I was told to talk about my parents as much as I wanted and I stopped panicking. The interesting thing was I seldom talked about my parents after that. Oh, I would point out how they would have enjoyed the sunset or the Christmas service at church. Mostly little memories. Once I knew I could talk about them if I wanted, I didn't feel the same need. And my life seemed more manageable after that."

She didn't know what it was like to lose a parent at three or four, but loss was loss, especially loss of a parent, and as she'd said to Dawson, Mattie could not erase half of her parentage and still be whole.

"I'm sorry for the pain of your loss." Dawson squeezed her shoulder.

She shuddered under his palm and then she smiled and calm came to her eyes. She leaned into his hand. "You see? I didn't have the fear that they would be snatched from my thoughts as they'd been snatched from my life." She settled back, her passion banked. "Maybe Mattie feels the same."

He dropped his hand to his side and eased back six

inches. "Except she doesn't have any memories. Violet spent hardly any time with Mattie."

"In which case, I would suggest she's had a double loss."

He stared at her. "Mattie doesn't even remember her mother."

"You do." Her words rang with accusation.

He groaned. "Not things I'd care to share with a six-year-old."

She rested a hand on his forearm, hoping to convey her sympathy that his memories were so bitter.

"Besides, I don't see what good it will do for you to talk about her mother when you know nothing about her."

"You could tell me about her." She read the refusal in his eyes and removed her hand. "You have to have some good thoughts about her. After all, you saw something in her that made you want to marry her. Don't you think you could share those with Mattie?"

He turned to stare at the building next door. "I'm supposed to be finishing the schoolhouse. I can't stop in the middle of the day to take Mattie home. It would upset Grandfather."

Her heart went out to him as she watched him struggle with his warring emotions.

Lord, I may not be the one to help him heal but please send someone into his life who can.

He sighed, signaling that he had given in to her request. "Very well. But promise you will only answer questions." The words were strained and she understood he had a hard time allowing this concession.

"I can promise that." She touched his arm again. "Dawson, believe me when I say I would never hurt Mattie."

His eyes remained guarded. "I believe you would not *intentionally* hurt her but sometimes adult choices have far-reaching consequences."

She shivered at the warning in his words.

Chapter Nine

Dawson worked on the end of the schoolhouse and had only to move to his right to see the doctor's house. When he heard the door slap shut next door, he leaned that direction and looked up. Isabelle carried out a bucket and dumped water on the bush. Done, she straightened and looked up at the blue sky. He saw only her profile but could tell she smiled as if enjoying the view. She slowly turned. He held his breath as her gaze came toward him. Their eyes connected with a jolt that shook his whole body. She lifted a hand in a wave and went back inside.

He jerked back. He'd chosen this position solely so he could keep an eye on Mattie when she came over after school, but that was hours away and he couldn't keep his attention off the house. If Grandfather could see him, he would point out how slowly the building was progressing. Dawson wanted to be done more than Grandfather could guess, and he set to work with complete concentration.

After school, Mattie stopped by on her way to see Isabelle. His daughter was still cautious around him and that stung like a thousand bees attacking.

"Have fun," he said as she sidled away, not letting him toss her in the air and tickle her as he usually did.

She nodded and crossed to the back door, where Isabelle opened the door and greeted her.

Dawson felt alone and tense when the door closed behind them. His thoughts were all tangled. Last evening Grandfather and Annie had kept up a running commentary on Isabelle's virtues and delivered a scathing assessment of Dawson's flaws in not seeing those virtues for himself.

Not that he wasn't aware of many of those virtues. She was gentle, kind, and from what he could see, she worked hard at keeping the doctor's house. None of that negated his fear of a city woman and his conviction that she would soon tire of Bella Creek and head back to the city and its attractions. What chance did a cowboy have against such things?

He pressed his hat tighter to his head. What was wrong with him? Why did he feel such a strong attraction to Isabelle? Did he have a character flaw that caused him to be drawn toward women who didn't fit into his life? He forced his attention back to his task. What did it mean if he did? That he should give up his dreams of having his own ranch and become a city dweller? He shuddered at the idea. All he knew was ranching. What would he do in a city but wither up and die?

Twice he was so distracted by his wandering thoughts that he had to cut another board because of a mistake. Good thing he was working alone or he might have had to explain himself. Not that he didn't wish some of the men around town would lend a hand on this project. After all, many of them had children. Didn't they want to see them in a proper schoolhouse?

He stopped pounding in a nail to tip his head toward the house next door, hoping for the sound of voices, but the windows were closed and he heard nothing. A trip to the stack of lumber allowed him to look at the house and he saw Isabelle at the stove. Was she making more hot cocoa? A good memory of her mother.

She had suggested he share memories of Violet with Mattie but there were no sweet memories. She had never made cocoa for Mattie. Had avoided as much as possible lifting her from her cot when she wakened. When Dawson was home, Violet never held Mattie on her lap. She'd never rushed to the door to welcome Dawson home or made him a cup of coffee. Nor baked cookies. Dawson had done his best to make up for Violet's lack of interest in their daughter. Thankfully, his mother had lived nearby and she gave Mattie the attention she deserved.

He worked steadily—if somewhat distractedly—for two hours, then went to the door and knocked.

Isabelle opened the door. "Come in. She's just getting her coat on."

"Smells good in here."

"We baked cookies. Would you like some? Mattie, bring your papa some of the cookies you made."

Mattie picked up a plate of misshapen objects and offered it to him.

"These look delicious." He chose two and bit into one. "They're as good as they look."

"They're snickerdoodles." Mattie choked back a giggle.

"That's a funny name for a cookie." He waggled his eyebrows and was rewarded with the flicker of a smile. He could wish for more but would take that as a sign that she would soon be back to her normal, cheerful self.

They went to the livery barn, got his horse and rode

home in silence—but not an uncomfortable one. She leaned her head against his back and he tucked her arms under his.

The next day Mattie eagerly prepared to leave. He knew school wasn't the draw… Visiting Isabelle was. Tension edged through his insides. He was allowing a lot to ride on Isabelle's time here. His fists clenched on the reins.

They arrived at the store and he dropped Mattie off to go to class, took the horse to the livery barn before he set to work on the school, where again he was the only man to show up. If Grandfather knew, he would likely ride to town and call a meeting in which he would make every man understand this to be a joint project…not a Marshall one. Dawson didn't mean to tell him. Besides, they'd all promised to work on Saturday.

Again he found his gaze and his thoughts turning toward the house next door. Isabelle went to the store once and twice came out to get wood.

Mattie again came over after school, this time allowing Dawson to hug her. Things would soon be back to normal between them.

Friday morning, he hoped they'd reached that place as Mattie clung to him on the ride to town. Maybe she was discovering it took too much energy to remain angry.

Something about those words accused him, but before he could analyze that thought they'd arrived in town. He left Mattie at the store and went to work. "Morning," he called to two men already working on the school. Finally some help, and having the other two there, calling out to each other, asking questions, standing side by side to muse over a problem, made it possible for him to keep his thoughts from wandering to the house next door. The day passed quickly until the time when Mattie skipped over after school.

She said hello to the others and gave Dawson a quick hug, in a hurry to go next door.

He stared after her. Would she and Isabelle sit and discuss Violet? Would Isabelle give Mattie an unrealistic picture of a loving mother? Wouldn't the truth destroy his daughter?

"Here, give me a hand with this."

He shook off his endless questions and focused on the work before him. But his concern returned with a hundred companions when he went to get Mattie.

Isabelle and Mattie both looked pleased. Mattie tucked something into her coat pocket. He couldn't see what and a warning bell tolled in his head.

"Thank you," he said to Isabelle.

"My pleasure," she said, a smile lighting her face. "She's a sweet child."

He waited, wondering if she had more to say. When it seemed she didn't, he agreed with her statement.

"I made something." Mattie pulled the folded papers from her pocket. "You want to see it?"

The warning bell increased in volume. "Of course I do."

"Come in and sit down." Isabelle indicated the chairs at the table.

He sat down and pulled Mattie to his knee. Isabelle sat in the chair beside him.

Mattie laid a little booklet on the table. "It's a story about my life."

He ground his teeth together. Her life, according to Isabelle, must include Violet.

Mattie turned the first page. She'd drawn a crooked barn with what he understood to be a horse beside it. Beneath she had printed the words *I live on a ranch*.

With a rattle of paper, she turned to the second page, a

picture of a table with several stick figures sitting around it. *I have lots in my family.*

Dawson's tension mounted with every turn of the pages. *Aunt Annie is a good cook. Grandfather reads to me. My papa hugs me lots. I like my kittens.* Each page had a picture drawn by Mattie. They came to the final page and he closed his eyes, afraid of what he'd read.

Mattie read the words aloud. "'God loves me lots.'"

Dawson opened his eyes and stared. Nothing about Violet.

Isabelle chuckled. "You needn't look so surprised."

He hugged Mattie. "That was a very nice book. You must show it to Aunt Annie and Grandfather and the others when they get back."

"I will."

"Now run outside and wait by Jumper."

She faced him. "Are you going to say something mean to Isabelle?"

"Of course not. Why would you think that?"

"'Cause you do."

Her words accused him. He wished he could deny it but he couldn't. Yes, he'd been harsh with her. If this booklet was any indication, he had perhaps been wrong. She could have used the afternoon to encourage Mattie to think about Violet. They could have drawn fancy clothes, big-city life. Instead, she'd guided the child into seeing how much she loved the ranch.

"I won't be mean. I promise."

"Okay." Mattie went outside. He waited until he could see her by the horse then turned to Isabelle.

"You surprised me."

She lowered her gaze. "I gathered that." Her dark eyes met his. "I hope it was a good surprise."

"It was. I half expected..." He shrugged.

She quirked her brows. "You thought I would want Mattie to talk about her mother. I only asked that I be allowed to answer any questions she had." She studied him a moment, her gaze sliding over him making him want something...a connection, a sharing, a—

He shook his head. He could not trust those feelings. Nor could he deny them.

Isabelle chuckled softly, further unsettling him. "Mattie is a very happy, content child. I have no wish to change that." She put her hand on his arm, gentle and warm. "Isn't it time you trusted me?" Her eyes were as dark as a new moon, full of kindness and something more. Something he recognized as an echo of his own heart. Longing for someone to share life with.

He covered her hand with his own. "Trust does not come easy for me."

"I understand that. But at least give it a chance."

Their look went on and on. He couldn't say what she saw or felt but he found a whole world of possibility. Possibility that both attracted and frightened. He had trusted before and paid an awful price. But Grandfather was right—he had to stop judging Isabelle to be like Violet.

The door opened and Mattie rushed in. "Papa, are we going home?"

"Be right there." He smiled at Isabelle. "Thank you again." He could almost wish tomorrow wasn't Saturday. Mattie wouldn't be attending school. He'd have no excuse to visit the doctor's house.

Dawson returned to the school the next day, glad to see a group of men ready to go to work. They looked to him for direction and he soon had them cutting wood and adding it to the walls. He paused a moment after he nailed a board in place and stood back, pleased to see how quickly the work proceeded with so many hands. At this rate, the school would soon be finished.

He'd be able to go check on his cows.

He'd have no more need to be in town.

But, of course, someone would still need to get Mattie after school. He would do that and perhaps be able to catch glimpses of Isabelle.

As if on cue, she stepped from the house to get firewood. He watched her pick up an armful. She turned and their gazes locked. A smile lifted her lips and lit his heart. The look went on and on until she ducked away as if embarrassed by his long study of her, and she slipped inside and closed the door.

The wood-chippy smell of freshly sawn wood mixed with the odor of men hard at work faded, replaced with the remembered scent of gingerbread and something more that tugged at his thoughts, settled deep into his heart—a delicate sweetness. He shut his eyes and let the memory of that scent fill his mind. It was Isabelle. He'd discovered a different sort of city woman in her... one who strove to learn the skills she lacked, one who cared tenderly for a little girl. One who—

"Hey, Dawson."

He turned at the familiar voice. "Johnny, when did you get back?"

"Two days ago." His smile flattened. "Pa isn't feeling well. He needs my help. Otherwise I would never have returned."

"Why not? Your friends are here." Dawson gave his pal a playful punch on his shoulder.

"And everywhere I turn, I'm reminded of Phebe." He stared into the distance.

Dawson nodded sympathetically. Phebe had been a friend of Violet's and had treated Johnny poorly...just as Violet had treated Dawson. A muscle in his neck twitched. Both were city women.

Isabelle came out again for more wood and Dawson watched her every move until she returned inside. Then he realized Johnny had observed it all. He swung his hammer. "Got to get back to work."

Johnny dogged his steps. "You fancy that gal?"

Dawson didn't have to ask whom he meant. "She watches Mattie for me after school."

"You didn't learn your lesson with Violet?"

"What lesson would that be?" He clenched the hammer so hard his knuckles whitened.

"Dawson, my friend, if you think a *rich* city girl is better than an ordinary city girl, you are headed for a lot of trouble."

"Rich? Why do you say that?"

Johnny snorted. "Because I have eyes. Do you?"

"Of course I do." He'd seen the black skirt and white shirtwaist Isabelle wore. Not unlike what many of the women wore. Perhaps a little better quality.

"I'm going to hazard a guess that all her clothes are extra fine and fit like a seamstress made them."

"I don't know how one could tell that by looking at her." Dawson's mind harkened back to the woolen coat she had arrived in, with its matching bonnet, to the blue dress she'd gone to the ranch in and to the dark purple dress she'd worn on Sunday. Yes, he might have noted that she wore fine clothes...city clothes. Did that make her rich?

"Seems to me you're asking for more heartache if you let yourself be interested in another woman like Violet."

"You're awfully quick to judge. Who's to say she's like Violet?"

"I got eyes. What did you say her name was?"

Dawson gave her name, again wondering why it seemed familiar. "Looks like I'm needed over there." He hurried away before Johnny could say anything more.

Was he repeating his earlier mistake of caring for someone who would hurt him? This time he had more than himself to be concerned about. He had Mattie to consider.

Isabelle wandered about the rooms. She'd tidied and dusted. She'd put meat and vegetables in the oven. Oven pot roast, the recipe said. Isabelle thought it too simple to justify a recipe…not that she minded. Or perhaps she had grown in her ability to make meals and run the house. The thought brought a pleased smile to her lips.

She'd been in and out of the house a number of times for different reasons and always stopped to watch the work on the schoolhouse. Eight or ten men had shown up bright and early. Soon the school would be ready. Sadie would be so pleased. So would Grandfather Marshall. Isabelle gathered he fretted at how slow the rebuilding progressed and chafed because he couldn't help.

Everyone who passed or who went to the store stopped to watch the progress, so Isabelle's interest could not be misunderstood. Even though she watched Dawson more than she watched the building. Surely she wasn't mistaken in thinking his gaze sought her and settled on her for a moment with a smile and nod.

But she couldn't stand about all day watching him, and she hurried back inside and found another chore to do.

The morning passed quickly enough but the afternoon yawned. Kate and the doctor were kept busy with patients. After dinner, the doctor was called away and Kate went with him.

Isabelle had to find a way to amuse herself without standing outdoors watching the men work…though she couldn't have said who any of them were apart from Dawson.

She picked up her book *A Guide to Practical Housewifery* and tried to concentrate on the chapter discussing gardening. No doubt Annie planted a big garden at the ranch. Could Isabelle plant a garden here? She'd ask Dawson. She chuckled. He'd be surprised at such a request, but then, he was slowly learning that Isabelle was not like Violet, apart from being from the city.

She chewed on her bottom lip. What would happen if anyone learned the truth about who she really was?

A wagon rattled by on the street.

Footsteps clattered on the front step. More people to see the doctor. But a knock sounded on the door to the living quarters. Before Isabelle could call out an invitation to enter, the door burst open and Annie rushed inside.

"Who wants to go to the river and see if the ice is breaking up?"

"But isn't the water already running? It was at the waterfall."

"Just underneath. Soon the entire ice surface will break up." Annie grabbed her arm. "Come on. I've never seen it even though I've always wanted to. Get your coat. Where's Kate?"

At least Isabelle knew how to answer that question. "She's helping her father."

"What about Sadie?"

"I saw her go into the store a while ago. I think she's preparing lessons."

Annie glanced out the window. "Dawson will see me if I go over there. I don't want him to know where I'm going."

Isabelle hesitated with her coat half on. "Why?" *Reckless* was a word spoken often in connection to Annie. Was she about to embark on one of those adventures?

"He thinks I should stay home and twiddle my thumbs. Just because Violet did foolish things and got herself killed. She was a city woman and never liked the ranch. But because of her, Dawson thinks everything I do that's fun is dangerous. *Phfft.* I'm only nineteen. I don't intend to be old just yet. Come on." She half dragged Isabelle out the door.

Isabelle pulled back. "Wait. I better leave a note so Kate will know where I've gone."

"Very well. But be quick." Annie watched out the window.

Isabelle studied her a moment. Was she afraid Dawson would see them? Would he forbid Annie to go? Isabelle almost snorted. Annie wouldn't heed Dawson if she had a plan of her own in mind, so Isabelle scribbled out a note. An adventure sounded like what she needed at the moment.

"Good. Now hurry." Annie raced down to the side street to where she'd left the wagon. Isabelle knew no one at the school would have seen it.

Annie had the reins in her hands before Isabelle could climb aboard and she scrambled to get to the bench before Annie drove off.

"Hi." Mattie jumped up from behind the seat, giving Isabelle a fright.

She laughed and returned the child's greeting.

"Did I scare you?"

"You did indeed."

"We're going to see the ice break up on the river."

"That's what your aunt says." They traversed the length of the street. Carly waited for them, mounted on horseback.

"I thought you changed your mind. Or Dawson changed it for you." She directed her comments to Annie.

"Nope," Annie replied, checking over her shoulder. "Now let's get going."

They headed to the east. Isabelle glanced back to town. What was going on? "Isn't the river behind us?" On their trip to Bella Creek they had crossed a narrow, frozen stream south of the town.

"That's just a little creek. We're going to the river that borders Carly's father's land. The Mineral River. Her father said he thought the ice would break up today."

The wagon rattled on at a pace that made Isabelle cling to the bench, and that made it impossible to carry on a conversation. Isabelle glanced back to make sure Mattie was safe. She clutched the back of the seat, her eyes flashing with sheer pleasure. Isabelle could only hope and pray none of them would be tossed from the racing wagon. They careened around corners and bounced over rocks. "Lord, keep us safe," Isabelle shouted in prayer.

Annie spared her a pained look. "You're sounding like Dawson."

Isabelle decided she respected Dawson very much at the moment.

She could see the river ahead. "Thank You, God." Now their frightening journey would end.

They jerked to a stop and Annie and Mattie jumped down. Carly was already on the ground waiting.

"Are you coming?" they asked in unison.

Isabelle ordered her hands to let go of the wood of the seat. She forced her shaking legs to climb off the wagon and followed the others toward the river. Well, she reassured herself, at least she wasn't bored.

Carly pointed out the water bubbling through the ice and spreading across the surface. "It will be soon now, if Father is correct."

Isabelle glanced up and down the bank. A dozen or more people watched the river. This must be a special event, though she was at a loss to know what was so special about watching water coming up from under the ice.

"You hear that?" Annie asked.

"That cracking sound?" Isabelle backed away, not knowing what it meant.

"The ice is breaking up. This is so exciting."

Mattie bounced up and down and edged closer to the bank.

"Is she safe?" Isabelle asked.

"Sure is." Annie squinted at Isabelle. "You worry too much. Just like Dawson."

More and more Dawson seemed a reasonable man with reasonable expectations.

The ice cracked again and again.

Annie pointed to the bend in the river. "It's breaking up."

Isabelle stared as slabs of ice twisted, churning around, driven by the water that roared past them. She couldn't tear her gaze from the show. Wondering if the others felt the same fascination, she darted a glance toward them.

Carly and Annie stood side by side, smiling.

Mattie teetered on the bank of the river, mesmerized by the show. Isabelle wanted to tell Mattie to stand back, but wasn't that up to Annie? Surely Annie knew if the child was in danger. Reassured, she watched the ice pile up against the riverbanks, twisting and turning.

"Isn't it exciting?" Annie asked.

"It's a great show." Isabelle shifted her attention to the river. The ice piled higher and higher.

"Ice jam!" The excited words carried up and down the riverbank among the spectators.

Isabelle couldn't decide if she shared the excitement or if fear pervaded her thoughts. But no one else seemed worried and they surely knew better than she if this was a dangerous situation.

The ice dam reached the same height as the riverbanks and water started to flow around it. Still no one moved. Just as Isabelle grabbed her skirts, preparing to run from the approaching water, the pile of ice broke free and frothy water careened toward them. Everyone cheered. Except Isabelle. Her heart still clutched to her ribs. Awesome power. But also frightening.

Mattie bounced up and down. "That was so good." Her foot slipped on the damp ground and one leg went out from under her. She stumbled, grasping for a handhold as she slid toward the rushing water.

Isabelle gasped. The waters pulled at the child's skirts. Isabelle leaped forward, grabbed Mattie's hand and jerked her back to safety. She pressed the child to her side. "I think it's best if you stay close to me."

Mattie leaned into her. "You saved my life."

"I wouldn't go that far, but I might have saved you from a good soaking." Even so, her shoes were wet and her skirts muddied.

Annie watched, saw that Mattie was safe and turned her attention back to the river as ice churned toward them.

Water sprayed their faces but no one turned away as the crest passed them and proceeded downstream.

Annie turned. "Wasn't that something? I've always wanted to see the ice go out. Seeing the jam was even better. Come on. Let's go."

Isabelle hurried back to the wagon, Mattie holding her hand. They climbed aboard. Rather than getting in the back, Mattie perched on the seat between Isabelle and Annie.

Isabelle thought they would return in the direction from which they'd come but, instead, they went up a little incline, passed through some trees and drew to a halt on top of the hill.

"I'm in no rush to get back home," Annie explained and jumped to the ground.

Carly joined her.

Mattie and Isabelle still sat on the bench.

"Mattie's shoes and skirt are wet. Don't you think we should take her home and get her dry things?"

"We were going to look for crocuses." Annie clearly didn't want to go back.

"Crocuses, yay. I'm fine." Mattie jumped down and waited expectantly for Isabelle. "It's just my shoes that are wet and I'm not cold."

Annie reached into the wagon for a bit of rug. "Here, dry yourself on this."

Mattie did so as Isabelle descended...still uncertain as to the wisdom of delaying their return.

"Crocuses," Mattie explained, "are purple flowers that came up first thing in the spring. Even before the snow is gone."

"Here are some." Carly called them over and Isabelle saw the fragile purple blossoms. She fell on her knees like the others and drank in the sight of a patch of flowers as big as the backyard in Bella Creek.

"How beautiful," she murmured and sat back on her heels to look about. Hills rose toward mountains on her left. The river sang to her right. A field of flowers was before her. Newfound friends were on either side. So many new and pleasant things that her heart felt ready to overflow.

Annie broke the spell by jumping up. "Let's eat."

Isabelle didn't immediately move. Mattie sat quietly at her side, studying her.

"Do you like the flowers?" Mattie asked.

"I do." Her throat seemed a little tight.

"What else do you like?"

Isabelle turned to the little girl. "The mountains are majestic. The river is powerful and awesome." Recognizing the hunger in Mattie's face, she caught the little chin in her hand. "But the best thing of all is your friendship."

Mattie lowered her eyelids, then slowly lifted them, her blue eyes wide and solemn. "I like having you for a friend," she whispered.

Her eyes stinging with unshed tears, Isabelle hugged Mattie. Affection for this child had found a ready and waiting welcome in Isabelle's heart. She got to her feet and held out her hand to Mattie. "Let's go see what your aunt Annie has for us to eat."

Carly and Annie sat in the back of the wagon, and Isabelle and Mattie joined them. The sun warmed them as they shared sandwiches and cookies.

Mattie finished eating and asked permission to go play.

Isabelle was content to watch and listen as Annie and Carly talked of people they knew.

She analyzed her feelings. She'd enjoyed the outing. Felt accepted by the others. Perhaps this was where she belonged...helping Kate and her father by taking care of the house, enjoying doing things with Annie and Carly, and spending time with little Mattie, who so eagerly accepted her hugs.

The idea seemed ideal. Then why did it leave her restless and anxious, as if she had overlooked something important? And why did Dawson's name and face rush to her thoughts? Would he ever come to see her as more than a city girl?

How long could she hide the truth about her inheritance?

Chapter Ten

Dawson looked up as the doctor and Kate returned. Maybe now Isabelle would feel free to come outside and watch the progress. He hadn't seen her since morning, but then, he had been rather busy helping put up the bell tower. A crowd had gathered to watch but Isabelle was not among them. He was certain of that.

They were about done for the day and men were cleaning up tools and bits of lumber.

Doc wandered over. "It will be nice when it's done and the children are in the school."

Sadie stood nearby. "I can hardly wait. I'm hoping there's lots of shelves for books. Dawson, do you know when the supplies are coming in?" Logan had ordered desks and books for the school but they had yet to arrive. "I'm a little short of reading material."

"I have a box of books," Doc said. "Why don't you have a look and see what you'd like to borrow."

Sadie seemed more interested in studying the building than getting books. "Dawson, would you mind going with the doctor and bringing back books you deem appropriate for the school? I can use them in the temporary classroom."

Glad of an excuse to go to the house, he readily agreed. "I suppose you don't want me to bring back advanced anatomy or a directory of medical conditions."

Sadie chuckled. "Perhaps not."

"I'll do my best." He accompanied Doc through the front door and into the doctor's examining room.

The door to the living quarters stood open but Dawson could see no one moving about. His curiosity grew as did a restless need to see Isabelle. He wished he could deny such an urge.

Doc indicated a crate. "I believe the books are in there." He lifted the lid, which was already loose. "Are these mine? I don't recall them."

Dawson opened the flyleaf of one of the books. "Says 'John Baker.' That's you."

Doc nodded, looking confused. He rubbed his head. "But I don't remember these books." He stared toward the living quarters. "Kate? Kate?" Doc's voice brought his daughter at a run.

"Father, what's wrong?"

"Why are we here?"

She drew his arm through hers. "You never think clearly when you're hungry. Come and eat something." She looked at Dawson, silently questioning his presence, and he explained about the books.

"Take what you need. I have to see that Father eats right away." She hurried them out of the room.

He could hear her murmuring to Doc as dishes rattled.

He hunkered down to look through the books.

A door opened and closed somewhere and Isabelle's

voice reached him. Excited, full of joy. He listened closely.

"Kate, I wish you had been free to join us today. We had the most wonderful trip into the country. What a beautiful place. I do believe I've fallen in love with it."

Dawson smiled. He understood the attraction of the rugged hills. Grandfather had done them good to bring them here.

"We saw the river break up."

Dawson jerked to his feet. That was Mattie speaking. Uninvited, he stalked into the kitchen.

Mattie practically hung from Isabelle's hand. Her shoes and stockings were wet.

Anger burned through his veins. He'd started to trust her, to know she would care for Mattie as carefully as he would himself. He'd even allowed himself to think she might consider staying in the area. After all, he'd seen her eagerness to learn the basic skills a woman needed and he'd heard her admire the countryside on more than one occasion.

His trust and hope had been misplaced. She didn't even know enough to protect a child from the icy, raging waters of a river.

Before he could think to couch his question in gentler tones, he confronted Isabelle. "What do you mean by taking my child out to the river? Don't you know she could have drowned? Look at her feet. Did she fall into the water?" A city woman out in the country. What did she know about the dangers? How could he think she would protect Mattie?

"Papa." Mattie's shocked voice dampened Dawson's anger. "Aunt Annie took us for a drive. Why are you so mad at Miss Isabelle? She didn't do anything bad. She—"

At the look on Dawson's face, Mattie stopped talking.

Dawson's anger shifted to his sister. What was Annie thinking to take Isabelle along on a trip with Mattie? He would have to make it clear it was not to happen again.

He spun on his heel. "I'll see to those books. Mattie, come with me."

"Yes, Papa. Goodbye, Miss Isabelle. It was a fine outing."

Dawson almost relented at the quiet sadness in her voice but there was far more to be concerned about than a momentary disappointment. He gathered up a few of the books, not bothering to finish going through the crate. "Let's go."

Before he reached the door, Isabelle spoke from behind him. "Mr. Marshall, I apologize for whatever it is I have done to offend you."

He stopped, turned slowly. "And I apologize for speaking so harshly."

They considered each other. Both had apologized, but did either of them mean anything by their words?

He grimaced a smile and continued out of the house. He'd make sure this didn't happen again. He carried the books to the back of the store. Annie and Carly visited with Sadie.

"You look like thunder," Annie said.

"He got mad at Miss Isabelle," Mattie supplied without prompting.

"Why on earth would you do that?"

Again Mattie answered. "He thought she took me to the river and let me fall in."

"I didn't say that." At least, not in those words, but he

had been harsh. And apologized rather insincerely. "But your feet are wet. How did that happen?"

Mattie hung her head. "The water rose over the banks and I slipped in it. Almost fell."

"I knew it." The words exploded from him. He closed his eyes and tried to control the flood of emotions raging through him. Anger. Fear. Regret. Regret? Yes, regret that Isabelle reminded him so much of Violet and his failure as a husband. "Mattie, go into the store and ask Uncle George for a candy stick. He can put it on my bill."

"I need something in the store, too." Sadie slipped away.

Dawson waited until they both left the room to confront Annie. "What were you thinking?"

Annie did not flinch before his demanding glower. "I knew it. You keep seeing her as another Violet. She's nothing like that woman. In fact, Isabelle was the first to see Mattie get too close to the water. When her foot slipped, Isabelle grabbed her." Annie gave a dismissive wave. "Not that she was ever in any danger. Do you think I'd let something bad happen to her?" Her eyes narrowed. "I have looked after her for three years. Have I ever done anything that would put her in danger?" She jammed her fists to her hips and squinted at him. "A woman who reminds you of Violet shows up and suddenly I'm not fit to watch her?"

"No, of course I didn't mean that." He rubbed at his neck. What did he mean?

"She's not like Violet, you know."

"I think she is more like Violet than you're ready to admit." How many times had he come home to find baby Mattie alone in the house? Untended. Her diaper soiled. He'd finally swallowed his pride and asked Ma to watch her. Violet had not objected when he'd said she was to take the baby over to his mother.

He'd been taken for a fool once by a city woman. He didn't intend it would happen again. "I'm taking Mattie home."

He stalked out the back door and stood in the afternoon sunshine. He'd tell Annie not to let Mattie near that woman. He'd tell Mattie the same thing. Except what could he say that didn't sound judgmental?

Isabelle dried her eyes. She'd had a little cry with Kate to comfort her. "I don't suppose I will ever fit in here." What she really meant was that Dawson would never see her as a capable woman. His opinion would sink even lower if he knew the truth about who she was and her pampered upbringing.

Kate set a cup of tea before her. "Drink this. It will make you feel better."

Isabelle chuckled. "I've never found a cup of tea solved my problems, but thanks."

Kate rubbed Isabelle's arm. "I don't mean to suggest it will. Only God can lead you to where you feel you belong."

Isabelle twisted her cup around. "I have asked Him to guide me and thought for a bit that I belonged." There was no need to add that she thought Dawson had accepted her. She gave her dear friend a miserable look.

Kate got a distant look in her eyes. "Sometimes He allows hard things in our lives."

"I'm sorry. Here I sit bemoaning my life when you've had to give up your dreams." Kate had hoped to follow in her father's footsteps and become a doctor, but after her father's accident she had given up the idea, saying her father needed her.

Kate smiled. "I don't mind. Father is all I have— besides you, of course."

Warmed by Kate's friendship, Isabelle began to relax. Yes, it hurt to be poorly judged by Dawson, but she had done nothing she regretted.

A knock came at the back door and Annie hustled in, Sadie in her wake. She rushed to Isabelle's side and hugged her. "I understand my brother scolded you royally. I apologize for him. Sometimes he is such a hard man."

"It's okay. He apologized."

"Good thing or I might be forced to drag him back by the scruff of the neck and insist he do so."

It was a picture that brought a burst of laughter from Isabelle. "That I'd like to see."

Annie shrugged. "Yeah, me, too. So, you want to bake a cake? I'll teach you how to make Ma's famous chocolate cake."

Isabelle hurried to her feet. "I can't think of anything I'd like better." A useful diversion was exactly what she needed.

Annie stood by as Isabelle followed her instructions. "You'll have to forgive Dawson. His wife was not suited to ranch life. She did all kinds of foolish things. I guess that's why he is always warning me not to take risks."

Isabelle wanted to know more but it wasn't her business and she didn't intend to pry.

Annie pointed to the cocoa needed for the cake. "She was killed when she raced her horse against some of the miners from Wolf Hollow and her horse lost his footing and threw her. She died instantly, which, I suppose, is something to be grateful for."

Isabelle measured the ingredients as Annie listed them. It amazed her that Annie could make a cake without written instructions.

"Ever since then, Dawson is cautious. I do wish he'd lighten up. He's only twenty-six and I think he's handsome, even if he is my brother. He needs to get married again for his sake as well as Mattie's."

Isabelle's hands stopped moving. Dawson would want a farm woman, a woman experienced in cooking, doing laundry, milking a cow and a hundred other useful things. The thrill of making the cake seemed suddenly very rudimentary. "I expect he'd be a good husband," she murmured.

Time to turn the conversation to something else… something that didn't make her feel so inept. "You have a lot of responsibility running a household of five men and caring for Mattie. I admire you for doing it so well."

"I appreciate that." Annie's smile thanked her more than words could. "Now, be careful as you break eggs into your cake. No one likes to eat eggshells."

The girls shared lots of good laughs as Annie taught Isabelle how to make the famous Marshall chocolate cake. It was baked before Annie departed. She left a bowl of frosting to be applied when the cake cooled.

"Join us for supper," Kate said to Sadie. "We have tons of food."

"Don't mind if I do." The three of them worked together to set out the meal.

Isabelle wrapped a sense of satisfaction around her. With some help from her friends she could learn to fit in here. Could that be enough?

Dr. Baker came from his bedroom, where he'd been napping. "Three girls in the kitchen is a pleasant sight for an old man."

Isabelle knew that kind of talk upset Kate and she squeezed her friend's hand.

They ate a generous meal. Then Isabelle served slices of the cake she'd made and frosted.

"It's excellent," Kate said.

"Indeed," Dr. Baker echoed.

Sadie nodded thoughtfully. "Every bit as good as Annie's was that first night."

Isabelle thanked each of them. "Might be because it's Annie's recipe and she supervised every step." But it was good to feel she had accomplished this.

They'd barely finished when someone banged on the front door. "Doc. Is the doctor in?"

Dr. Baker hurried to the door. "What's the problem?"

"It's my wife. She's having a baby and it's taking too long. Can you come and see her?"

"Certainly. Let me get my things." He stepped into the examining room.

Kate scrambled to her feet and rushed after her father. "I'll go with you."

Seconds later a wagon rattled away with the doctor and Kate.

Sadie and Isabelle stared at each other, then grinned. "We're on our own," Sadie said. "I'll help clean up."

The two girls worked together. When the kitchen was clean and the food put away, the evening stretched out ahead of them. Isabelle couldn't think what she would do on her own.

"Why don't you stay and keep me company?" she asked Sadie.

"I'd love that. I wish I'd brought my chessboard with me. Do you play chess?"

"I do, and I happen to have my own board." She went to her trunk and returned with the game set. Soon they were immersed in the game.

A rattle outside sent a rush of fear through Isabelle's veins. "Did you hear that? Is that a normal sound?"

Sadie's eyes were wide. "I heard it. It sounds like someone is out there."

"Maybe it's someone looking for the doctor. But why don't they come to the door?" The possibilities drew the blood from her face. Someone might be so injured they couldn't make it to the door. Or—

Sadie put words to Isabelle's fear. "Maybe it's a prowler."

A muffled grunt gave substance to her suspicions.

"What do we do?"

Sadie looked about. "Do the doors lock?"

"I have no idea." One of them would have to tiptoe forward to see. Isabelle sucked in air. Sadie was a guest. That left it to Isabelle.

Trembling from head to toe, she eased to the door. No key. She looked about. There. A key hung on a nail by the door. She grabbed it, stuck it in the keyhole and turned it.

Her breath whooshed out.

But what about the front door? And the door to the doctor's waiting room? She scurried into the sitting room. Again a key hung near the door and she turned it into place, then hurried through into the waiting room and locked that door, as well.

Meanwhile, Sadie pulled the curtains across the windows so no one could see them. Then the two of them huddled in the dark sitting room, whispering.

"How long before he goes away?" Sadie asked.

"I don't know. And how will we know when it's safe? How will you get back to your room? You'll have to stay here."

They listened. Were those footsteps approaching the door? They clutched hands. Isabelle forgot how to breathe.

"It was an honest mistake and I apologized." Dawson grew tired of Annie's sorrowful sighs and Mattie's refusal to look at him. Even Grandfather scowled continually after hearing Mattie and Annie's version of the day's events and what he'd said to Isabelle. If only Pa and Dawson's brothers would return. Surely they would be on his side.

"A mistake you made because you misjudged the poor woman," Annie insisted. "I know she'd been crying when I went over to teach her to bake a chocolate cake, though she did her best to pretend all was well."

"I have to say," Grandfather said with enough accusation in his voice to make Dawson wish he could slide under the table, "that I'm glad neither your grandmother nor your mother are alive to see this."

Dawson closed his eyes and longed for the peace of a bedroll in the midst of a snow-clad bunch of trees.

"I don't know why you don't like her." Mattie blinked back tears. "I like her."

"I never said I didn't like her."

Three pairs of eyes challenged his words.

"I didn't." He only wanted to protect Mattie—and, yes, himself—from a rich city woman. Thankfully, no one could read his thoughts to ask what he needed to protect them from, though he would have had an answer… From the risk of being hurt by allowing himself to care about her.

Tears pooled on Mattie's bottom eyelids, threatening to overflow.

Dawson jerked to his feet. "I'm going to town."

"Good. You need to make things right with her." Grandfather seemed to think he knew Dawson's plans.

Dawson wished he could tell the old man his assumption was wrong. Without answering, he went to the cloakroom, planted his hat on his head, grabbed his coat and strode to the barn. Muttering to himself about how foolish and unnecessary all this was, he saddled Jumper and rode to town in the dark.

He passed the wagon shop and blacksmith on his left. Both buildings were darkened but a light glowed in the back of the second in the living quarters attached to the business. The livery barn on his right had a lantern shining from a hook by the door to invite late-night travelers. He resolutely turned left at Ore Street and rode down the alley. He passed the blackened ashes of the burned-out businesses and reined in at the doctor's residence. A lamp glowed in the kitchen, but the curtains had been pulled across the window, making it impossible to see inside.

He knocked and waited. And waited. He knocked again and tried the door. It was locked. "Hello. Is anyone there?"

The hurry of footsteps came toward him.

"Dawson?"

He recognized Isabelle's strained voice. "I need to talk to you."

The key turned in the lock. The door eased open. "Please, come in."

He stepped inside and she pushed the door closed behind him. Rather hurriedly, it seemed.

"I'm certainly glad to see you." The welcome in her voice surprised him.

"Really?" That was quite the opposite of the reaction he'd expected. "Where is everyone?"

"The doctor and Kate have gone to a birthing. Sadie is here. Sadie?"

Sadie came slowly from the sitting room, her eyes wide.

Dawson looked from one to the other and considered the locked door and drawn curtains. "What's wrong?"

"We heard someone outside," Isabelle answered as Sadie hovered in the doorway, ready for a quick escape. "Would you mind checking? It might be someone injured and looking for the doctor. Or—"

"Or?"

"An intruder."

An intruder? This was Bella Creek. People didn't lock their doors. The sheriff patrolled the streets to make sure any rambunctious miners went to Wolf Hollow to be rowdy. But what did he expect from a city woman? "I'll look." He lit the lantern by the door and went outside to check.

A bit of burned paper from the fire fluttered in the leafless fire-scarred tree in the yard. The men had decided to leave it standing. Give it a chance to see if there was still life in it after the fire. *Give it a chance.* The words echoed Grandfather's admonition about Isabelle.

The paper made a rattling sound. Perhaps the girls had heard that, because no one lingered in the shadows.

A piece of firewood had rolled from the stack. He replaced it. No doubt one of the neighborhood cats had wandered by and dislodged it. That might have been what they heard.

He returned to the kitchen and explained about the paper and the cat. "That was your intruder."

Sadie and Isabelle looked at each other. He guessed from their expressions that they weren't convinced.

"Thank you for checking," Isabelle said. "Can I offer you tea and cake?"

"Thank you, yes." Words would come easier if they all sat down and got comfortable. A chess game had been pushed to the side. "Were you two playing this game?"

"We were." Isabelle filled the kettle and set it to boil. She cut three slices of cake and put them on china plates, then poured the hot water over the tea.

He studied her covertly. It didn't surprise him that Sadie played chess. Why should it surprise him that Isabelle did? Perhaps, as Annie and Grandfather said, he'd jumped to conclusions regarding the woman.

He watched her every move. As if he'd never seen a woman make tea before! He jerked his gaze away. Nothing could change the fact she was a city gal and, if Johnny wasn't mistaken, a wealthy one. Or at least she came from a well-to-do family. Again he tried to remember why the Redfield name seemed familiar.

Sadie still hovered in the doorway. "Come, sit down." Isabelle's words shifted the woman into action and she hurried to the table.

Isabelle sat across from him. "Now, what did you want to speak to us about?"

He tasted the cake and made appreciative noises. "Annie said you made this cake."

"With her help, yes, I did." That cautious note in her voice crackled along his nerves. As if she expected to be scolded again.

"I'm afraid I jumped to conclusions this afternoon. Mattie explained how you pulled her back from the river. I should have thanked you rather than berating you. I again apologize and I hope it's not too late to say thanks."

"You're welcome."

She wasn't making this easy for him, which made him feel he had to explain.

"I'm protective of her." Where did he mean to go with this? He didn't want to talk about Violet and they probably didn't want to hear about her.

Silence filled the edges of the room.

Sadie spoke. "The more I look around, the more I am stunned by the extent of damage from the fire. It must have been frightening."

"Seeing the flames jump from building to building and fearing the fire might take the whole town was the most frightening thing. It was hard to get water enough to put it out. A few of the townspeople suffered frozen fingers."

"What started it?" Isabelle asked, a note of relief in her voice.

He wished he could undo the angry words he'd spoken earlier, wished he could erase the wariness in her face. "Fires aren't uncommon. It started in the lawyer's office. Perhaps he left the fire burning too briskly. Or left papers where they could light from the stove." He shrugged. "He might even have forgotten to turn off the lamp when he closed the office for the day."

"The fire has affected a lot of people." Isabelle looked thoughtful. "But it seems everyone is pulling together to rebuild. That's nice."

"Everyone but the owner of the dry-goods store. He's even gone so far as to suggest the Marshalls started the fire in order to eliminate competition. Little does he know how much this fire is costing the Marshalls."

Isabelle looked surprised. "How is that? Is your family footing the costs?"

He'd only said what everyone in town already knew. "Everyone has contributed what they could, but Grandfather feels responsible for the town. He sees himself as the overseer of it since he started it in the first place. Many of the buildings belong to the Marshall family and are rented out."

"I see."

He wondered if she truly did. "It's called Bella Creek after my grandmother. Her name was Annabelle." Like Grandfather said, Isabelle's name was similar to his grandmother's. The town might have been named for them both.

"That's sweet." Isabelle said the words but Sadie added her sigh.

"I know. So romantic."

He rolled his eyes, having heard that sentiment many times in the past.

Both women chuckled softly. He knew he had correctly guessed what they thought.

The cake was gone, the teapot drained. It was time to leave. Yet he lingered.

A knock at the door jerked all three of their gazes to the door.

"Would you get it?" Isabelle's voice quivered.

He shoved back and went to do so. "Hello, Sid. If you've come to see the doctor, he isn't here right now."

"Not needing the doc. I'm looking for my milk cow. Any of you seen or heard her?"

Dawson glanced over his shoulder. "I think we found your intruder." He turned back to Sid. "She was here an hour or two ago, but I didn't see her when I had a look around."

"Thanks. I'll keep looking."

Chuckling, Dawson closed the door and grinned at the ladies.

The three of them shared a laugh over the runaway cow.

"I should be getting home," he said, with a great deal of reluctance. "Or do you want me to stay until the doctor returns?" He addressed Isabelle.

Her gaze searched his as if evaluating his words for a hidden meaning…as if expecting him to be standing in judgment on her. Perhaps Grandfather was right. He had been making a quick assessment. Just like Johnny.

Isabelle hesitated a moment as if considering the idea, and then she shook her head. "No. I'm certain I am quite safe. No one else in town needs a guard. Neither do I, but thank you."

Sadie rose quickly. "Would you be so good as to escort me across the street? I know you said there was no prowler outside but I'm nervous after hearing something out there."

"Certainly." He grabbed his hat and coat from where he had hung them upon being invited in for tea and strode into the sitting room. He waited while Isabelle unlocked the door. She would be alone when he left. Was she frightened at the thought?

"Good night, then," Sadie said.

"Good night," Dawson echoed.

"God bless." Isabelle closed the door and turned the key in the lock.

He escorted Sadie to the hotel and waited until she climbed the stairs and went to her room before he left. Isabelle might have refused his offer but he wasn't going home until the doctor returned. Not that he didn't think she was perfectly safe, but her comment that no one else needed a guard made him realize that no other woman was so alone. Yes, there were one or two who lived by themselves, but they had friends and neighbors nearby. Isabelle didn't.

He circled to the back of the doctor's quarters, found himself a piece of firewood to sit on and settled down to stay as long as necessary.

From where he sat, he could see the glow of the lamp and the occasional shadow crossing the light as Isabelle moved about.

Cold settled into his limbs and he pulled his coat tighter. He'd light a campfire but that would alarm Isabelle as well as the town residents, everyone being more than a little nervous after watching the fire that consumed a whole block of buildings.

His horse waited patiently for him to decide to return home. "I'll give you extra oats," Dawson murmured in the deepening night.

A bump and clatter from farther down the alley brought Dawson to his feet. Was there really someone lurking about? He heard a meow. Just a cat. He stretched and yawned, then settled back again on his narrow log seat.

A wagon rattled up the street and pulled to a halt in front of the house.

"Thanks, Doc."

"Good night," Kate and the doctor called.

Dawson waited until Isabelle unlocked the door to let them in, until he saw shadows moving about in the kitchen, until the light left the kitchen and moved to the bedroom before he swung to the saddle and headed back to the ranch. He smiled at nothing in particular except to wonder what Isabelle would say if she knew he'd kept watch for the better part of an hour. She need never know, but he was content that he'd done the right thing in making sure she was safe.

It struck him before he was a mile from town. Why did he allow himself to feel responsible for her when, at the same time, he told himself he wanted to forget he'd ever met her?

Chapter Eleven

$\sim$

Sunday morning, Isabelle prepared for church with mixed emotions. Dawson had apologized, but did that mean he'd changed his mind about what sort of woman he thought she was? Did he still see her as city versus him as country? Did he still see her as being like Violet? And, as such, a danger to his child?

She could have told him he was wrong on all scores, but telling him wouldn't make him believe it.

She, Kate and the doctor walked to church. They were joined by Sadie and greeted at the door by Mattie and Dawson. Mattie grabbed her hand and pressed to her side. Dawson smiled down at Isabelle. Something in his eyes brought a rush of heat to her cheeks. She told herself it was only her imagination.

He indicated they should make their way to the fourth-from-the-front pew and stood back to let her go in. Mattie slipped in next to her and Dawson sat beside his daughter. Mattie held both their hands and beamed from one to the other.

Isabelle looked at Mattie's hand in hers. Would Dawson accept her for who she was? How could he, when she wasn't being entirely honest? She kept her head lowered. She wasn't ready to tell him the truth and risk changing everything.

Slowly she brought her gaze to his and saw both welcome and caution. She ignored the caution and let herself bask in the welcome. Once he truly believed she was a capable woman, she would tell him the truth.

Pastor Arness took his place at the pulpit.

"Today I want to speak to you of hope and loss, and how the two go hand in hand." He paused before he continued. "I once had a wife."

Isabelle heard Annie suck in a rush of air from where she sat on the other side of Dawson.

"We had a little boy. Rather, we *have* a little boy. My wife left me to go with another man to the gold fields and took our son. I've come here hoping to find him. So far I have not learned anything that would lead me to his whereabouts. That is my pain and my loss." He raised his voice. "But that is not the end of my story because I have hope. Hope in a God who loves me, who loves my son even more than I do, and I trust His goodwill in helping me to find my boy."

He went on to speak more of his trust in God, but Isabelle could only think of how dreadful it would be to be missing a child, and she wrapped her arm about Mattie's shoulders.

Dawson, perhaps feeling the same way, did the same and neither of them shifted away.

Mattie smiled from one to the other.

Isabelle tipped her head enough to see Dawson's expression and their gazes crashed together. She knew he would move every obstacle to find his child should she disappear. She gave a tiny nod, not wanting to distract

those around her. But her silent message was that she
would risk life and limb for Mattie, as well.

Their gazes locked and held, full of a shared love for
this child and so much more, though she feared to give
words to what she thought she saw…hoped she saw.

Someone behind them coughed and Isabelle jerked
her attention back to the pastor.

This feeling between them was too new for her to
know what to call it.

As soon as the service ended, Mattie rushed both
Isabelle and Dawson out. "I want to show you something," she said.

Isabelle dared a glance at Dawson and, seeing his
amusement, let herself be urged along. They went to
the side of the church, to the small cemetery. She immediately noticed that Dawson's jaw muscles bunched
and he no longer looked amused.

"Mattie?" he warned.

"I just want to show her Mama's grave."

Isabelle stopped, causing Mattie to jerk on her arm.

"Come on. You want to see, don't you?"

She didn't care to, but could see that it meant a lot
to Mattie. She turned to Dawson. "I don't wish to in-
trude. I won't go further without your consent." Why
did she feel like she asked for much more than a visit
to his wife's grave?

"Please, Papa. You heard the preacher. We 'cept our
pain."

Dawson looked stunned. He gave his head a little
shake. "I don't know what you have in mind but we'll
go with you."

Mattie rushed ahead, and Dawson and Isabelle followed more slowly. She had to make herself clear. "If this makes you uncomfortable…?"

"I'm fine."

Mattie had reached a simple granite headstone and fell to her knees.

Isabelle hung back, but Mattie waved her forward. She went slowly, cautiously, and knelt beside the child when Mattie indicated she should.

"The preacher said we should hope. He said we should ask God and trust Him. I'm going to ask Him right now." Mattie bowed her head, clasped her hands together. Her lips moved but no sound came out.

"Amen." She beamed with trust and faith and joy. "You want to know what I prayed?"

Isabelle didn't say yes or no, half-afraid of what the child wanted.

Mattie pulled Isabelle close and whispered in her ear. "I prayed you would be my mama."

Little did the child know that life wasn't that simple when other people were involved. Closing her eyes against the rush of tears, she hugged the child and whispered in her ear, "God loves you enough to do what is best for you. You must believe that."

Mattie sat back and studied Isabelle. Disappointment and hurt filled her eyes, and then she blinked and hope returned. "I know he'll find his little boy. God will help him."

A few minutes later they left the cemetery.

"Was she worried about the preacher's boy?" Dawson asked as Mattie skipped away to join Grandfather Marshall.

Relieved that he hadn't asked her to reveal what Mattie had said, she answered, "She seemed to have listened attentively to what the preacher said and trusts that God will help him find his son."

Dawson's eyes darkened. "I hope all the talk about God helping us doesn't give her false hope. Sometimes we don't get what we pray for."

"I know." She soothed, rubbing his arm in an attempt to lighten his mood. "That's the trust part of the equation, isn't it?"

She felt the tension ease from him. And her own dissipated when he smiled.

"Sounds like you were listening carefully, as well."

"As were you, to recognize that as part of the sermon." They smiled acknowledgment at each other then parted ways, he to take his grandfather and daughter home, she to join Sadie and Kate as they walked back along the street.

Hope and trust went hand in hand. Dawson mused about the words the next day as he returned to work on the school. If he could embrace both, would it give him the courage to follow his heart and court Isabelle? He had to consider more than his own wishes. What was best for Mattie? Was Isabelle's obvious fondness for Mattie enough?

He was still pondering those questions when the sheriff strode toward him. "Can you spare some time to come with me? I could use your help."

Jesse had been Conner's best friend since Jesse had moved into the area with his grandmother. He hung around the Marshall place so much he was like Dawson's third brother. "What's going on?"

"Someone rode in and informed me they'd been by

the Brown place and found the whole family dead in their beds."

"I'll come." It wasn't the sort of task a man should face alone. "Just give me a moment to inform Miss Redfield. Mattie goes there after school."

He hurried across the adjoining yards.

Isabelle looked surprised to see him.

"I'll be away for a little while helping Jesse—the sheriff."

Her eyes widened. "Nothing dangerous, I hope."

He tucked that little bit of concern into a secret vault deep inside and explained the situation.

Her eyes widened ever more. "That's awful. What happened?"

"Jesse didn't say. He perhaps doesn't know yet. But I can't let him face it alone."

Isabelle shuddered. "Of course you can't." She looked about to be ill. "I hate the smell of death."

He knew her words hid a story but he didn't have time to ask about it. He squeezed her shoulder, felt her lean into his hand and almost pulled her to his chest. To comfort and reassure her only. Determinedly he resisted the urge, regretting the missed opportunity even as he did. With a murmured "Goodbye. See you later. Take care of Mattie," he strode to the livery barn to meet Jesse.

His thoughts grew more and more muddled. Was she the sort of woman he should let himself care for?

Isabelle watched until Dawson was out of sight. *Lord, give them both strength to deal with this situation.* She tried not to remember seeing her parents dead in their beds. Tried not to recall the antiseptic smell of a sickroom. But the memory of those days twisted through her mind like a tornado. She groaned and tried to distract herself. It would be several hours before school let out. She must get her thoughts under control before Mattie got there.

Perhaps a walk would help.

She donned her coat against the chilly air, but as she reached for the door handle, someone knocked on the other side. She drew back, her heart pounding in alarm. *It's okay*, she told herself. No one was bringing her bad news.

Unless Dawson had been hurt. Maybe an evil man was going about killing people. Or Mattie was... Her stomach recoiled.

She sucked in air as the knock came again. Her imagination, mingling with memories, was getting away from her. Calming herself, she opened the door.

One of the older schoolgirls faced her. "Miss Young asks if you will come and get Mattie. She's sick."

It was just like Mama and Papa.

"She thinks Mattie should lie down."

"I'll come right over and get her." Isabelle almost tripped on the girl's heels as they hurried over to the store. Without looking to the right or left, she passed through to the schoolroom.

Sadie rushed over to greet her. "The child is running a fever and feeling quite miserable. She shouldn't be here."

"I'll take her home." One look at Mattie and Isabelle forgot all about her fear of illness and rushed to her side to hug her. "Honey, you come home with me and I'll take care of you."

Mattie nodded miserably and raised her arms. "Carry me."

Isabelle lifted the child, staggering under the unexpected weight. But she didn't want to put Mattie down any more than Mattie wanted to get down. The child clung to Isabelle's neck, her face hot. She was a sick little girl.

Isabelle hurried as best she could, taking Mattie in through the front door to the kitchen, where she parked her on a chair, removed her coat and had a good look at her. She knew nothing about childhood diseases but certainly the runny nose, red eyes and slight cough on top of the fever couldn't be good. "You wait here and I'll get the doctor to look at you." She rapped lightly on the door connecting to the examining room.

Kate cracked the door open. "Do you need something?"

"I'm sorry to bother you, but Mattie is here and she's sick. I don't know what to do."

"Sick how?"

Isabelle relayed the symptoms.

"I'll look at her." Kate stepped from the room, pulled the door closed behind her and went to Mattie. "I'm sorry you're sick." She felt Mattie's forehead and pulled down her bottom eyelid. "Open your mouth for me." Kate peered into Mattie's mouth. She straightened and turned to Isabelle. "I can't say for certain what it is yet, but you need to send her home."

Isabelle's heart stalled and refused to start again. The skin on her face grew taut. "You suspect something."

Kate began to say something, then closed her mouth and shook her head. "She needs to be home, where she can rest properly. Go get Dawson."

Isabelle left Mattie slumped on the chair and drew Kate into the other room. "He's gone with the sheriff." She explained the situation.

Kate sighed. "More work for Father. Listen, Isabelle. Mattie might have measles. She can't stay here. It's far too communicable."

"Measles? How dangerous is that?"

Kate smiled. "Children get it. So do adults." She grew concerned. "You've had them, I hope."

"Yes, I remember," she answered, her thoughts on Mattie. "I'll get her home. Can you stay with her while I rent a driver and a buggy to take us?" She headed for the door even before Kate responded in the affirmative.

Never mind being taught that a lady didn't run in public. Isabelle lifted her skirts enough to ensure she wouldn't trip and ran as fast as she could to the livery barn. "I need a buggy and a driver." She could barely speak as she panted from the exertion.

"Huh? I don't have anyone sitting around waiting to be hired as a driver."

"Mattie Marshall is ill." She'd not say it might be measles for fear it would be reason enough to be refused. "Her father has gone with the sheriff and I have no other means of getting her home. Of course, you could just rent me a buggy. I can learn how to drive on the way out there."

He snorted. "Never mind. I'll find someone."

"Excellent. Have them pick us up at the doctor's house." She didn't wait to hear any more but hurried back to the house.

Kate had settled Mattie on the couch in the other room, pulling the drapes to darken the room. As soon as Isabelle returned, she gave her instructions. "Tell Annie to keep her in a dark room. Keep the fever down. Give her water to drink."

Isabelle shivered, hoping Kate wouldn't notice. She

shouldn't be so relieved to turn Mattie over to Annie's care, but ever since her parents' deaths, sickrooms and doctor's office odors had filled her with such dread she could barely function.

The clop of horse hooves stopped in front of the house. Kate looked out. "Your chariot awaits."

Isabelle bundled a blanket around the child and carried her to the buggy. She managed to get her aboard and, despite Mattie's protests, drew the blanket over her face. "Kate says to protect your eyes against the light."

Mattie snuggled into Isabelle's arms on the trip to the ranch. The driver helped her down. "Wait while I take her to her aunt. Then I'll need a ride back."

She carried Mattie inside and through to the kitchen, where she lowered her to a chair. "Annie?" she called.

Grandfather Marshall hobbled in on his two canes. "What's going on?"

She explained Mattie was sick. "Kate thinks it might be measles, so she couldn't stay there. I have instructions for Annie." The young woman had still not made an appearance. "Is she not home?"

"She went upstairs after dinner and hasn't come back down. She must be sewing or something. Run on up and fetch her. I'll stay with little Mattie."

Isabelle had some notion of the layout of the upper floor from her previous visit when she had tucked Mattie into bed. A day full of promise and possibility. How quickly both had narrowed. She stopped at the top of the stairs. "Annie."

A groan came from one of the rooms.

"Have you hurt yourself?" Isabelle hurried into the room without knocking.

Annie lay on her bed, curled into a ball, shivering and moaning.

"You're ill." Isabelle squatted by the bed for a closer look. Annie had red, watery eyes, a fever and a dry cough. "You have the same symptoms as Mattie."

Annie blinked as if to bring Isabelle into focus. "Where's Mattie?" she croaked.

"Mattie's just fine. Don't you worry." She pulled the shades to darken the room. "I'll be back in a bit." She took the stairs at a pace she'd never before used.

"Grandfather— May I call you that?"

The man chuckled. "Beats calling me 'old man.'"

"Do you know if Annie has had the measles?"

He rubbed his chin, a gesture so like Dawson's that Isabelle smiled despite the seriousness of the situation and allowed herself a moment of missing Dawson. He'd know what to do. He'd be calm and steady, not all flustered as she was.

"You know," Grandfather said, "I don't believe she has. Why do you ask?"

"Because I think she has them now. She's upstairs with a fever." A sick child, a sick woman and the only other adult was a crippled man. She could not in good conscience leave them. Mentally girding up her loins, she knew she must overcome her fear of illness and stay with these people until appropriate help arrived.

"I'll send the driver away and take care of Mattie and Annie." Did the words sound as solid and sure as she hoped, or did they reveal her trepidation?

She returned to the waiting driver. "I don't need a ride back. Would you take a message to the doctor's daughter? Tell her I'm remaining here until..." How long before anyone returned? "Until further notice."

He agreed to do so and she handed him some coins, not having any idea if she'd paid too little or too much, but he seemed happy enough as he drove away.

Back inside, she helped Mattie upstairs, found a nightgown and helped her change into it then tucked her into bed under a light cover and drew the shades. Ignoring the fear fluttering in her heart, she trotted back to Annie's room, did the same for her and went back downstairs at a rate that left her breathless. Explaining what she needed, she located a basin with Grandfather's help, and clean washcloths and towels, and she carried them, along with a jug of water, back up the stairs.

Annie seemed the sickest, so she went to her first. Isabelle insisted the woman drink a glass of water then dampened a cloth and washed her face.

"Why are you here?" Annie asked.

"I brought Mattie home. She's sick, too."

"I need to take care of her." Annie groaned and tried to sit up but sank back. "I'm dizzy."

"I'll take care of her. I promise." At least until help came. But how long would it take Dawson to help Jesse? She shuddered. Death and illness hovered in her mind like dark shadows.

"You rest." She drew a sheet over Annie and hurried to Mattie.

Mattie sobbed into her pillow.

Isabelle sat on the edge of the bed and pulled the child into her arms. "Honey, what's the matter?"

"I thought you had gone. I thought everyone was gone." Each word rode a sob.

"I'm not leaving you until your papa comes back."

Mattie's arms tightened about Isabelle's neck. "Don't go. Not even when Papa comes. Promise me."

Isabelle hesitated. How could she give such a promise? This was not her home. She wasn't good around illness, and most of all, Dawson might resent her intrusion. It was one thing to have the child coming over after school, and even being granted permission to talk about her mother. Quite another to move into his house even temporarily.

But wouldn't it be wonderful to be able to spend time with him? To be needed? Wanted?

"I promise I'll stay until you feel better." Even if someone told her to leave, she would stay until she fulfilled that promise.

Chapter Twelve

Dawson rode beside Jesse as they returned to town. With no sign of sickness or injury to any of the dead family, Jesse had looked at the chimney. "Just as I thought. It's blocked." And the odorless fumes had killed them all.

"At least they didn't suffer," Dawson said, finding a sliver of relief in that fact. It didn't, however, make the details left to deal with any less difficult. They had to take care of the bodies, make sure any stock was tended and a dozen other necessary tasks.

He couldn't wait to get back to town and Mattie and Isabelle. He'd hug his little girl close and allow himself to accept whatever comfort Isabelle offered. Would she touch his hand as she had before? Smile with eyes so gentle it reminded him of Mattie's comment, soft as kitten fur. Maybe she'd even make him hot cocoa and serve him cookies.

By the time he'd helped Jesse with turning the bodies over to the undertaker, who was also the blacksmith, he ached for the solace of family. It didn't even seem odd to him that he thought of the doctor's house and not the big Marshall house on the ranch.

He used Jesse's quarters behind the jail to wash up, hoping he did not carry the smell of death with him.

No one answered his rap on the front door at the doctor's house. Should he go around back and knock? But surely they would have heard him. Instead, he went into the waiting room and tapped on the inner door.

Kate opened the door. "You're looking for Mattie." The waiting room was empty and she joined him there. She explained how Mattie had been sent home from school with a fever. "It looks like measles, so she couldn't stay here. It's far too contagious. Isabelle took her to the ranch."

"She did! How?"

Kate chuckled. "You underestimate my friend. She can do most anything she sets her mind to. She hired a driver and buggy. The driver came by some time ago to say Isabelle had stayed there."

"She did. Why?" His ability to think and speak had shriveled to a few words.

"I don't know. No doubt you can ask her yourself when you get there."

"Of course." Then the facts hit him. Mattie was sick. He left the waiting room without a backward look and trotted over to get his horse. He rode homeward at a gallop.

If anything should happen to Mattie—

He wouldn't think of it. But at least Isabelle was with her. Why did he draw strength from that thought even though he tried to tell himself he shouldn't?

He quickly unsaddled the horse and crossed the yard at a lope to throw open the door. "Mattie? Where are you?"

Grandfather called from the sitting room. "She's upstairs."

Dawson hurried to the stairs.

Grandfather stopped him. "She's in good hands. Isabelle has been tending to both of them. She's a fine gal, just like I told you."

Dawson didn't have time to think whether or not he agreed with Grandfather. "Them? Who else?"

"Annie's sick, too. She never had the measles when you boys did. But it appears she has them now."

Dawson clattered up the steps three at a time and went to Mattie's room first.

Isabelle held Mattie, cradling her so tenderly that Dawson skidded to a halt and stared.

Mattie's eyes came to him. "Hi, Papa. I'm sick but Isabelle is taking care of me." She pressed her cheek to Isabelle's shoulder and looked as contented as a baby in her mother's arms.

Dawson brought his gaze to Isabelle's. Saw both worry and affection…affection for his child. Did that affection extend a little toward him, as well, despite how hard he had fought it?

Her smile trembled on her lips and did not reach her eyes.

He crossed the room and sat beside her on the bed to cradle his arm about Mattie. "I hate to see you sick, little one." His forearm pressed against Isabelle's arm, his shoulder against hers. Tension lifted as if he'd shared it with her.

"Aunt Annie is sick, too," Mattie said, her words muffled against Isabelle.

"So I heard." He needed to check on his sister, but

he couldn't tear himself from his daughter or this feeling of connection.

"I need to see how Annie is," Isabelle said and shifted Mattie to his lap. She smoothed the child's hair and pressed a kiss to her forehead.

Her hair tickled Dawson's face. He closed his eyes against the flood of unfulfilled dreams washing through him. Dreams that had been quenched at the failure of his marriage to Violet. Or so he'd thought before they burst into life again. All this time, they had only lain dormant. Starved and stunted. As Isabelle hurried from the room, he tried in vain to push them back underground. They could not spring to life with a woman such as she. That was sheer foolishness.

You underestimate my friend, Kate had said. Dare he cling to hope?

"Isabelle promised she would stay with me until I'm better," Mattie murmured, half-asleep.

"Did she?" He certainly would remain at Mattie's side while she was ill. Did that mean they would be here together, caring for his child? Sharing love for her? Again those dormant dreams pushed at the surface, trying to emerge.

Mattie had fallen asleep, and he gently laid her on the bed and pulled the sheet over her. He kissed her cheek and watched her a moment. Then he went to Annie's room.

Isabelle had her hands on Annie's shoulders, holding her in bed. "You must rest."

"I can't." Annie tried to get up. "I have to take care of Mattie. And who will make the meals?"

"I will."

Dawson moved to the side of Annie's bed. "Annie, we have things in hand. You relax and rest."

Annie struggled against Isabelle's hand.

Dawson pressed her back. "Everything is okay."

"Are you sure?" At his further assurance she sighed and closed her eyes.

Isabelle rose and stood at his side. "She is afraid of disappointing everyone."

Did he see a question in her eyes? As if she wanted to know what would happen if Annie didn't do all the things she normally did. "Do you think we can't manage?" He liked saying *we* for some reason. Those silly, stubborn, dormant dreams again.

"I've no doubt we can." But the unasked question filled the air.

He scrubbed at his chin. "Isabelle, if Annie never leaves this bed again, it won't change our love for her. She doesn't have to work to earn it."

Isabelle's gaze held his, the air between them heavy and still as she appeared to assess his answer. Finally she nodded. "She's a blessed woman."

He released a breath he hadn't realized he held. She seemed to approve of his answer, yet her eyes remained troubled. He wished he knew why, but Grandfather called. "Is everyone okay?"

"He's waiting for a report." He caught Isabelle's elbow and guided her down the stairs.

Grandfather looked at them. "You both look like something hung out to dry in a cold wind."

Dawson led Isabelle to a soft chair and let her sit. "He means we look worn out."

"That's what I said. How are the girls?"

Dawson answered. "Fevered. Their eyes look sore."

He couldn't sit with his insides clenched, so he walked to the window and looked out, though he saw nothing past the glass. He spun about and faced his grandfather. "Miss Baker said she suspects measles. That's not serious, is it?"

"Dawson, my boy, you survived. I expect your sister and daughter will, as well. But it's good to have Isabelle here to care for them."

Belatedly he realized he hadn't thanked her. "I appreciate how you've tended them both. Thank you."

"Boy, go make her some tea."

Isabelle sprang to her feet. "That's not necessary. I told Annie I would take care of things and I intend to." She was halfway to the kitchen when she turned. "I also promised Mattie I would stay until she's feeling better."

Dawson could not have missed the challenge in her voice if he'd tried. For certain Grandfather didn't, and the look he gave his grandson warned him he best have the right response.

"I have no objection. Whatever Mattie wants she can have. Within reason, of course."

The look Isabelle gave him caused his toes to bunch up. As if his answer had been far from adequate. Then she disappeared into the kitchen.

Grandfather grunted. "Boy, sometimes you have all the charm of a rattlesnake."

"I don't know what you mean." And he didn't.

"If that's so, I have failed badly to teach you to be the sort of man you should be."

"Huh? Why don't you say what's bothering you?"

"What Mattie wants? As if you only tolerate the woman for Mattie's sake. I can't believe you are so unkind. Let alone blind. I've said it before and I'll say it again—you're wrong to continue to see her as a repeat of Violet." He picked up the paper on his lap and snapped the pages in front of him.

Good. Dawson didn't want to hear any more of this conversation. "Guess I'll go see if she can use some help." He ignored his grandfather's *harrumph* as he left the room.

In the kitchen, Isabelle had filled the kettle and pulled out the makings for tea. She had the cupboard door open and was examining the contents. She turned at the sound of his footsteps.

"I need to get back to town for my things if I mean to stay. And I do." Her words were firm and full of warning.

He'd had enough of everyone thinking him unwelcoming. "Isabelle, I'm glad to have you stay." Saying the words made him realize how true they were, even though he had tried so hard to pretend otherwise.

She studied him long and hard, assessing his sincerity. "You mean it?"

"I do." He let her continue her study until she was satisfied.

"Well, good."

He chuckled.

"What?"

"Tell me what you would have done if I'd said I was taking you back to town to stay." His words were teasing but his heart called for something more. He couldn't say for sure what, perhaps recognition. Or acceptance?

"I would have had to refuse." She said it with such calm assurance that he laughed, delighted at such firmness and—

Commitment?

He sobered. Commitment was something that had been missing in his marriage.

"I can't take you to town, though. It would leave Annie and Mattie alone except for Grandfather, and he can't navigate the stairs."

She turned back to looking in the cupboard. "Very well. I'll make the best of it."

Again, her attitude, this time of acceptance and unconcern, both baffled and amazed him.

"But why don't I ride back to town and ask Kate to prepare whatever you need?"

"That would be fine. You can inform her I will be staying until Mattie is better. Wait. I'll write her a note."

He got paper and a pencil from the other room, ignoring the way Grandfather again snapped his paper.

She wrote quickly, folded the paper and handed it to him. "I appreciate this."

His fingers closed on the paper but he didn't immediately take it. Instead, the two of them held the note between them, their fingertips touching and their eyes meeting. "You have no need to thank me. I'm grateful for your help."

She spoke not a word. Yet a whole world of communication passed between them. Mutual gratitude, but much more. The promise of discovery, the hope of reaching each other—

He jerked the bit of paper away and hurried out to the barn. How could he possibly think he knew her thoughts? What's more, how could he expect this to turn out well?

And yet he felt not fear, nor caution regarding Isabelle's visit. If not for Mattie and Annie being ill, he would even admit he looked forward to spending time with her in his home, on the ranch. It didn't hit him why there was something frighteningly familiar about those words until he saw the house he'd lived in as a married man.

Those were the exact words he'd thought when he brought Violet out here the first time.

Isabelle needed her book *A Guide to Practical House-wifery* to help her prepare meals. However, she didn't have it and wouldn't until Dawson returned. In the meantime, it grew late and she needed to make supper. Something simple for the ill ones upstairs. A broth, she supposed. Though she had no idea how to make such.

She stood staring into the cupboard, waiting for inspiration and enlightenment, when Grandfather Marshall thumped into the kitchen.

"My wife, God rest her soul, always gave our boys barley water when they were ill. Said it contained healing qualities."

"Can you tell me how to make it?"

"I surely can. Do you see a jar of barley in the cupboard?"

She laughed. "It could up and hit me in the face and I wouldn't know it."

His chuckle came from deep inside and made her happy to hear it. He hobbled over and pointed to the jar. "Rinse a generous handful, then cover it with water and boil it."

"Sounds easy enough." She followed his instructions. "I suppose everyone thinks I'm useless because I don't know how to do anything."

He chuckled again, bringing a smile to her lips. "Did

you ever stop to think that no one is born knowing any-thing? Everything we know, we have learned."

"But usually before my age."

"I don't see what age has to do with it."

For the first time since she had stepped off the stage in Bella Creek, she didn't feel like an ostrich at a chicken farm. "You're very encouraging."

"My Bella was a city woman and there wasn't any-thing she wouldn't tackle and succeed in doing."

"You named Bella Creek after her?"

"I did. Young lady, you remind me of Bella. She'd have liked you."

"That's a wonderful compliment." Her pleased smile slid sideways. "Not everyone shares your opinion."

He snorted. "You mean Dawson. I love that boy but sometimes he is so thickheaded. Just because he un-wisely fell in love with Violet, that's no reason to be so gun-shy."

"I think it's more woman-shy," she said with a touch of irony.

Grandfather laughed. "Don't you worry, though. He's smart enough to know a good woman when he sees her, even if he'll fight it to the last possible moment."

"Is that right?" She dared not ask if Grandfather had a particular woman in mind.

But the old man didn't leave her in doubt. "You're just the sort of woman for him, and sooner or later he'll come to the same conclusion. You just wait and see."

Her cheeks burned so hot she wondered if she ran a fever.

Grandfather chuckled. "Forgive an old man for see-ing things you young folk might not see. It's because I've lived long enough to understand life better than I did fifty years ago. Now if you look in the pantry, you'll find ham and potatoes left from last night. Fry them up for supper."

"Thank you."

"For telling you about the pantry or for telling you about Dawson?" His eyes twinkled.

"I can use all the help I can get." Let him decide what that meant. But if he asked, she would say with making meals. She wouldn't admit she had enjoyed hearing about Dawson, too. Or that Grandfather had given her hope that he would see her for who she was...or did she mean, for who she wanted to be?

And not her money.

An icy tremor raced across her neck. How long could she hope to keep the truth about herself hidden? How would learning she was an heiress change how people viewed her?

She had the ham and potatoes chopped neatly, ready to toss into the frying pan, when she heard Dawson's return. By the time he came in from caring for his horse, they were already browning.

He dropped a bulging satchel on the floor and sniffed. "Smells good in here. I've been so busy I forgot about eating, but now I realize I'm starved to a shadow."

Grandfather had kept her company throughout the preparations, often offering a word of advice. He gave his grandson a disbelieving look. "Boy, it would take a long time to turn you into a shadow."

"Guess I can blame you for my size." He snagged a bit of ham from the pan. "You haven't seen the others," he said to Isabelle. "So you wouldn't know the Marshall men are all tall like Grandfather."

"Are they all as blond as you?" Oh, my, where had those words and that admiring tone come from?

His eyes sparkled. "We're all blond but I'm the best-looking one of the bunch."

"Also the most humble," Grandfather said with such despair that Isabelle laughed. It was a pleasure to listen to their good-natured teasing.

"How are the girls?" Dawson glanced toward the ceiling.

"I checked on them a few minutes ago and they're both asleep." Annie had been a little restless but Isabelle had washed her face and arms and it seemed to make her more comfortable. According to Kate, it would help reduce the fever.

She stirred the ingredients in the frying pan. They were golden just as Grandfather said they should be. "Supper is ready, such as it is."

"Good, nourishing food," Grandfather said as she served up the meal. "I'll say grace."

She bowed her head as the older man prayed.

"Father, we thank You for Your many blessings. We are indeed most grateful that Isabelle can help us out in our time of dire need. She is indeed one of Your blessings to us. Bless her as she has blessed us. Oh, and thank You for the food, prepared by Isabelle's capable hands. And help our girls to get better real soon. But not so soon we don't have time to enjoy Isabelle's company."

Isabelle's face grew hotter with each word.

Dawson cleared his throat.

"In Jesus's name. Amen," Grandfather finished hastily.

"I thought we might starve to death before you quit." Dawson handed the bowl to Isabelle.

She dared not look at either of them.

"How can you be so impatient?" Grandfather managed to sound hurt. "It was my sincere prayer."

"Oh, I'm sure it was." Dawson took the bowl and filled his plate. He looked around the table, then rose and went to the pantry, found a jar and brought it to the table. "Tomato chutney. My mother's recipe. Makes everything taste better. Try it." He spooned a generous amount onto his plate and passed the jar to Isabelle.

"Save some for me," Grandfather said. "And the recipe came from my Bella." He sounded aggrieved that Dawson had failed to mention that.

Isabelle took a scant spoonful and handed the jar to Grandfather, who, like Dawson, took a very generous amount.

But after one taste, she could understand why. "This is delicious. I'll have to learn to make it." If she was still here come fall, and she hoped beyond hope that she was.

"It's a family recipe. Not shared with others. But if Dawson doesn't remain stubborn, you will be getting the recipe soon."

"Grandfather." Isabelle and Dawson protested together.

She couldn't lift her eyes from her plate as embarrassment burned through her.

"I'm not getting any younger," Grandfather said, not at all repentant. "It's time my grandsons got married and gave me a bunch of great-grandchildren to enjoy while I still can."

"You have Mattie," Dawson pointed out, all annoyed, which did nothing to ease Isabelle's state of mind.

"And I love the child dearly as you well know. But she's lonely. Time you and your brothers fixed that."

Dawson sighed long and hard. "Isabelle, pay him no mind. He's old and thinks that gives him the right to say anything that pops into his mind."

"Now wait a minute. Don't you be apologizing for me. I'll do my own apologizing when it needs to be done. And right now it doesn't. I spoke the truth." Grandfather harrumphed. "One never needs to apologize for the truth."

Dawson harrumphed right back.

Isabelle could not help herself. She burst out laughing.

Both pairs of blue eyes came to her full of surprise.

She tried to contain her amusement. "I'm sorry," she gasped. "But I grew up an only child. Mealtimes were always quiet and serious." She laughed again, tears streaming down her face.

Both pairs of eyes narrowed.

"Are you saying we're loud?" Grandfather said.

"Are you suggesting our table manners could use improvement?" Dawson demanded, his eyes less friendly than his grandfather's.

She sobered. "I've never before enjoyed this kind of teasing around a table. I think it's special. The way families ought to be."

Both men relaxed and smiled at each other.

"She likes it," Dawson said.

"Of course she does. Like I've been trying to tell you—"

Dawson pushed back from the table before his grandfather could finish. "I do believe I will go check on the girls."

Isabelle got up, too. "I'll be there as soon as I clean up."

Grandfather sighed. "No one wants to listen to my advice."

Isabelle chuckled softly and bent to kiss the old man's leathery cheek. "You've made your opinion very clear."

He brightened and caught her arm to pull her close and kiss her cheek. "I did, didn't I?"

Isabelle chuckled again as she quickly cleaned the kitchen and hurried upstairs to check on Annie and Mattie.

Grandfather's opinion was indeed very clear but it wasn't his that mattered.

Dawson was in Mattie's room, so she checked on Annie first.

Annie opened her eyes. "Is Mattie okay? Is Grandfather okay?"

She washed Annie's face and arms again. "Everyone is fine. You rest and let us take care of you and the others."

Annie closed her eyes as the cloth rubbed her face. "That feels so good. Thank you." Her eyes opened. "What do we have?"

"Kate thinks it's the measles. Says we'll know for sure if you get a rash."

"Oh, lovely."

Isabelle grinned at her tone.

Annie's eyes drifted closed and Isabelle slipped away to Mattie's room. Two chairs had been placed by her bed and Dawson sat in one, talking to his daughter.

Mattie smiled and reached out her hand as Isabelle entered.

Isabelle sank to the chair next to Dawson. Apart from the fact Annie and Mattie were sick, it was pleasant to sit together beside the child.

A shiver crossed her shoulders. But wasn't she living a life of pretense? Pretending she was someone she wasn't? When was she going to tell Dawson the truth about who she was, and more important, how would he react?

Chapter Thirteen

"Where's Isabelle?" Mattie's voice thinned with her misery. "Did you make her leave?"

"She went to see Aunt Annie." Dawson couldn't still a little thread of annoyance making its way through his brain at Mattie's worry as to why Isabelle wasn't with him, and then her eager welcome when Isabelle stepped into the room. Annoyance at himself. He could handle the disappointment when Isabelle left or determined she didn't care for any more ranch life. But his daughter would be hurt and he could only blame himself. From the beginning he'd warned himself to ignore the way his heart opened to her. To his credit, he'd tried to put an end to any contact. Yeah, he thought with self-mockery, he'd given a halfhearted attempt, more than a little relieved when Mattie had insisted she stay with Isabelle after school.

And now look where they were. The two of them side by side, tending Mattie and Annie.

Mattie sat up and leaned toward Isabelle, who sat beside him. Had he purposely positioned the chairs so close their arms brushed? He allowed he might have.

"Does everyone get the measles?" Mattie asked.

Dawson felt Isabelle's startled look come to him and turned to meet it.

"I don't know," Isabelle admitted. "Do they?"

Dawson shrugged, barely able to remember the question at the way he felt drawn into her dark, bottomless eyes. He felt himself swimming through a warm, fragrant mist, heading toward a place that promised the fulfillment of all his dreams.

"Did you have them?" Mattie asked.

Dawson jerked his attention back to his daughter. "I did, along with both your uncles." Though he wondered if he was mistaken and had spiked a fever at this very moment. That would explain his foolish imaginings.

"Did you?" Mattie asked Isabelle.

"Yes, I did." Something about the sweetness in Isabelle's tone brought Dawson's attention back to her. But, thankfully, she looked at Mattie, saving him from himself. "I remember my mama sitting with me, her long black hair in a thick braid. I liked to hold the braid and feel the silkiness of her hair."

At Mattie's soft sigh, Dawson shifted his gaze back to his daughter. Her eyes were wide, filled with dreamy thoughts. "Your mama loved you."

"Yes, she did. I had a nanny but Mama insisted on taking care of me herself when I was ill."

"Tell me stories about your mama."

Isabelle darted a look at Dawson as if gauging his reaction to all this talk about mothers. Then determination replaced inquiry. She meant to say what she thought Mattie needed to hear.

He had granted her permission to talk about Mattie's mother. He just hadn't thought he'd have to be in attendance but he had no intention of leaving this room. Though, he reasoned, Mattie had asked to hear about Isabelle's mother, not her own. He should feel relieved. He wasn't sure he did.

"What sort of stories do you want to hear?" Isabelle took Mattie's hand as she talked.

"What did she look like? Did she play with you?"

"My mama was beautiful. She'd been born in Spain and had the dark eyes and dark hair of her family."

"Like you." Mattie touched a strand of Isabelle's black hair. "You must look like her. You're beautiful, too."

Red stained her cheeks. "Thank you, but my mother was very, very beautiful. And she had the sweetest voice. I wish you could have heard her sing."

Another soft, lonesome sigh from Mattie. The almost imperceptible sound ached through Dawson. He remembered Mattie's distress when Violet had disappeared from her life but he'd never considered the ache had remained.

Isabelle continued. "Mama told me stories about life in Spain. About the horses her family raised. How the family would gather under the olive trees for the midday meal. The trips to the Mediterranean Sea every summer. But the stories I liked best were of the games she played as a child."

"What sort of games?" Mattie tensed in anticipation.

"*Rayuela* was one Mama taught me. It's like hopscotch. I loved it when she played with me. She was very good. She never lost her balance."

For a few minutes, Mattie sat mesmerized as Isabelle recounted tales about growing up with a loving, attentive mother.

Dawson, too, felt himself carried along by her words,

imagining an idyllic childhood full of love…the sort of life he had dreamed of for his own child.

Mattie looked away from them. "I wish I could remember my mama."

"Your mother was beautiful." The words came from behind a door thrown open by Isabelle's stories. She was right. Good memories were healing and he would do his best to give some to Mattie. "I remember the first time I saw her. She had come to town with some others. Strange, I can't even remember who she was with. But the first time I saw her, I was smitten."

"Smitten?" Mattie sounded confused. "What does that mean?"

He chuckled. "It means I liked what I saw."

"What did she look like?"

"She had eyes like yours, as green as they were blue. And your hair is almost the same color as hers—like gold in the sunlight."

Mattie had a pleased smile on her lips.

Isabelle leaned closer, pressing against his arm. Was it intentional or did she think only of Mattie? He liked to think she had both of them in mind.

"All the young men were smitten. Even Uncle Jesse."

Isabelle shifted, putting several inches between them, something that he regretted. "The sheriff is your brother?"

"He's Conner's best friend and has spent so much time here Mattie took to calling him Uncle Jesse." He suddenly realized something. "We see a lot less of him now that he's sheriff."

"Did Uncle Jesse like Mama?" Mattie sounded concerned, as if she imagined rivalry between Dawson and Jesse.

"Like I said, everyone was smitten, but your mama

picked me to be her beau." In hindsight, he wondered if Jesse and the others had seen Violet for who she really was and had not pursued her for that reason.

Mattie giggled. "'Cause you were the handsomest of them all."

He dared not look at Isabelle as heat crept up his neck at his daughter's adoration. He couldn't speak for a moment as he considered the facts. Violet might have thought him handsome to begin with, but then she found reasons to complain about him. He was too big. His big boots got in the way. He took up too much space. Why had he let her comments bother him? With a start, he realized they no longer did. Perhaps it was Mattie's admiration that took the sting from those words. Or it might even be the touch of Isabelle's arm against his.

"Tell me more," Mattie begged.

He found he could talk of Violet without pain and only mild regret. After all, she'd given him this precious child. "She was so full of life. So eager for excitement."

It was more than that, he realized now. She was restless and unhappy and blamed everyone around her for her state of mind. The truth was, he saw so clearly now that he wondered how he'd ever believed otherwise, something inside her had seemed to be missing and she'd sought it in all the wrong ways—excitement, adventure, new activities. His mind at ease in a way he'd almost forgotten existed, he told Mattie how her mama chose pretty bonnets for Mattie as a baby and how she liked to brush Mattie's hair and do special things with it.

Mattie's eyes began to droop.

"It's time for you to rest."

She protested weakly.

Isabelle sponged Mattie's face and arms, then tucked her into bed with a kiss.

"Can you sing to me, like your mama did?" Mattie asked.

With a half-apologetic glance at Dawson, she sat on the edge of the bed.

Why should she feel sorry? To his regret, he admitted he'd given her every reason to feel he didn't want her spending time with his daughter. To his shame, he'd even suggested she was unsuitable simply because she was…what? A city woman? A newcomer? Beautiful?

All those things could mean danger. Or they could mean nothing.

He wasn't sure he had changed his mind, but it became harder and harder to remember his reasons.

Isabelle crooned a song in Spanish.

He sat, as mesmerized by her sweet voice as Mattie was. In a distant corner of his brain, a warning voice called, reminding him how caring for Isabelle could end in disappointment and wrenching pain. The voice was drowned out by the sound of her voice and by the blossoming of his distant dreams.

Mattie's eyes drifted shut.

Isabelle brushed her fingers over Mattie's face, from forehead to chin. She leaned close and kissed each cheek. "Sweet dreams, little princess."

The word jolted clear through Dawson. *Princess.* Was that how Isabelle saw his child? His throat tightened. His eyes burned. So many people loved and cared for Mattie but something about Isabelle's tender touch and sweet words felt different.

She rose from the bed.

Dawson stood up, too, and they faced each other, so

close he could watch her pupils narrow, see the way her black eyebrows thinned to a point at the outer corner of her eyes. He could feel her breath go in and out, and he inhaled the scent of sandalwood and honey.

Their look went on and on. The air seemed to shimmer between them. All his doubts and fears flew out the door. He lowered his gaze. At this moment, he was acutely aware of everything she seemed to offer—beauty clothed in tenderness, tenderness wrapped in love. A never-ending circle.

With a half smile she sidestepped him. "I'll check on Annie, then see if your grandfather needs anything."

His lungs emptied with a whoosh as she left the room. He heard her speaking to Annie, and then her footsteps returned. She paused outside the door. "Are you staying here?"

It would be the best thing for his state of mind and yet he caught himself answering, "No, I'll come with you." And his feet carried him down the stairs at her side.

Grandfather sat in the parlor, his book open on his lap and his head hanging down.

"He's asleep."

Grandfather's head jerked up. "I was resting my eyes." He didn't even try to hide a yawn.

"Would you like tea?" Isabelle asked, her voice calm, as if unaffected by the minutes spent tending Mattie with Dawson at her side.

Dawson wished he could get himself even halfway back to unaffected.

"I'd like that," Grandfather said and started to struggle to his feet.

Dawson knew better than to offer help.

Isabelle waved at him to stay sitting. "I'll bring tea in here."

"If it's not too much trouble."

"None whatsoever."

Dawson followed her into the kitchen. He thought to assist her but how many hands did it take to fill the kettle and wait for it to boil, gather together cups and set them on a tray? Besides, he kind of liked watching her move about as if she knew her way around the kitchen.

The thought slapped him on the side of the head. One of his disappointments with Violet was her inability to manage a kitchen, let alone a home, and yet here was Isabelle bustling about, making tea for them as if she'd done it all her life.

He leaned his elbows on the top of the table, rested his chin on his hands and watched.

She poured water over the tea leaves and set the pot on the tray, then went to the cupboard by the stove. "I think I saw some cookies in here. Yes, here they are. Do you think Annie will mind if we eat them?"

"I'm sure she won't mind at all."

"I'll bake some tomorrow to replace them." She glanced over her shoulder as if to make sure he understood her intent. She grew confused. "What? Did I do something wrong?"

He sat up. "No. Why would you think that?"

"Because you were staring at me as if I'd made a mistake."

"I wasn't. If you must know the truth, I was admiring how easily you took over running the kitchen."

She turned to face him full on. "You were?"

"Why are you so surprised?" It stung that she misjudged him. "Do you think me so critical?"

Her little laugh seemed more doubtful than mirthful. "Let me see, perhaps because I heard you say I was unsuitable for anything useful." Each word rang with accusation and hurt. "Maybe because you said I couldn't be around Mattie."

"Then, if you care to recall, I changed my mind."

She went on as if he hadn't spoken. "Or it might be because you took me to the waterfall, treated me like you enjoyed my company then turned all cold and dismissive. It might even be all of those things and even things you didn't say but communicated clearly."

When she reached for the tea tray, he took it but didn't immediately carry it through to where Grandfather waited. "Isabelle, my experience with women may have left me a little jaded."

"Only a little?" She marched into the sitting room.

What could he do but follow and sit with a cup of tea while she gave Grandfather a report on the girls upstairs?

"Annie is the sicker of the two but she was resting when I left."

Grandfather ate a cookie and drank his tea then pushed to his feet. "It's time for this old man to go to bed. I'll leave you young ones to make sure the girls are okay. Don't hesitate to waken me if they get worse. I wouldn't want to sleep through their need. Good night." He gave Dawson a look no doubt meant to instruct him to treat Isabelle right before he trundled through the door to his bedroom.

Dawson and Isabelle sat in silence, concentrating on the contents of their teacups as if they could avoid each other.

Isabelle broke the awkward silence first. "Thank you for telling Mattie about her mother. I know it meant a great deal to her."

Dawson thought to point out how odd it was for her to thank him, when Mattie was his daughter and his concern. But he knew Isabelle shared a love for his child. "I should never have married Violet."

"So you've said. I'm sorry your marriage was so unhappy."

"I thought her excitement would translate into eagerness to care for a home and family."

"And it didn't?"

He shook his head. "She was spoiled. Her parents gave her everything she wanted."

"What do you mean?" Despite the bitterness he couldn't keep from his voice, she sounded calm, sympathetic.

"She had everything money could buy."

"But, Dawson, money can't buy everything. It can't buy affection or time or satisfaction."

He didn't care to hear Violet defended. "She was dissatisfied."

"Then she doesn't sound spoiled so much as deprived."

He gave her a look loaded with disbelief.

Her smile was gentle. "She might have everything she wanted but did she have what she needed?"

His eyebrows rose.

"Could it be she was looking for meaning in things, possessions, and even new experiences? Perhaps searching for something to fill the emptiness within?"

"You're saying love, a home and marriage weren't enough?" He wasn't enough? But then, he already knew that was how Violet had felt. But it stung to hear it from Isabelle.

"I believe a person has to find meaning and satisfaction within, not from outside influences." Seeing his confusion, she continued. "I remember something my mother told me often. She quoted a verse, 'Man shall not live by bread alone but by every word that proceedeth out of the mouth of God.' She urged me to not look for satisfaction in the fleeting things of life."

"So you look to God for satisfaction and meaning?" He'd been taught much the same but it didn't always seem to apply to his situation. "What about when things go wrong?"

"Sometimes it's hard to trust, but God is ever faithful." She spoke with such calm assurance.

"Have you found everything you want in life, then?"

"For the most part. I know what is important to me." She searched his gaze. "What about you?"

"I've always known who I am…a Marshall and a cowboy. And I know what I want. My own ranch. In fact, I bought a herd of my own last fall. Sank all my savings into them." He glanced toward the door as if he could see his father and brothers. "Pa and the others are out right now seeing how well the animals fared through the winter." He hoped for a good report soon and not just on his animals. He brought his gaze back to her and found himself telling her more of his dreams. "I've always wanted a family of my own and now I have Mattie."

Her gaze searched his. He kept his lost dreams and wishes behind a barrier so she couldn't guess at them.

"So, you have everything you want?"

He had to answer honestly. "Not quite." If she asked he'd have to tell her how he still longed for a home and family of his own. Before she could voice the question rising in her eyes, he asked one of his own. "What happened to your parents? I don't believe you've ever said."

Her eyes filled with such darkness he wished he could pull the question back.

* * *

Isabelle's heart hung somewhere between the pain of her past and the joy of the moment when she had sung a familiar lullaby to Mattie, successfully made a meal and earned surprised approval from Dawson. She didn't want to ruin the mood by talking about her parents. Yet, strangely, she found she ached to tell him of their deaths.

"They had a strange fever. No one ever told me what it was exactly. Maybe the doctors didn't know. They got sick within days of each other. Nurses and doctors were in and out of the house constantly. Their rooms became hospital rooms." She shuddered. "To this day I can still recall the smell of antiseptic." She shuddered again.

"That's why you fled from the doctor's examining room, isn't it?"

She nodded. "The smell of any kind of illness fills me with such dread I can barely breathe." She paused to gather herself. "The doctor and nurses kept reassuring me that my parents would get better. They were wrong. So very, very wrong. Mama died first. I was at her bedside holding her hand. She smiled at me, made me promise to always do as she had taught me. Then her hand went limp."

Isabelle's muscles twitched so she couldn't sit still, and she went to the window to look out into the dark. "I didn't realize she'd passed away until the nurse took me by the shoulders and led me from the room. Papa died that evening. I never got to say goodbye to him." She hugged her arms about herself, wishing for the comfort of her mother's touch.

She hadn't realized Dawson moved until his hands rested on her shoulders. "You were very loved. That's something that can never be replaced."

A sob tore up her throat and pushed against her teeth.

He turned her about and pressed her head to the hollow of his shoulder. "I'm so sorry for your loss."

The tears came in a hot flood. She clung to Dawson, needing his comfort. He held her close and let her cry until she was spent.

"I've soaked your shirt." She hiccuped.

"I don't mind."

She leaned into him, so weak from her bout of crying she didn't know if she could stand on her own. "I feel like I should apologize."

"Absolutely not. I think you needed that." With his thumb he gently wiped away the last of her tears.

His touch reached a place deep inside that, until this very moment, had been dry and barren but now sprang into full, flowering life. "If I helped in any way, I couldn't be happier." His thumb continued caressing, stopping at the corner of her mouth. "Though it hurts to see you cry." His voice deepened. "I would take your pain if I could."

She smiled. "In a sort of fashion, you did." She wiped at the wet spot on his shirt then brought her gaze back to his.

Neither spoke, though she wondered how he could not hear the cry of her heart. Something about this man broke down the barriers she'd erected to protect herself. His touch, his tenderness reached inside.

His blue eyes brightened, flashed understanding. Or at least that was what she allowed herself to believe. He lowered his gaze to her lips then brought it back to her eyes, silently questioning her.

She smiled, as much with her eyes as her mouth, and tilted her head in invitation.

He needed no more than that as he bent his head and claimed her lips in a gentle-as-dandelion-fluff kiss.

She leaned into his embrace, pressed her palms to his muscular back and let every pain, every disappointment, every lonely thought disappear.

He lifted his head, ending the kiss.

She ought to step from his arms but he again pressed her head to the hollow of his shoulder. The wet spot from her tears dampened her cheek. His chest rose and fell; his heart tattooed a rhythm against her ear. She had not felt so safe and cherished since her parents died.

He turned her to his side. "Come, let's check on the invalids." They walked up the stairs together, his arm about her.

They checked Annie first. She lay curled on her side and moaned.

Isabelle left the safety and comfort of Dawson's arm and sat on the edge of the bed to sponge the fevered girl. Dawson waited with her until Annie settled again. Then they checked on Mattie. She slept peacefully.

They tiptoed out of the room.

"She isn't as sick as Annie," Isabelle said, stating the obvious. "I'll sit up with her. Why don't you get some sleep?"

He glanced down the hall to three more doorways. "I suppose there's no point in both of us sitting up, but I'll take the first awake shift. You can use Pa's room. Next to Annie's."

"I couldn't—"

"I insist."

"I was about to say I couldn't sleep yet. I'm not tired."

"Nor am I."

They smiled at each other.

She couldn't sleep with their kiss so fresh in her mind. Was he having the same reaction? Her cheeks burned and she turned away lest he see and guess the reason.

Dawson took Isabelle's arm and led her back to Mattie's room to sit side by side. "We might as well be comfortable," he said. "As soon as you're tired, feel free to go to bed."

"Okay." She wondered how long it would take for her emotions to wane.

A lamp glowed from the hallway. They checked on Annie regularly, but other than that, their voices low, they talked as the night deepened. Isabelle couldn't seem to stop talking about her parents. Little stories from her memories. Dawson encouraged her with questions and comments.

Finally she stopped. "I'm sorry. I've monopolized the conversation. Tell me about what your life was like as a boy."

She listened eagerly as he talked about growing up on a ranch, about the first calf his pa had given him, the first horse he'd owned. "As the oldest, it seemed I always had to prove I was as good as or better than the others." He chuckled softly, mindful of the sleeping child nearby. "Sometimes it got me into trouble."

"What kind of trouble?" She had a yearning to know every detail of his life. Not only because it was so vastly different from her own upbringing but because it was Dawson's and she longed to know more about the man.

In the low light of the room, his teeth flashed as he grinned. "Well, I could tell you about the time I roped a porcupine to prove to the boys it could be done. I forgot to take into account that I would have to face the quills to get the rope back."

She gasped. "Did you get them in your hand?"

"Nope. I managed to loosen the loop enough to let it escape. I wasn't so fortunate when it came to a skunk." He didn't explain.

Realizing he teased her, making her beg for more, she sighed dramatically. "You roped a skunk?"

"Not quite. We had an old hired man at the time and he was always telling us of his escapades and filling our heads with all sorts of lore. He told us if we picked up a skunk by the tail, it couldn't spray."

"Really? I didn't know that. And I can't think of any reason I would need to."

"Unfortunately, it isn't true." The way Dawson drawled the words tickled her insides.

"How do you know?" She couldn't keep the teasing laughter from her voice.

"I tried." He wrinkled his nose. "I got sprayed in the armpit. Phew. My eyes water just remembering it. I had to bury my clothes, and Ma made me eat and sleep outside for two days. And bathe in the horse trough using tomato juice." He watched for her reaction and it came swiftly.

She covered her mouth to silence her chuckles.

He grinned. "Yeah, it's hard being oldest. Always having to prove myself. Always being the first to learn valuable lessons while the others stand by and take notes."

Her shoulders shook with laughter and she escaped into the hallway before she wakened Mattie.

Dawson followed. "It's not kind to laugh at my misfortunes." He sounded hurt, which she did not believe for one moment.

She patted his arm. "I only wish I could have been there." Her grin filled her eyes.

He looked down at her, the lamplight making his features even more strong than normal. He brushed his curled finger against her cheek. "I wish you could have been there, too." His voice deepened.

They faced each other. He pulled her close and she tilted her face toward him, inviting another kiss.

"Isabelle?" A soft call came from Annie's room. "Are you there?"

She turned from Dawson's arms and hurried to his sister's room. "I'm here."

"I'm so itchy."

Dawson brought the lamp into the room so they could see Annie better. A dull pink rash covered her face and neck.

"I'll get something to ease your discomfort." Isabelle hurried downstairs to mix up a paste with oatmeal and water according to the instructions Kate had given her.

As she worked, she fought an inner battle. Dawson had begun to accept her as capable and trustworthy. He might even want to get to know her better…maybe even see her in his life long term.

Before any of that could happen, she needed to be honest about who she was. But if she told him she was an heiress, would he suddenly become more interested?

She couldn't bear the idea. No, it was too soon. Time enough to reveal the truth after she was certain of his feelings toward her. Thankfully, he could not find out until she chose to tell him. But keeping a secret from him made her jittery inside. She longed to tell him everything about herself and judge his reaction. If she didn't guard her tongue, she would blurt out the truth.

Chapter Fourteen

Dawson held the lamp as Isabelle spread a paste over Annie's rash. He turned his back as Isabelle pulled the neck of Annie's nightgown lower to apply it to her chest and back.

"That should help." Isabelle's voice soothed.

"It does. Thanks. How's Mattie?" Annie asked.

"Still a bit fevered but you seem to have gotten the worst of it."

Dawson hoped it was so. Not that he wasn't worried about his sister.

"I'm okay now," Annie said.

"Don't hesitate to call," Isabelle said as she straightened. Without the need to speak their intent, she and Dawson went to check on Mattie.

"No rash yet," Isabelle said after looking closely at Mattie's skin.

They sat together at Mattie's bedside. Conversation lagged as the evening wore on. He hoped it was only because Isabelle was tired, not that she regretted the tender moments they'd shared. As if to reassure him that was the case, her head drooped.

She jerked upright.

"Go lie down for a bit," he whispered.

She made a protesting sound.

He took her hand, pulled her to her feet and led her to Pa's room. "We'll take turns resting," he said, as she stared longingly at the bed.

"You'll waken me if anything changes?"

"Of course."

"Very well. I'll rest a couple of hours. Then you can rest."

"Have a good sleep." He backed out of the room and returned to Mattie's side.

The next thing he knew, someone tapped him on the shoulder. He jerked awake. "Huh?" It was Isabelle, smiling down at him. He smiled back. Nice to wake up and see her at his side.

"I had a sleep. Now it's your turn."

He would argue, but all he could do was yawn.

She took his hands and pulled him to his feet then pushed him toward the door. "Have a good rest."

He paused in the doorway to look at Isabelle bent over Mattie, checking her fever and looking for signs of the rash. It was a pose he would cherish forever, a mother–child tender moment even though they were not mother and child.

He hurried to his room and threw himself on the bed to stare at the dark ceiling. Mattie needed a mother. More correctly, a stepmother. Was it possible? Did he want it enough to court Isabelle? Or was he simply courting pain and rejection?

Morning light spilled through the cracks around the window blind and he came to his feet in a jolt. How long had he slept? Far too long. He strode from his room straight to Mattie's.

Isabelle leaned over the child, just as she had when he left. Had she not left Mattie's side?

She heard his footsteps and looked up. "Annie's rash has spread. I've made her as comfortable as I can. Mattie now has a rash."

"Look, Papa. I'm all red." She scratched at her chest. "And itchy."

"Try not to scratch." Isabelle smoothed oatmeal paste over her rashy areas then sat down.

He sank to the chair next to Isabelle. "You shouldn't have let me sleep so long."

"You only slept a couple of hours."

"Really?"

"Check the clock if you don't believe me."

"It seemed longer," he added lamely.

She pushed to her feet. "I heard your grandfather moving about. I'll go make breakfast." She headed for the door.

He thought she might want to spend a few minutes with him and was on his feet instantly, following her. "I didn't mean to offend you."

She spared him a smile. "You didn't. And if I sounded prickly, it's because I'm tired and concerned about Annie and Mattie."

His nerves tensed. "Is Annie worse?" He took a step toward her room.

"No, but I'm not good in sickrooms." She ran a weary hand over her brow. "I kept thinking of my mama and papa."

Regret edged his thoughts. "I'm sorry. I shouldn't

have left you alone, especially after you told me about them." He pulled her to his chest.

Her shoulders sank. He could almost feel the tension leaving her as she rested her head against him. In the exact spot where she had cried her heart out and soaked his shirt. He might always think of that spot as hers. A smile curved his lips at such sentimental nonsense.

She eased back. "I'm okay now. Thanks again." Her gaze rose no farther than the collar of his shirt.

He caught her chin and tipped her face upward.

Her eyes lifted, pausing at his chin, then his mouth. She swallowed hard and he allowed himself a tiny bit of joy that she likely recalled last night's kiss. Her gaze finally reached his and he hoped his smile relieved any lingering tension. "You should have wakened me to keep you company."

She nodded. "You don't know how many times I thought of it." She straightened and squared her shoulders. "But I had to prove I could do this on my own."

"Who did you need to prove it to?" He asked out of curiosity and concern, but more so out of regret that he had given her cause to feel the need to prove anything.

"To myself, of course." She ducked her head. "And maybe to you."

He crushed her to his chest again. "I'm sorry I ever suggested you were incapable of anything. You know, your friend Kate warned me I underestimated you and she was right."

Isabelle leaned back. "I hope you continue to believe it."

"I see no reason I wouldn't. Grandfather informed me my grandmother was a greenhorn and he never had any reason to complain." He closed his eyes as he realized how self-serving those words sounded. He didn't mean them that way. "All I'm trying to say in my faltering way is that you've changed my mind about...women." He finished weakly, not sure what he meant.

She stepped back. "Good."

He wondered at the caution in her eyes. Had he not explained himself sufficiently? "Are you not willing to forgive me for my foolish assessment of earlier?"

She patted his hand. "I forgive you. Now I must see about breakfast."

He watched her descend the stairs. Something bothered her, and if not his earlier judgment, then what? He turned back to check on Annie. She was red with the rash.

"I know I look a fright but please don't stare."

"Can't help it." No wonder Isabelle seemed a little standoffish. No doubt seeing Annie like this and watching the rash break out on Mattie brought back the shock of having her parents die in their beds. He should never have left her alone. He would not do so again.

A few minutes later, she called up the stairs. "Breakfast is ready."

He trotted down and joined Grandfather and Isabelle at the table. Grandfather demanded a report on Annie and Mattie. They gave him the details. He added a prayer for their recovery to his grace.

Both Isabelle and Dawson murmured, "Amen." Their gazes caught and they shared a moment of sweet understanding.

Finished, Grandfather moved to the sitting room to enjoy the sunshine.

Isabelle jumped to her feet. "I'll take something up for the girls."

He smiled at how quickly she'd picked up Grandfather's way of talking about Mattie and Annie.

"I need to run out and take care of the chores. Will you be okay while I'm gone?"

She spun about to face him fully. "Are you still questioning my ability to cope?"

He groaned at his stupidity. "That's not what I meant. But I know it's hard for you to face the sickroom. I wouldn't leave you alone again except there's no one else to do the chores." He crossed to her side and touched her cheek. "I believe, like Kate said, you can do anything you put your mind to."

Her gaze came to his, full of soft lights and golden thoughts.

He congratulated himself on making his meaning clear for a change.

"Thank you," she whispered. "It means a lot to hear you say that."

"I thought I already had in my muddled way."

She grinned widely. "It can't hurt to say it more than once."

He lowered his head, kissed her forehead and hurried to the cloakroom while he could still remember he meant to do the chores.

Isabelle fairly danced as she cleaned the kitchen and prepared barley water and fingers of bread and jam for the girls upstairs. Dawson thought her capable. He no longer saw her as incompetent. Moreover, she understood his initial reaction to her. His wife had wounded him deeply.

She hummed as she took the tray upstairs.

Her well-being lasted throughout the morning as she and Dawson cared for the girls. Annie was restless and uncomfortable, and she took much of Isabelle's time while Dawson tended Mattie.

By noon, Isabelle had run up and down the stairs a dozen times or more, had sponged Annie several times and applied oatmeal paste. She'd made tea for the girls and for Grandfather.

Dawson stopped her on yet another trip, this time carrying fresh water. "Isabelle, I can do that." He took the jug from her. "You don't have to do everything. You have nothing to prove."

She sucked in a deep breath. "Is that what I'm doing? Trying to prove something?"

"Sure looks like it to me. The girls aren't that sick. Now let me give them fresh water to drink. You go sit down somewhere and rest a bit."

When she hesitated, he pointed toward the stairs.

"Fine." She returned to the kitchen and found the makings for dinner.

He came into the kitchen and stared at her. "Is this how you rest?"

She laughed, delighted by his concern, and if she'd been the least bit tired, it fled at his words. "I'm hungry. How about you?"

He tried to look uninterested.

She laughed again. "You are. I can tell. So I made dinner."

Grandfather wandered in and joined them.

After the meal, Dawson insisted on washing the dishes while she dried, surprised at how good and right it felt to be working side by side.

* * *

By midafternoon Mattie was fussing with the itch of her rash but Annie seemed to be more comfortable.

Isabelle applied paste to Mattie's rash and tried to soothe her discomfort with gentle words.

"I'm itchy all over," Mattie complained.

"I know you are and I wish I could do something about it." Dawson's voice behind her made Isabelle's hands grow still. More and more it seemed as if they shared the same dreams and wishes, and she felt—hoped—he saw her as capable.

The evening came and they were kept busy tending to the girls.

"You should go sleep," Dawson said. "We'll take turns again."

She wanted to protest. Partly because she worried about Mattie and partly because she didn't want to lose a moment of this sweet accord with Dawson, but she was tired enough to have a headache. "I guess I could rest a bit." She went to his father's room and lay down, intending only to rest her eyes, but she fell asleep almost as soon as her head hit the pillow.

The room was dark when she jerked awake and she tiptoed from the room.

"Papa, sing to me like Isabelle does." Mattie's voice stopped Isabelle in the hallway. She smiled, wondering how Dawson would handle Mattie's request.

"I can't sing like she does," Dawson protested.

"You sing in church."

"Where my voice is drowned out by others. Besides, I don't know any little-girl songs."

"Please, Papa." Mattie sounded weepy.

"Okay, I'll do my best." He cleared his throat. "O

little doggies, settle down. No more roaming until the dawn."

Isabelle leaned against the wall and listened to the deep rumble of his voice as he sang a song surely intended for a herd of cows. The absurdity of it so tickled her funny bone that she covered her mouth to stifle her laughter.

Dawson stopped singing. "Isabelle, is that you?"

She straightened, sucked in air to stop her amusement and stepped into the room. "I'm awake."

His eyes narrowed. "How long were you out there?"

She managed to keep her expression flat but knew laughter filled her eyes. "Not long."

"Long enough, I'm guessing."

She grinned. "You'd be right." She pulled her gaze from his to Mattie. Her rash had spread. The child looked quite uncomfortable. Isabelle sat on the edge of the bed across from Dawson and stroked Mattie's forehead. "How are you?"

"I'm itchy." She squirmed and scratched her face.

"I'll be right back with some fresh paste." Isabelle hurried down the stairs and into the kitchen, where a lamp burned low. She quickly mixed up the concoction and returned upstairs to apply it to Mattie's rash. "Does that help?"

"A little." The child was understandably peevish.

Isabelle turned to Dawson to whisper, "I can manage. You should have a rest."

He hesitated. "I hate to leave her."

"I'll call if she gets worse or if she asks for you."

After a moment's hesitation, he nodded and left the room.

Isabelle checked on Annie, relieved to see her sleeping.

She returned to Mattie's room and did her best to keep the child comfortable. It seemed Dawson had hardly left when he returned, but already dawn had grayed the sky. Where had the night gone?

Mattie remained fussy most of the day.

"Would you like to have a kitten visit you?" Dawson asked.

Mattie brightened. "Could I?"

"I'll fetch one." He was gone, his words following him down the stairs.

Isabelle was as excited as Mattie.

Dawson returned with a tiny furry bundle in variegated colors. He placed it on Mattie's chest and she petted and crooned at the animal.

Isabelle put out a tentative finger to touch the cat. "It's so soft. I've never before seen such a little kitten."

"You can hold her." Mattie put the kitten in Isabelle's arms.

Isabelle rubbed her cheek against the fur, laughing at the tiny rumble coming from the kitten. "I've never seen anything but wild, mangy cats scrounging through the garbage. Nothing as sweet as this."

"You've never had a pet?" Mattie asked the question but Dawson looked equally shocked.

"No, never."

"Then you can have one of these when they are big enough to leave their mama, right, Papa?"

Dawson nodded. "Right."

A little later, he said he must take the kitten back to the mommy cat.

Mattie's eyes closed and she rested.

Isabelle went to the kitchen to prepare a meal, surprised that the day was more than half gone.

Dawson returned and leaned against the door frame, watching her.

She paused and faced him. His gaze held hers, on and on. She waited, her heart drumming against her ribs, wondering what he thought.

"I'm glad you're here with me…" He paused a beat then added, "With us."

She continued to wait, not knowing how to respond. Did he mean simply that she helped or did he mean more?

"You aren't what I thought you were."

"What is that?"

He gave a slight shrug. "I'm not even sure. I suppose Grandfather and the others were right when they accused me of seeing Violet in every woman. I'm cautious about believing they'll be what they appear to be." He crossed the floor and took her by her arms, holding her so close she could feel him in every breath. "You're real." He caught her lips in a gentle, promising kiss.

It was time to be honest with him about who she was. How would he respond? But before she could find any words, Grandfather hobbled into the room and the opportunity was gone.

Dawson felt a sense of peace and rightness he had not known in so long he had forgotten it existed. Isabelle fit his dreams. Honest, capable, loving… She made the anxious hours of Annie's and Mattie's illness more bearable.

That night and the next day passed in pleasantly shared tasks of caring for the girls, taking care of meals and taking turns sleeping.

By Saturday morning, the girls seemed over the worst of it. Annie insisted on getting out of bed. As soon as Mattie heard Annie get up, she wanted to be up, too, and they both traipsed down the stairs.

Grandfather took one look at Annie and chuckled. "You're all blotchy."

She didn't answer but swept by him to the kitchen.

"Can I sit on Grandfather's knee?" Mattie asked.

"Of course you can." Grandfather lifted her to his lap and smiled at the flushed child. "Sure hope your rash goes away soon."

Mattie snuggled into his arms and looked pleased with herself.

In the kitchen, Annie began to open cupboard doors as if she meant to make the meal.

Dawson was about to tell her there was no need when Isabelle went to Annie's side.

"You need to rest yet. I can manage for now but don't worry—as soon as you're fit to take over I will bow out."

Annie sighed. "Am I that obvious?"

"Only to someone who understands."

Dawson stared in surprise. How had Isabelle known what Annie needed to hear? She surprised him more every day. Capable, understanding, tender…

Everything required to make his dreams come true.

Isabelle had supper preparations under way when horses thundered into the yard.

He glanced out the window. "Pa and the boys are back." Now he'd find out if his herd had survived. If it had he could afford to start his own place. If not…

He'd need to start over.

"They'll be here for supper," Grandfather said.

At Isabelle's almost inaudible gasp, Dawson turned. "All you need is more potatoes. I'll help you with that." It would occupy his mind while he waited for the news.

He didn't have long to wait until the outer door opened and the three men clattered in. He could picture them removing their hats and coats and pulling off their muddy boots. Then the connecting door opened and Pa stepped into the kitchen followed by Conner and Logan.

Pa stopped and the boys had to sidestep around him. "We got company."

Dawson suddenly remembered Isabelle had not met the rest of his family and sprang forward to introduce everyone.

Pa greeted her warmly. Dawson knew he'd measured Isabelle and he wondered what his father thought of her.

Logan bowed over her hand. "Pleased to meet you. You might be happy to know not all the Marshall boys are as dour as Dawson." He gave Dawson a challenging look.

Conner, always more restrained than their youngest brother, greeted Isabelle with proper courtesy but revealed nothing of his opinion.

Annie and Mattie, with Grandfather between them, stood in the far doorway.

Pa looked at the girls. "What's wrong?"

Grandfather and Dawson spoke at the same time. Annie held up her hand to silence them.

"We have the measles."

Pa crossed the room in three strides to grab Annie by the shoulders. "Are you okay?"

"I'll survive. And so will Mattie."

Pa squatted down to Mattie. "Can't go away without something happening, can I?"

Dawson protested, "Nothing has gone wrong and Isabelle has helped with the girls."

The three men turned again to consider Isabelle.

If Dawson wasn't mistaken, she edged closer to him.

He wondered if any of them noticed how his chest swelled to know she looked to him for safety.

She gave an uncertain smile. "Supper is ready."

There followed a general shuffling as everyone found a place. He made sure Isabelle sat next to him, where he could take care of her.

Wouldn't she be annoyed to know he thought she needed it?

He waited until Grandfather had said grace and the food was passed before he asked the question that burned on the tip of his tongue.

"Did you find all the cows?"

Pa and his brothers stopped eating and looked at one another.

He looked only at Pa to relay the news.

Pa put his fork down. "We found them." The words hung in the air like a wet banner.

Dawson set his fork down, too, and planted both hands beside his plate. "Sounds like you have bad news."

Pa nodded. "Good news and bad news. First, the good. We found the main herd had wintered well. A few old cows missing but that's to be expected. However—"

Dawson braced himself for the bad news.

"Son, we found your herd in a box canyon. I don't know how long they'd been trapped there." He let that sink in.

Dawson swallowed hard and nodded. "How bad was it?"

Conner spoke. "We spent the better part of two days digging them out."

"How many?" Dawson persisted.

Conner shook his head. Logan refused to look at him.

He brought his gaze back to Pa. "Pa, give me the bad news."

"It's bad all right. There were only a dozen still alive."

Dawson sat back with a thud. A dozen? He'd lost his entire savings. He'd have to start again. It would take, what? Ten, fifteen years to recoup his losses?

"Son, you will always have a place here," Pa said. "You're a part of this." He waved his hand to indicate he meant the ranch.

"I know." That had always been the case, but he'd wanted something uniquely his. A herd of cows with his own brand, not the Marshall Five brand. He'd planned this since he'd married Violet. For the first time he admitted to himself the truth of his plans. He'd wanted to prove to a woman that he had something of his own to offer her. He'd hoped he would have that to offer Isabelle. Now he had nothing.

Funny, in all their discussions he'd never thought to ask about her finances. Mostly because he assumed she came from a rich family and because he hoped he could point to his thriving herd as proof she would lack nothing if she should ever consider ranch life. Perhaps she would be content with the life he now lived. A partner in the Marshall Five Ranch but with nothing truly his own. She wasn't like Violet, who had made him want this independence to prove his worth to her. He would not go on judging her by Violet's behavior.

He was nothing if not a persistent dreamer.

Chapter Fifteen

Isabelle wished she could reach for Dawson's hand and let him know she understood how much this loss hurt him, but with so many people watching, she settled for leaning toward him just a little. Whether or not he noticed she could not say.

They finished the meal. Mr. Marshall and Dawson's two brothers described the work they had done. Grandfather, Annie and even Mattie listened with keen interest. Dawson appeared distracted. She couldn't say for sure what he was thinking but suspected it was about the loss of his cows.

She had money. She could replace them without even noticing the amount. Was now the time to tell him of her inheritance?

But if she did and he accepted, how could she ever be certain his interest in her wasn't dependent on money? No, she'd wait and see if his interest continued without the added benefit of her bank account.

Annie insisted on helping clean up even though Isabelle tried to persuade her it wasn't necessary. Mattie helped, as well.

The men disappeared into the sitting room, deep in conversation. Except for Dawson. When she glanced into the room, he sat alone, staring into the distance, the skin on his face taut.

It was on the tip of her tongue to say she could help him, but again she felt the need for caution and didn't speak.

A knock came on the door. Annie called out for the caller to enter.

A weathered man of indeterminate age stepped into the kitchen.

"Hi, Jimbo."

Mr. Marshall introduced Isabelle. "Jimbo is one of the hired hands. He's been here so long I think he might have come with the land."

Jimbo chuckled, a dry, crackly sound. "Brought the mail from town like you asked." He handed Mr. Marshall a bundle of papers.

"Thanks." Mr. Marshall was looking at the bundle before Jimbo got the door closed. "Lots of newspapers. Good. I feel the need to know what's going on outside our little corner of the world." He turned to the other room. "Boys, we have newspapers."

Logan and Conner hurried in and each took a paper their father handed them. Grandfather followed and received a section. Dawson came last, showing little interest, but he sat down and opened up the section placed before him.

She wished she could go to him and tell him how much it hurt to see his shock and disappointment, but she was far too aware of the others and how they would read such a move.

Not that she knew how to interpret her desire except

to admit she felt she and Dawson had entered into a new understanding and appreciation of each other. Her heart rate increased with anticipation of their friendship developing even further. Finally, a man who saw her simply as Isabelle Redfield. A tremor skittered across her shoulders. Sooner or later she would have to tell him the truth about herself. "Girls, do you want to catch up on the news?"

"I do." Annie sat down. "Isabelle, join the fun."

Somehow the only empty chair was at Dawson's side, so she sat there and began to read the pages she had.

She gasped as she read the story before her. Too late she realized she should have hidden her surprise. Now she had Dawson's attention.

"What is it?" he asked.

She couldn't answer and knew it was too much to hope he wouldn't see the story that caught her attention. She knew the moment he found the paragraphs.

He read the story aloud. "'Where is the Redfield heiress? She has not been seen in days.'"

He glanced at the dateline. "This paper is ten days old." He continued. "'Queries to Miss Redfield's lawyer have led to no information. He refuses to disclose her whereabouts. Her cousin, with whom she has lived since her parents' untimely deaths, refuses to speak to this reporter. Speculation is rampant. Has something happened to Miss Redfield? If so, what will become of the Redfield–Castellano fortune?'"

Isabelle stared at the page, not seeing anything.

"Is that you?" Dawson asked.

She nodded, feeling every pair of eyes on her.

"What's a hair-is?" Mattie demanded.

Grandfather recovered enough to answer the child. "It means she has a lot of money."

Not until I marry or turn twenty-five, she silently protested. Though her allowance was more than generous. But she would not say that. It was like sending out an invitation for every eligible man in a hundred-mile radius to submit a marriage proposal.

"Isn't that good?" Mattie sounded confused.

"It can be," Grandfather added.

"Not always." Isabelle managed to squeeze the words from her constricting throat.

"Why didn't you say who you were?" Dawson made it sound like she'd tricked him.

She lifted her head to face him. "Would it have made a difference?"

Confusion and anger filled his eyes. "No." He shook his head. "Yes. Yes, it would. Do you think I would have let you play nanny or nursemaid if I knew you were one of the richest women in America?" He banged the heel of his hand to his forehead. "I knew I'd heard that name somewhere. I've been such an idiot. Twice tricked by a city woman." He banged his forehead again as if trying to drive the words into his brain.

With every ounce of self-control she'd had drilled into her head during her many lessons on proper deportment, she rose to her feet. "I see we are right back where we started. I'm again a rich city woman with no practical skills. Totally unsuited for life in western Montana." She had the guilty pleasure of seeing her accusations hit home, but then his expression again hardened and she understood he would not forgive her for not telling him the truth. Though, by his own mouth, he'd said he would never have allowed her to take care of Mattie if he'd known. "If you'll excuse me, I'll pack my bag and return to town." Ignoring Annie's and Mattie's protests, she swept up the stairs.

Not until she reached the room where she had snatched bits of sleep the last two nights did she let her pain explode. She sank to the edge of the bed and leaned over her knees, waiting for the pain gripping her insides to abate. For a few days she'd been free to live the life she desired. How foolish of her to think it could last.

Conversation rose and fell downstairs. She caught enough of it to know both Grandfather and Annie scolded Dawson for being so judgmental. She couldn't make out his words but knew from the tone that he protested.

Annie and Mattie rushed up the stairs and plopped down on either side of her.

"You can't go," Mattie said.

"Don't let Dawson's attitude affect you," Annie said. "He doesn't know what's good for him."

She hugged Mattie. "I can't stay." She smiled at Annie. "Thank you for your loyalty and friendship."

"What are you going to do?" Annie asked.

"Will I still be able to come to see you after school?" Mattie's tears were very close.

Isabelle would give anything not to hurt this dear child. "I can't say. For either of your questions. Everything has changed now. I will never be treated the same." She sighed, determined not to feel sorry for herself. Yes, she'd dreamed things could be different, but being an heiress had always been a burden to her.

Tears were very close to the surface. Annie must have realized it, for she reached for Mattie's hand. "We'll leave you alone to consider your options." She took Mattie's hand and they returned downstairs.

Her options? She had none. Already Dawson looked

at her differently, judged her as useless. Useless and rich. What a combination. Was there no place she'd be accepted as more than an heiress, no one who would see her as more than that?

The last few days, when she'd felt as if Dawson saw her as more, had only been pretend. Wishful thinking. She pushed her few belongings into the valise Kate had sent. She held her book in her hands. *A Guide to Practical Housewifery.* A mocking title. Signifying everything she wanted and was doomed never to enjoy.

She jammed the book on top of her other things, closed the valise and headed for the stairs. She paused as regrets and wishes washed through her. Leaving her valise at the top of the stairs, she went to Mattie's room and stood in the doorway. Two chairs still sat by the bed. For a little while she had been what she wanted to be...valued for herself, dreaming of belonging in a family.

It was not to be.

She returned to where she'd left her valise and took a moment to gather together her courage.

Downstairs she heard Grandfather's canes as he hobbled into the sitting room, announcing, "I'll have none of this speculation."

She made out Dawson's father's voice. "I've had enough, too. I'll go get the wagon in case Miss Isabelle is set on going to town." The outer door opened and closed.

One of the brothers spoke. She didn't know them well enough to recognize their voices. "Dawson, she's practically made of money. Why not ask her for a loan to buy some more cows? From what I've read of her, she can well spare the money."

The other brother added his opinion. "Seems like it was meant to be. You and her all friendly already. From the way she was looking at you when we first came in, I'd say she was ready to do most anything for you."

Anything but be seen in his eyes as a source of money.

"Guess there might be some truth in that."

Dawson's words scalded clear through her, leaving a trail of pain. How easily he began to regard her as a rich opportunity. Not waiting to hear more of what he would say, knowing she couldn't take much more of this kind of talk before she broke down, she hurried down the stairs and into the kitchen.

The three of them had the good grace to look embarrassed at her entrance.

"I'm ready to go." She crossed to the floor and put on her coat, then stood at the door.

Dawson sprang to his feet. "I'll take you."

Thankfully, his father came through the door at the same time. "The wagon is outside. I can take you."

"Thank you very much."

Mattie and Annie hovered nearby. She hugged them both. "This has nothing to do with either of you. Remember that."

Both girls turned accusing looks at Dawson.

He stood at his chair, rubbing his chin, looking as hurt and confused as she.

She slid her gaze past him. This was not a time to show weakness simply because of all she had thought possible in this home. "Goodbye. Nice to have met you all." She nodded toward the brothers.

Grandfather returned from the other room, his face drawn as if in pain. Likely because he had crossed the two rooms at twice his usual pace. "Anyone who would let you go," he said, "is about as smart as an old fence post." He glowered at Dawson.

His words amused her but she was so close to crying she didn't dare laugh, knowing tears would follow all too quickly. "You're a good man, Grandfather. It's been a pleasure."

Grandfather's eyes grew teary.

She must leave before she broke down in front of everyone and she reached for her valise but Mr. Marshall took it. She followed him to the wagon and let him help her up. A cold wind blew from the north and she huddled into the protection of her coat for the ride to town.

She would have been content to utter not a word nor hear one on the trip to town but Mr. Marshall had other ideas.

"I think I can safely say that you have grown fond of Dawson and he of you."

She made a sound he could take as agreement or disagreement.

"Dawson was somewhat surprised to learn who you are."

That stung. "Am I not the same person now I was before he knew of my inheritance?"

"Of course. I didn't mean otherwise. Maybe what I meant is that his wife taught him to be cautious about taking a woman at face value, so to discover you have such a big secret has thrown him for a loop."

"You might say that to realize that it matters so much to him has thrown *me* for a loop." She vowed she would say no more on the subject, and it appeared he was of like mind, for they made the rest of the journey in silence.

He pulled up to the doctor's house, helped her down and carried her valise to the doorway.

"Thank you for the ride," she said, wanting nothing

more than to rush into the house and have a good cry in the privacy of her room.

"Thank you for taking care of my girls and befriending Dawson. I refuse to think it's over."

"Goodbye." She stepped inside and closed the door. She had no wish to be rude but neither could she stand on the step and discuss the possibility of a continuing friendship with Dawson. His father had not heard the plan Dawson and his brothers were cooking up to turn their friendship into monetary gain.

She didn't wait to hear him drive away before she fled toward the sanctuary of her room, but she came face-to-face with Kate, who took one look at her and gasped.

"What's wrong? Mattie? No—"

Isabelle calmed her turmoil to deal with Kate, who had taken her upset for something to do with the measles. "Mattie and Annie are both on the mend."

"Annie, too? Tell me all about it." She led Isabelle to a chair, and too wobbly inside to protest, Isabelle sat. She looked around the room.

"Where's your father?"

"He was up all night with two men injured by a raging bull. He's sleeping now. I hope he gets an undisturbed night. But what about you? Was it awful looking after two patients?" Kate knew of Isabelle's fear of sickrooms and apparently assumed it to be the reason for the way she clenched her hands together so tightly the fingertips were white.

"It wasn't bad." Isabelle marshaled her thoughts and began at the beginning. "Dawson helped me tend the girls. I got to know him better and understand him more." Or so she'd thought. Maybe that was what hurt the most… that he seemed to care for her when she was only a city woman. But as soon as he discovered she was rich, his opinion had changed from friendship into something more mercenary.

"And grew to admire him more?"

"I believed so. He talked about his dreams and plans. He's always wanted his own ranch. His own cows." A bitter note crept into her voice. "Turns out that's all that matters to him."

"Surely you mean apart from Mattie."

"Yes, of course." She'd give him that. "He bought a herd of cows last fall and was concerned they might not have made it through the winter. He had reason to worry." She repeated the news his pa and brothers had brought. "Even before he learned who I was he must have realized I came from a well-to-do family. Like you pointed out, my wardrobe gave it away." No doubt he'd seen the possibilities of her family's bank account from the beginning. It hurt to know his interest had all been self-serving. Her heart twisted so hard she felt faint.

"Wait a minute. Did you say he knew your secret? How?"

"Would you believe from reading an old newspaper his father got in the mail?" She filled in the details for Kate. "He accused me of deceit. But that's not the worst. Before I left the house he and his brothers were already scheming how to get money from me." Her voice crackled. "Why can't anyone accept me for myself?"

"I do." Kate's voice was reassuring. She alone knew how Isabelle struggled to find acceptance.

"I know you do and I truly appreciate it." She unlocked her fingers and reached over to squeeze Kate's hand.

"You want more though, don't you?"

"Don't think me ungrateful but—" She choked on her tears. She wanted home, family—love. "I thought Dawson—" Why had she let herself begin to hope and dream? She couldn't go on and Kate pulled Isabelle to her side as she wept.

A little later, her tears spent, Isabelle sat up. "I let myself believe I had found what I wanted here in Bella Creek."

"What is it you want?" Kate asked, gently.

Isabelle smiled, though it was more a gesture of regret. "To be simply Isabelle Redfield, an ordinary woman with an ordinary life."

"Is that possible, given your inheritance?"

At Kate's question, Isabelle sat up straighter. "Perhaps it is, but maybe I need to make it happen." She wondered if she could. "I have an idea but I need to think on it a bit."

Kate studied her. "I'm not sure what you're planning but I hope whatever it is, you'll stay here."

"I like Bella Creek just fine." She could say nothing more until she had worked out a few details. "I'll keep you informed of my plans." With a murmured apology she hurried to her room, pulled out a piece of paper and began to work out how she could achieve her goals.

Dawson couldn't think over the racket of his family.

Grandfather scowled. "Boy, you've made the worst mistake of your life."

He didn't think that possible. Violet had the dubious honor of being his worst mistake.

Logan and Conner spoke at the same time. "You should have asked her for money to buy more cows. How often does such an opportunity come your way?"

Annie sputtered. Fire flashed in her eyes as she confronted her brothers. "Is all you see about her is her money? Shame on you." She turned to Dawson. "Shame on you, too. She cared about you. I wasn't too sick to overhear much of what you said."

"Well, shame on you for eavesdropping." It sounded defensive, even to his own ears.

"I saw the way she looked at you. And how you smiled at her."

Mattie crossed her arms and stood resolutely by Annie. No mistaking what side she placed herself on, and the knowledge that she didn't choose him added to the burning in his heart.

"I heard, too," she said. "You were real nice to each other until you read that paper about her. I don't understand why you're angry at her just because she has lots of money. Grandfather is always telling us that what's important is how a person acts. Isn't that right, Grandfather?"

Grandfather smiled adoringly at Mattie. "I'm pleased at least one of my offspring listened to me."

"I always listen to you."

The noise of all the comments and judgments filled Dawson's head. He couldn't think. He had to get away from all this. "Annie, I know you're sick but could I leave Mattie here a few days? I need to get away." Taking her consent for granted, he stepped into the cloakroom and pulled on his coat, boots and hat.

Annie, his brothers and Mattie crowded into the cloakroom after him, all talking at once. Only a few words could be understood and they were the very ones he didn't want to hear.

"You can't run away from this."

What did he want? He couldn't decide at the moment.

Or maybe he couldn't face the idea that he couldn't have what he wanted.

Grandfather called from the kitchen. "She isn't Violet, you know."

But who was she?

Only one of the many questions mattered and that was Mattie's. "Pa, are you going to let her go?"

He lifted Mattie and pressed his face to hers. "I want to check on what remains of my herd. I'll be back in a few days. You be good for Aunt Annie." Mattie's rash had faded but she still had the measles. Was he being foolish to leave her before she was fully recovered? He had to believe she was well on her way to recovery or he couldn't go, and right now he felt a burning need to leave all this behind and figure out what to do next.

He gathered up supplies for a few days and a tent. If he'd hoped to be able to prepare in peace he was sadly disappointed. Logan and Conner dogged his every step, blasting him with questions.

"What about the work in town?" Logan asked.

"The schoolhouse is about three-quarters finished." He threw the saddle blanket on Jumper. "I saw to the completion of the doctor's residence and welcomed the newcomers. The school was your responsibility, Logan. Take care of it."

"Yes, sir." Logan saluted.

Conner cleared his throat.

Dawson bent over to catch the cinch, knowing it was too much to hope his brothers would leave him alone. He straightened. Yup, Conner was waiting to say his piece.

"Were you and this Miss Isabelle interested in each other?" His low voice hid a lot of meaning but Dawson wasn't interested in pursuing any of it right now.

He faced his brother. "You stay away from her, hear?"

Conner smirked. "Guess that answers my question."

Dawson fitted the saddlebags, bedroll and tent to the saddle and swung to Jumper's back. "I'm on my way."

Logan caught the bridle and stopped the horse. "Care to tell us where you're going?"

"I'm going to check on my cows." He jerked the horse away and galloped from the yard.

He let the pounding of Jumper's hooves fill his brain, mile after mile until flecks of sweat peppered his face and he realized how hard he worked his horse. He slowed the pace and patted Jumper's neck. "Sorry, old fella. I wasn't thinking." Or, perhaps more accurately, he was trying not to think.

He crested a hill and looked down on a sorry-looking bunch of cows. With a start, he realized they were what was left of his herd…his dreams. He studied them. Shouldn't he feel more than this regret that so many had perished? And the survivors were thin? But they were on good grass now and would soon put on weight.

He reined away in a different direction. An hour later he considered his options. A line cabin lay to the north, a pretty valley to the west. After the briefest of pauses, he headed west and didn't stop until he reached a grove of trees on the hillside overlooking the grassy basin.

He dismounted and removed his supplies and the saddle. He brushed Jumper and left him to enjoy the grazing. Dawson sat down on the hillside. He had only the birds and bugs for company. There on the grassy slope he laid his dreams and disappointments out before God. "Help me understand what it is I really want. And need."

He looked at every aspect of his life, honestly seeking God's guidance.

His cow herd was decimated and yet it mattered less to him than learning of Isabelle's secret. Why should that be?

Because it felt too much like Violet, pretending one thing while living another. Committing to marriage, while yearning for activity and excitement. Was that all this trip to Bella Creek was for Isabelle—the thrill of something different?

Why had he been so attracted to Isabelle even though he knew from the first day what she was?

His brain churned with far more questions than answers.

That night he spread his bedroll on a sheet of canvas and slept under the stars. Or, more correctly, he lay awake watching the stars and searching for understanding.

The next morning he ate a hurried breakfast, but when he reached for the saddle, his eyes caught the pale purple of a patch of crocuses and his thoughts went back to the day Isabelle had gone to the river with Mattie and Annie. He dropped the saddle to the ground and stared at the wildflowers. Even back then he had fought his attraction to her, seeing her as an unsuitable girl.

An unsuitable girl who cared for his daughter.

An unsuitable girl who proved she could tackle anything from housework to nursing.

An unsuitable girl who didn't want anyone to know she was an heiress.

Why? Why would she keep such a secret from him?

He returned to saddling Jumper, mounted and spent the next few hours riding around the ranch, hoping to find answers.

That night he again lay under the stars. He felt like the answer hovered just beyond his grasp and he determined he would not go home until he found it.

Dawn had only begun to lighten the sky when Dawson wakened, cows on his mind.

He'd lost his investment. Lost his dream of starting his own place. Strangely, it didn't matter. As he'd ridden across the rolling hills, through the trees and along the river, one thing had become clear. This land, right here on the Marshall Five Ranch, was part of his heart and soul. Besides, he thought with a wry chuckle, how could they call it the Marshall Five if he left?

He didn't want to leave.

Why had it seemed so important just a few days ago? What did he want?

It was somehow connected to Isabelle. Wasn't it?

He jerked to a sitting position. No, not Isabelle. It was connected to Violet and her restless nature. Something she'd said had stuck in his craw and wormed into his mind to stay there all these years.

What would you know about adventure? You're stuck here. You don't even have anything of your own.

Even the house wasn't enough for her. And thus the need to have his own place had been born. Except it wasn't what he wanted. He liked it here. His roots went deep into the bedrock of the land. He wanted Mattie to enjoy the love and support of a large family.

There was only one thing he lacked. A wife and family of his own. The pain he'd felt at learning Isabelle's secret stemmed from knowing she hadn't been completely honest with him.

Why?

He banged his fist to his forehead. Because as soon as everyone knew who she was their opinion changed. Well, maybe not everyone. Not Grandfather, Annie or Mattie.

A troubling thought blasted through his mind. She'd come down the stairs as Logan and Conner were pointing out the benefits of knowing a woman with lots of money. Had she overheard them? Did she think he shared their opinion? It couldn't be further from the truth. He didn't care if she was an heiress or poor as a blackbird. They had shared something that went beyond belongings and possessions. As Grandfather said, what mattered was how a person lived.

A smile filled his heart. He liked the way Isabelle lived. She was gentle and understanding with Mattie, she did a good job of whatever she tried and she had kissed him.

What more did he need? He sprang from his bedroll and broke camp in record time. The sun was just peeking over the horizon as he made his way back to the ranch. He arrived in time for breakfast and a noisy welcome.

"As soon as we've eaten I am going to town to find Isabelle and tell her how I feel."

Grandfather harrumphed. "And how is that?"

"First, I don't care an ounce about her money. She can do whatever she wants with it. All I care about is her friendship."

"Friendship?" Logan mocked.

Dawson gave a dismissive shrug. "I wouldn't object if it went further."

Mattie clapped. "Papa, you are doing the right thing. Can I go with you?"

He chuckled. "I'm glad to meet with your approval, but, no, this is something I can handle on my own."

The meal over, he strode from the house and swung back into Jumper's saddle. His ever-so-helpful family crowded around him, offering advice. He ignored them and repeated, "I can handle this on my own."

His heart raced ahead of him into town. He rode to the back door of the doctor's residence and dismounted. His lungs fought to find enough air as he stood before the door. He brushed the dust from his trousers, took his hat off, ran his fingers through his hair to make sure it was halfway neat and knocked.

Footsteps crossed the floor and he held his breath, quickly rehearsing the words he'd practiced on the way to town. Kate opened the door. Her mouth fell open.

"Howdy." He glanced past her. "Is Isabelle in?"

"I'm afraid not. She's gone."

The words took several seconds to register. "Is she at the store?" He would go find her.

"She's left town."

He stared at Kate as the words sifted through his brain. "Left town. For where?"

"She said she had business to attend to. I'm sorry. I wish I had better news."

Was it like Violet all over again? Running after something new? But this was not Violet. This was Isabelle and she was different in all the best ways possible. "Is she coming back?"

"I can't say."

What did that mean? That Kate knew but wouldn't say or that she didn't know. "Tell me where she went. I will go after her."

Kate's study of him caused him to squirm.

"I need to tell her something."

"Like what?"

It wasn't any of her business but he understood Kate wouldn't release the information he needed unless she approved of his reasons. "I need to tell her I care about her and I want her to stay here. She's more than a rich city woman. She's a person who matters to us—me and Mattie."

Kate nodded. "She's in Great Falls."

"Thanks." He grabbed Jumper's reins and led him to the Wells Fargo station where he could purchase a ticket to ride the stagecoach. If he wasn't mistaken, the stage-coach from Great Falls would arrive this afternoon. It went as far as Wolf Hollow then turned around for the return trip to the city. He would be on the stagecoach. He would go to Great Falls and find her. And somehow he would convince her of his feelings.

Chapter Sixteen

Isabelle leaned out the window as the stage drove down the street in Bella Creek. This was where she wanted to belong if people would accept her for who she was. Mostly she hoped Dawson would see her as a person who belonged. The past two days had been very busy. She'd wired her lawyer and he'd agreed to let her sign papers with a lawyer in Great Falls. She'd come away from those intense meetings feeling free as never before.

A wagon rumbled by on one side. She caught only a glimpse but was almost certain she'd seen Mattie between Grandfather and Annie, and a smile caught her lips. Mattie had been the first person she saw when she arrived in town. And then Dawson. She sat back. Besides Mattie, he was the person she most wanted to see again.

The stagecoach pulled to a halt. She sat back, suddenly afraid, wondering if returning was the right thing to do. Of course it was. Hadn't she prayed about it? And wasn't that what all her planning led her to?

The door opened and the driver reached up to assist her down. As soon as her feet reached the ground, she looked up and right into the surprised blue eyes of the very man she missed so much her insides felt hollow. "Dawson, what are you doing here?" Now, if that wasn't a stupid question. He had every right to be anywhere he wanted in town.

"I didn't expect you." He stood so close she could barely breathe. Did he have any idea of how his presence affected her? Of course he didn't and she should be grateful. It saved her pride from another fall.

She managed to pull her gaze from him and look beyond. Mattie, Grandfather and Annie stood to the right. Mr. Marshall, Logan and Conner stood to the left. What was this? A Marshall reunion? Several other townspeople stood about. Time to get on with the business that had brought her here. "I've come to stay. I intend to help Dr. Baker and Kate in the clinic."

Mattie clapped. "I can go to your place after school." Her eager smile fled. "If Papa will let me."

At his name, Isabelle brought her attention back to him.

"I was about to get on the stage," he said.

"Oh, I'm sorry." She had been blocking the door and stepped to one side.

"I was coming to find you."

"Oh." She could think of nothing more to say. Then she recalled the words his brothers had spoken, how Dawson should take advantage of a rich woman's funds. She stepped farther to the side, putting enough distance between herself and Dawson that she wasn't overly distracted and speaking loud enough for everyone to hear. She wanted them all to be very clear as to her financial situation.

"My name is Isabelle Castellano Redfield. And, yes,

I was sole heiress to the Castellano and Redfield fortunes."

There was a surprised intake of breath from those standing nearby.

She could not look at Dawson, nor his brothers. Instead, she focused on Annie. Out of the corner of her eyes she noted Kate join the crowd and then Sadie slipped from the store to see what was going on. Feeling as if she were supported by her friends, she continued.

"However, I am no longer rich. I have turned all the money into foundations for the less fortunate." She'd arranged for a board to supervise the operation of various charities—a hospital in the heart of St. Louis, an orphanage in Montana and an educational fund to provide teachers and books to areas that couldn't afford to pay for them. The lawyer had insisted she continue to receive a modest allowance but she wasn't about to admit that in public.

She finally brought her attention back to Dawson. "I have no money to buy cattle or ranch land."

The look he gave her was direct and challenging. "I don't care about your money. Give away every last cent if that's what you want."

"What about your dreams of your own ranch?"

"It wasn't really my dream."

She glanced around at the interested observers. Perhaps she'd get a chance at some point to ask him what his statement meant…a time and place with no one else to hear what he had to say.

He closed the distance between them and took her cold, trembling hands. "Isabelle, I don't care about your money. All I want, all I need, is you and you alone."

She gaped at him. "Why?"

His grin tilted to one side. "Isn't it obvious? I love you."

She swallowed noisily. "Love me?" The words echoed in her head. Could it be possible her most precious dream could be coming true?

"I love you in every way a man can love."

She digested the information, and as the words became clear in her brain, her heart did a happy dance. "You do?"

"With my whole heart."

The sheriff had joined Dawson's brothers and called out, "Miss Isabelle, put the poor man out of his misery."

"Yes, please do," Dawson begged. "Tell me you forgive me for being such a dunce and you'll give me a chance to prove how much I love you."

She closed the final few inches between them and wrapped her arms about his neck. "I do believe I'd enjoy that. You could start by kissing me."

"Here?" His eyes widened.

"It's a good place to start." Before the friends and family she hoped would be her friends and family as well as his.

He caught her lips in a gentle, sweet kiss that filled her with such joy she laughed.

The crowd clapped and cheered. Mattie ran to Dawson and Isabelle and wrapped her arms about their waists. Dawson lifted her and they hugged her between them.

Annie, Sadie and Kate all pressed close, happy for the promise of their love.

The sheriff and Dawson's brothers slapped him on his back.

The preacher strode to the crowd and chuckled. "Looks like I'll soon be conducting my first wedding in this town."

Dawson gladly, joyfully accepted everyone's good wishes. But there was one problem. Despite Preacher Hugh's assumption, Dawson had not asked Isabelle to marry him. Not yet. And for one reason only. She had not said she loved him.

Was it an oversight on her part? Or was he jumping ahead of himself? He had to find out but it took him most of an hour to pull her away from the others. By then he felt ready to explode.

"Let's go for a walk." He would sooner take her for a drive out of town where he could be certain they'd be alone, but it would take too long to arrange a buggy. He simply couldn't wait any longer. He sent Mattie to stay with Kate and pulled Isabelle's hand into the crook of his elbow, wanting to keep her as close to his side as possible.

He led her south past the trees and houses to Mineral Creek, which flowed by town. The trees had not yet leafed out. The creek ran high as the snowmelt filled it. The sound of the rushing water had a pleasing sound he'd never before noticed. Likely because of the anxious hope in his heart.

There was no place to sit. Later he'd see that a few benches were placed along the shore for future use. He led her to a cluster of trees where they were mostly out of sight and turned her to face him.

"I'm glad you came back," he said.

"What did you mean that having your own ranch wasn't really your dream?"

He told her how he'd discovered he had mistaken what Violet thought he should want for what he really wanted.

"What do you really want?"

"A home and family of my own. The place isn't important, though I like to think of being surrounded by family and friends."

"I like that, too. That's why I came back."

His heart thudded sluggishly. "Is that the only reason? Do I figure into your plans at all?"

Her laughter trilled through the air. "It was the main reason." Her eyes shone. "And you made my dreams come true by meeting me at the stagecoach and declaring your love." She trailed a gentle finger across his cheek. "Thank you."

He caught her hands and held them between them. "There's only one thing missing." He could hardly squeeze the words out.

"Really? I can't think of anything." She looked puzzled.

"Isabelle." His voice was suddenly hoarse. "Put me out of my misery as Jesse said. Tell me how you feel about me."

Her eyes widened. Her mouth formed an O. "I guess I thought I had." Her expression softened. She slipped her hands from his and cupped them to his face. "Dawson Marshall, I love you in every way possible. With my whole heart."

He pulled her closer and claimed her mouth as his heart overflowed with love and gratitude. He lifted his head, ending the kiss. "There is one more thing."

Her eyes were soft as kitten fur. "Really?"

"Isabelle Castellano Redfield, will you marry me and make me the happiest man on earth?"

"Yes, I will, and I will be the happiest woman."

They sealed their promise with a kiss.

Epilogue

Isabelle waited in Annie's bedroom at the ranch house. A view from the window allowed her to watch wagons, buggies and horseback riders arrive. She smiled. Dawson was right. She closed her eyes as she recalled the conversation.

"I don't want a big wedding," she'd said. "If I sent invitations to all the people I should invite, word would surely get out. The last thing I want is for reporters to show up for the marriage of the mysterious missing heiress." The papers had continued with speculation as to her whereabouts along with reports of a new hospital and orphanage funded by an anonymous donor. So far, no one suggested the two events were connected and she hoped they never would.

Dawson had kissed her gently. "I want all my friends and family to attend and witness my joy at finding the most beautiful, most suitable, most amazing woman in the world."

She laughed and tried to look both surprised and hurt. "I might like to meet this paragon of a woman. Though I warn you I can be very jealous."

"You know I mean you." He had smiled so adoringly

it had brought tears to her eyes. "Trust me, the sort of big wedding I have in mind is nothing like the high-society event you mean."

So she had agreed to follow his plans. But it was only fair, seeing as he'd given in to her desire to change the date of their wedding.

After she'd agreed to marry him, they'd had a long discussion about their future.

"I want you to be completely certain this is the right thing to do," he'd said.

She'd tipped her head from side to side as she studied him, wanting to be clear as to his meaning. Her heart went to him as she realized he harbored a little fear that she might, like Violet had, regret settling down as a married woman on the ranch. "I'm not going to change my mind. This is the sort of family I have dreamed of, wished for and prayed for since my parents died."

"A family is one thing," he'd murmured. "Life on a ranch is another." He'd pulled her close and looked deep into her eyes. "If you ever grow tired of it, simply say so. Mattie and I can learn to live in the city if that's what you need."

She had hugged him so tightly he grunted. "You are a noble, generous man and I thank God for bringing you into my life." She gave a little laugh that caught in her throat. "I am so blessed."

He'd pressed his head to her hair. "I believe you were brought into my life. Not the other way around. And it is I who am blessed."

They'd kissed, her heart so full of joy and gratitude she clung to him, never wanting to let him go. But if it gave him peace of mind to wait to marry, she would agree. They had set a date four months away.

Only saying goodbye grew harder and harder. She

ached to begin life with him and Mattie. To have her own home and her own family.

After two weeks, she had begged him to change the date. "I'll never be more sure of what I want to do."

His eyes had shone like a sunny summer sky. "If you're certain. What did you have in mind?"

"Next Saturday?"

He'd laughed. "You think we could manage that?"

"How long does it take to send messages to those you want to attend? Cousin Augusta won't want to travel so far, so she won't mind if she simply gets an announcement of the wedding. Other than that, all my friends are right here."

"Then let's do it."

As she watched people arrive, she couldn't help but be amazed so many showed up on such short notice.

Annie stepped into the room. "You look lovely."

"Cousin Augusta was right when she said a person never knew when they might need a special gown." Her dress of palest pink silk floated about her like a cloud reflecting the sunrise. "It's very generous of you to lend me your mother's veil." The simple veil of tulle, trimmed in lace and held in place with an ivory comb, hung to her elbows.

"My mother would be honored." Annie's voice caught. "Knowing you're wearing her veil makes it almost feel like she's here."

Kate and Sadie crowded into the room. Like Annie, they wore pale gray dresses that each had in her wardrobe, and Isabelle had gladly agreed to go with that color for her bridesmaids.

"Where's my flower girl?"

"Here I am."

All eyes turned to the door as Mattie came through it. A little while ago, Isabelle had styled the child's golden hair into a fall of ringlets. Annie had discovered a pink dress that fit her. She held a basket full of wildflowers, their scent filling the room even as joy filled Isabelle's heart.

Isabelle leaned down to Mattie's level. "You are pretty as a picture."

"Will Papa be surprised?"

"He certainly will. In fact, he might forget to look at me."

Mattie giggled. "No, he won't. I'm just a little girl. Besides—" her eyes glistened "—no one is as beautiful as you."

Isabelle kissed the child on the forehead. "Thank you."

Mattie tugged on Isabelle's hand and pulled her down to whisper in her ear. "Can I call you Mama now or do I have to wait until after you and Papa get married?"

Not caring if it rumpled her dress or pulled her veil crooked, she hugged Mattie. "Now is just fine."

"Mama. I like the sound of that. You're my mama."

Isabelle couldn't say who smiled the widest—she or Mattie.

Sadie turned away from the tender scene to look out the window. "Preacher Hugh has arrived."

Annie hurried to join the teacher and said, "I don't think I've ever seen a man more handsome in a black suit."

Isabelle looked at her soon-to-be sister-in-law. Did Annie have feelings for the preacher? It hardly seemed possible. Annie was much younger than the man.

Dawson's pa, or Grandpa Bud—as Isabelle had gotten used to thinking of him—called from the stairs. "We're ready whenever you are."

Isabelle looked about at her little gathering of friends.

Kate returned the look, her gaze full of warmth and love. "This is an answer to your prayers."

Isabelle nodded. "Can we have a word of prayer before we go down?" She reached out her hands to Kate on one side and Mattie on the other, taking agreement for granted. After all, she was the bride and today got to say what she wanted and expect her wishes to be fulfilled.

Sadie and Annie joined hands and they became a circle. Isabelle's throat tightened. A circle of friends who saw her only as Isabelle Redfield, soon to be Isabelle Marshall, an ordinary woman. She blinked back tears, cleared her throat and prayed. "Dear God, I am so privileged to have these friends, to be welcomed into this family and soon to become Dawson's wife and Mattie's mother. I thank You from the bottom of my heart for these blessings. May the day go well." As a last-minute thought, she added, "And may these friends of mine find their own love to enjoy. Amen."

Sadie, Kate and Annie protested at the same time.

"I won't marry. My father needs me." Kate's words, full of unexpected sadness, made Isabelle ache for her friend.

"I refuse to believe God can't provide a man especially suited for you. Now, let's go."

One by one, her friends went down the steps. Mattie waited, as if reluctant to leave Isabelle. They joined Grandpa Bud at the top of the stairs.

"'Way you go, little one," Grandpa Bud said and Mattie went demurely ahead of them.

Isabelle took his arm. "I'm pleased you agreed to walk me down the aisle."

Grandpa Bud patted her hand. "I am honored. My son deserves a woman like you."

Her throat closed off at his kindness.

Then they began their descent into the waiting crowd. The table and chairs had been removed from the dining room, leaving space for the gathering. Isabelle tried to take in the many people, wanting to recognize them when she saw them in the future. But her eyes were drawn toward the front. Her friends stood to one side. Dawson's attendants stood to the other side—his two brothers and Sheriff Jesse.

At last, she allowed herself to meet Dawson's bright blue eyes, so overflowing with love and admiration that she might have stumbled if not for Grandpa Bud's firm arm.

She made it to Dawson's side, received a kiss on her tulle-sheltered cheek from Dawson's father as he released her to Dawson's arm. She heard the words of Preacher Hugh, answered the questions correctly, but it felt like a dream, viewed through a gossamer curtain.

And then Dawson lifted the veil and kissed her.

Suddenly, everything became clear as a sparkling windowpane. She was Mrs. Marshall, wife to Dawson Marshall, mother to Mattie Marshall, and she couldn't have contained any more joy.

She smiled as Dawson introduced her to friends and neighbors. She smiled as ladies of the church served tea. With part of her mind, she took in the greetings, the welcome and the warmth of the room. With a much larger part, she yearned for everyone to leave so she and Dawson could cross the yard to their own home.

A secret pleasure filled her as she recalled the first time she'd seen the house. It fulfilled all her dreams. A big kitchen where she could imagine cooking and serving family meals with Mattie's help. A cozy sitting room. The furniture in it sparse, as if the room had rarely been used.

"I can see two comfy armchairs with a side table beside them right here," she'd said to Dawson. "A bookshelf filled with books and journals and pens. I'm going to keep a journal of all our happy moments." She'd laughed. "It will be full within a few months."

Dawson had held her close. "I can't wait to share every moment with you. I'll hold your hand through the bad ones and rejoice with you through the good ones."

Her throat clogged now at the memory, just as it had when he'd spoken the words.

"Tell me what else you see in this room."

She'd described Mattie playing nearby, a warm fire and golden lamplight. "And at Christmas, we will invite our friends over and share our joy."

Her tour of the house had led her to the nursery, where Mattie's cradle still stood.

"I hope we are blessed with many children." She'd spoken softly. They had discussed the matter. She was pleased to learn he yearned for lots of little ones.

Her thoughts returned to the gathering as people began to depart, again extending congratulations and best wishes.

Finally Dawson looked around. "We can go now." Only family and close friends remained and they had settled in for a long visit.

She and Dawson slipped away across the yard to their own house. At the threshold he scooped her up in his arms and stepped into their new home. He didn't put her down until they reached the sitting room.

"Welcome home, Mrs. Marshall."

She kissed him.

"Have a look around."

She turned to examine the room. "Oh, Dawson." He'd moved in furniture and arranged it exactly as she had described the room to him.

"I want this house to be your home. It was never Violet's. She was never the woman of my dreams…only of my youthful foolishness. You are the woman I dreamed of as my wife, my friend and the mother of my children."

She went eagerly into his arms. "In you I have found what my heart has wanted all my life. You are my husband and I will do my best to do you good all the days of my life."

With a lingering kiss they began their life together as man and wife.

* * * * *

If you liked this tale of romance and family drama,
pick up these other stories from Linda Ford.

A DADDY FOR CHRISTMAS
A BABY FOR CHRISTMAS
A HOME FOR CHRISTMAS
THE COWBOY'S READY-MADE FAMILY
THE COWBOY'S BABY BOND
THE COWBOY'S CITY GIRL

Find more great reads at www.LoveInspired.com.

Dear Reader,

I visited Kootenay Falls near Libby, Montana, and sat on a rock to watch the water rumble and roar. I knew it was a perfect place for characters in my book to share important revelations. Little did I know it would be a child who would be the one to reveal a secret. Secrets can be the source of shame, pain and embarrassment. But revealing them can also be healing. That's what happens in this story.

I hope and pray that if any of my readers have secrets that are hindering them they will seek help and allow God's healing love into their hearts.

You can learn more about my upcoming books and how to contact me at www.lindaford.org. I love to hear from my readers.

Blessings,

Linda Ford

"There's the land office," Simon said, nodding to a whitewashed building ahead. He strode to it, shifted Nora's case under one arm and held the door open for her, then followed her inside with his brothers in his wake.

The long, narrow office was bisected by a counter. Chairs against the white-paneled walls told of lengthy waits, but today the only person in the room was a slender man behind the counter. He was shrugging into a coat as if getting ready to close up for the day.

Handing Nora's case to his brother John, Simon hurried forward. "I need to file a claim."

The fellow paused, eyed him and then glanced at Nora, who came to stand beside Simon. The clerk smoothed down his lank brown hair and stepped up to the counter. "Do you have the necessary application and fee?"

Simon drew out the ten-dollar fee, then pulled the papers from his coat and laid them on the counter. The clerk took his time reading them, glancing now and then at Nora, who bowed her head as if looking at the shoes peeping out from under her scalloped hem.

"And this is your wife?" he asked at last.

Simon nodded. "I brought witnesses to the fact, as required."

John and Levi stepped closer. The clerk's gaze returned to Nora. "Are you Mrs. Wallin?"

She glanced at Simon as if wondering the same thing, and for a moment he thought they were all doomed. Had she decided he wasn't the man she'd thought him? Had he married for nothing?

Nora turned and held out her hand to the clerk. "Yes, I'm Mrs. Simon Wallin. No need to wish me happy, for I find I have happiness to spare."

The clerk's smile appeared, brightening his lean face. "Mr. Wallin is one fortunate fellow." He turned to pull a heavy leather-bound book from his desk, thumped it down on the counter and opened it to a page to begin recording the claim.

Simon knew he ought to feel blessed indeed as he accepted the receipt from the clerk. He had just earned his family the farmland they so badly needed. The acreage would serve the Wallins for years to come and support the town that had been his father's dream. Yet something nagged at him, warned him that he had miscalculated.

He never miscalculated.

Don't miss
CONVENIENT CHRISTMAS WEDDING
by Regina Scott, available November 2016 wherever
Love Inspired® Historical books and ebooks are sold.

www.LoveInspired.com

LIHEXP1016

Love the Love Inspired book you just read?

Your opinion matters.

Review this book on your favorite
book site, review site, blog or your own
social media properties and share your
opinion with other readers!